P9-CUK-857

# POWER CHALLENGES

# POWER CHALLENGES

## Ben Bova

CAEZIK
SF & FANTASY
ARC MANOR
ROCKVILLE, MARYLAND
*
SHAHID MAHMUD
PUBLISHER
www.CaezikSF.com

This is a work of fiction.

Cover art by Christina P. Myrvold; artstation.com/christinapm

ISBN: 978-1-64710-018-6

First Edition. 1st Printing. May 2021.
1 2 3 4 5 6 7 8 9 10

An imprint of Arc Manor LLC

www.CaezikSF.com

**To the men and women who will return humankind to the Moon—this time to stay.**

We choose to go to the Moon in this decade ... not because [it is] easy, but because [it is] hard, because that goal will serve to organize and measure the best of our energies and skills, because that challenge is one that we are willing to accept, one that we are unwilling to postpone, and one which we intend to win ....

President John F. Kennedy
*12 September 1962*

# Contents

# Book One: Spring

## Reagan National Airport

Jake Ross sat in the airport's VIP lounge, his elbows on his knees, his head in his hands, and stared at the flight information screen.

*Cancelled. Cancelled. Delayed. Cancelled.* Every flight in or out of Reagan National was either cancelled or delayed. In the posh surroundings of the VIP lounge he couldn't see the rain pouring outside, but he saw its results. No flights in or out.

Tami's stuck in New York, he told himself. Well, if you've got to be stuck someplace, New York isn't so bad. Turning to look at the weather map on the wall beside the ARRIVALS/DEPARTURES screen, he saw that the storm was swerving eastward: New York City wouldn't get much more than a few showers.

The lounge was nearly empty; only Jake and a handful of others sitting around morosely, staring at the information screen or quietly sipping drinks.

Outside, Washington was getting drenched by the heavy springtime downpour. With a sigh, Jake pushed himself to his feet. His wife wasn't going to get home tonight, he admitted reluctantly.

Jacob Ross stood just short of six feet tall, his body on the lean side, but solid. His hair was dark and unruly, his face too long and horsey to satisfy him. But he was the science advisor to the vice president of the United States. And he had responsibilities.

As he walked slowly out of the VIP lounge, struggling to pull on his trench coat, his cell phone buzzed. For a few comical moments he flailed with the coat as he reached with his free hand into his jacket for the phone, knowing that only Tami and a handful of others knew his private number.

"Tami?" he said into the phone, still thrashing with the trench coat.

"Jake!" Even in the phone's minuscule screen he could see that she was smiling. Her voice was strong, vibrant.

"How are you?" they said in unison.

Jake couldn't help laughing. "I'm okay. At the airport."

"My flight's been cancelled," she said.

"I know."

Tami's smile faded; she looked halfway between glum and resigned. "I'm going to get a room at the airport motel. Catch the first flight out tomorrow morning."

"You sure?"

She broke into a grin. "It's all set. Got my ticket. Helps to be a TV news personality."

Jake nodded as he walked out of the lounge, worming his free arm into the trench coat's sleeve. He said, "I've got a meeting with Frank at 8:00 A.M."

"Duty calls," she said. "Yes, dammit."

"That's okay. I can find my way home."

"Wish you were here," he said.

"Me too."

"Stay clear of the bar. Those other news guys can be frisky."

"Jealous?"

"Damned right I am."

"Good!" Her smile returned and it lit his heart.

Reluctantly, Jake said, "See you tomorrow night, then."

"Tomorrow. Sleep tight."

"Uh-huh."

Suddenly there was no more to say. Jake stared at his wife's image for a few seconds, then said, "Goodnight, hon."

"Night, sweetheart."

The screen went blank.

## ■ Offices of the Vice President

The morning dawned bright and cheerful. But Jake awoke slowly. He labored through his morning ablutions, pulled on a suitably drab, dark suit, fussed with his tie, then headed down the elevator to the apartment building's parking garage and got into his Dodge Dart GT.

The traffic on his way to the White House was fairly light; Jake almost always rose early enough to be ahead of most of Washington's snarls and tie-ups. He got past the uniformed guards at the gate and parked in the underground lot, then hustled up to the vice president's offices.

Although the desks were less than half occupied this early in the morning, when Jake stopped at the vice president's open office door, B. Franklin Tomlinson was already at his desk, in his shirtsleeves and bright-red suspenders, deep in earnest discussion with his chief of staff, Kevin O'Donnell.

"Come on in, Jake," called the vice president, his voice strong, melodious.

B. Franklin Tomlinson was the scion of the wealthiest family in Montana, and he looked it. Tall, golden-haired, tan, and handsome in a rugged, outdoorsy way, Tomlinson also had a keen intelligence and a burning drive—instilled in him by his late father—to become president of the United States.

O'Donnell, on the other hand, was a rake-thin bundle of nervous energy, his light-brown hair thinning badly, suspicious dark eyes peering out of his pinched face. A longtime Beltway insider, he was sharp and incisive, wise in the ways of Washington's intricacies.

The office décor had been directed by Amy, Tomlinson's wife, dominated by a broad cherrywood desk big enough almost to land a helicopter uon, sweeping silvery drapes across the windows that looked out at the Capitol dome, and comfortable leather chairs in handsome burgundy.

Jake took the seat next to O'Donnell. The vice president eased back in his mahogany-toned swivel chair and said, "This farm bill is going to be troublesome."

"Aren't they always?" Jake quipped.

"It's not funny," snapped O'Donnell, his voice sharper than usual. "The Big Chief wants the bill passed, and the Democrats want to tack a half a zillion amendments onto it."

"Not my territory," said Jake, raising his hands shoulder high.

"Could be," said the vice president. "They're bringing up the ethanol question again."

"Again? I thought that was settled years ago."

"So did we," O'Donnell groused. "But the other side wants to reopen the matter."

Surprised, Jake said, "Farmers should grow food, not capital gains for the energy companies."

"Try telling that to the energy companies," O'Donnell muttered.

"And to the people who represent them in the Congress," Tomlinson added.

Jake shrugged. "Doesn't look like a science problem."

"The hell it doesn't," O'Donnell snapped. "We need a solid scientific argument to show that ethanol is nothing more than a boondoggle for the energy corporations."

"We made that argument when the energy bill was before the Senate."

"Well, we'll have to make it again," said Tomlinson.

Jake asked, "Where's the president on this?"

"Where he usually is," said O'Donnell sourly, "squarely on the fence."

With a shake of his head, Jake said, "I guess we can dig up the arguments we made about ethanol when we got the energy plan approved."

"Maybe," O'Donnell replied carefully, drawing the word out. Then, "But McMasters and his people will have some new counters for that, most likely."

The vice president nodded in agreement.

"I'm working on the Project *Artemis* plan now," Jake pleaded.

"The space plan?" O'Donnell's doubt came close to contempt.

A frown clouded Tomlinson's handsome face. He said, "Better put *Artemis* on a back burner for now."

"But I can't just—"

"Back burner, Jake. Just 'til we get this ethanol question settled."

Jake bit back the bitter reply that sprang to his mind and nodded his acquiescence. When the veep gives you a direct order, he said to himself, you salute and do your duty.

But he didn't like it.

Back in his own office, on the far side of the vice president's suite, Jake pulled up the history of the ethanol debate. It was still in his desktop computer, buried in the voluminous files of his energy plan—the plan that had gotten B. Franklin Tomlinson elected to the U.S. Senate more than eight years earlier—which then helped propel him into the vice presidency.

Ethanol creates more problems than it solves, Jake said to himself as he scanned the old debate. Dammit, we won this fight nearly eight years ago. Why is McMasters bringing it up again?

Because it can hurt President Sebastian, of course. And cripple Sebastian's backing of the *Artemis* program.

Jake shook his head. Don't imagine that everything is keyed to the space plan, he told himself. Yet in his heart he feared that it was. Jake's plan called for a return to the Moon, building a permanent base there, and beginning to use the resources in space to create whole new industries for the people of United States—and the rest of the Earth.

Vice President Tomlinson backed the plan one hundred percent. But there was plenty of opposition. Tomlinson was nicknamed "Captain Moonbeam"—even by Kevin O'Donnell and others on the vice president's own staff—although never within his hearing.

Is McMasters's move really an attempt to sink the space plan? Jake asked himself. Or am I getting paranoid?

There was one person who might help him answer that question, he realized. Isaiah Knowles.

# Isaiah Knowles

Isaiah Knowles was a former astronaut, a man who had been in space more times than Neil Armstrong and all the other Project *Apollo* heroes.

Now he worked for the Space Futures Foundation, a small non-profit outfit that represented the scattered, struggling private corporations trying to earn a living from space operations.

"Been a while," said Knowles, as Jake slid into the booth on the other side of its narrow table.

They were in the Old Ebbitt Grill, a favorite watering hole for the locals. Corporate executives and government bureaucrats could meet there and share a few drinks while they told each other their problems. As usual, the place was jammed, with plenty of young women crowding the bar.

Which ones are the hookers? Jake wondered. Then he realized, with a pang of conscience, that they all were—one way or another—including himself.

"How are you, Ike?" Jake asked. He had to raise his voice considerably: the babble from the bar filled the air.

"Fair to middlin'," Knowles noncommittaled. He was a Black man, usually serious, straight-faced. It had taken Jake years to break through the man's natural reserve and make something of a friend of him.

A harried-looking waiter came up and asked Jake for his drink order. Jake asked for ginger beer, as usual. The waiter scribbled on his pad, then disappeared into the crowd, mumbling to himself about big drinkers.

"Been a while," said Knowles. "Whatcha been up to?"

"The *Artemis* plan, mostly."

Knowles broke into a grin. "Artemis, sister of Apollo."

With a shrug, Jake replied, "One of Piazza's PR guys thought it up. Kind of poetic."

"Gonna take more than poetry to get your big-time space operation going."

Jake felt his brows hike up. "Why? Have you heard anything . . .?"

"It's what I haven't heard, pal. There isn't much enthusiasm for your Project *Artemis*. Not where it counts."

"Has it affected you?"

A rare smile brightened Knowles's face. "Your fancy space plan has brought some business to my door. Every little pissant private space outfit in the world wants to get on the gravy train."

"It's not a gravy train," said Jake.

"That's what I tell 'em, but they don't believe me. They see a big government program and they want to get in on the freakin' gold rush."

Jake shook his head. His space plan was based on funding from private sources—backed by a government guarantee. If everything worked right, the taxpayers wouldn't have to shell out a penny for it, Wall Street investors would pay the bills.

If everything worked right.

The waiter struggled through the crowd with Jake's drink and swiftly departed again. Knowles, who had been sipping on what looked like ginger ale, leaned slightly across the booth's table.

"So what's your problem, Jake?"

"McMasters wants to renew the ethanol additive for gasoline."

Knowles's brows hiked up. "What's that got to do with space?"

"It might be a ploy to unravel the plan before it really gets started."

"You're getting a Washington disease, pal."

"A Washington disease?"

"Paranoia."

Despite himself, Jake grinned at the ex-astronaut.

The waiter came back and asked for their luncheon order. Both men asked for burgers—rare.

Once the waiter disappeared again, Jake hunched forward and shook his head. "Even paranoids have enemies, Ike."

Knowles made a skeptical face.

"But it's not paranoia, really," Jake explained. "McMasters wants to be president. He's willing to trade the ethanol subsidy to collapse the space plan, which would be a slap in Sebastian's face."

"And Sebastian would be perfectly willing to scuttle your Project *Artemis*."

"He's never thought much of it. Agreed to back it in exchange for Frank's settling for the vice president's slot instead of fighting him for the top job."

"Politics," Knowles said, as if it were a dirty word.

"This could get nasty," said Jake.

Knowles shrugged. "Well, I haven't heard anything about this wrinkle. All my pigeons are flocking around, looking for easy money."

Jake felt his teeth clenching. With an effort he said, "I thought you ought to know."

"Like I don't already have enough to worry about."

"Keep on the lookout, will you, Ike? Please."

Knowles's grin reappeared. "For you, Jake, sure. No sweat."

Somehow Jake recalled a memory of Winston Churchill's words, "I have nothing to offer but blood, toil, tears, and sweat."

# Tamiko Umetzu

In a sense, Tamiko Umetzu was more American than George Washington. Tami was a fourth-generation American, descended from Japanese immigrants and born in the United States, near Fresno, California.

She had left her parents and siblings right after graduating from UCLA and gone to Washington, DC, where she was hired as a news reporter for the Reuters news agency. She was fired from that job at the insistence of Senator Mario Santino, then chair of the Senate Energy Committee. The "Little Saint" had gotten furious over an exposé Tami wanted to make public.

Jake had met Tami while she worked for Earthguard, an environmental lobbying firm, after she'd been effectively blackballed by Santino. They soon fell in love and married. Now they lived near Dupont Circle, in the heart of the city. With Jake's help, Tami had landed a position as weekend anchor for a news program at WETA-TV, the Washington-based PBS station. Santino had retired from the Senate by then, to spend his last days in a suburban nursing home.

As Jake pushed through the front door of their apartment, he couldn't resist the old cliché from early television, "Honey, I'm ho–ome."

Tami called from the kitchen, "I'm in the scullery!"

He dropped his slim briefcase on the table next to the door and strode toward the kitchen. Tami came out to greet him: an elfin, dark-haired woman not quite as tall as his chin, with lovely high cheekbones and deep brown, almond-shaped eyes. She was wearing a pair of cutoff jeans and an old, rumpled T-shirt. Still, to Jake, she looked lovelier than a movie queen.

She threw her arms around his neck, he grasped her by the waist, and they kissed mightily.

"I missed you," Jake said, once they came up for air.

"Ditto, darling."

"How was New York?"

"Pulsating," she said. "Makes you realize how sedate Washington is."

"Sedate? First time I've ever heard this town called sedate."

Arm in arm, they headed for the kitchen.

Jake set dishes and silverware on the tiny foldout kitchen table while Tami put the final touches on a platter of raw fish. Jake often teased her that if sushi counted as cooking, he was going to make steak tartare—raw hamburger—next time it was his turn to prepare dinner.

But he had to admit that Tami's sushi was delicious, even though he still had trouble handling the chopsticks.

Tami grinned at him as he struggled with the fish. "Damned thing's not dead yet," Jake grumbled.

"You want a fork?" she asked.

Jake gave her a dark look. "Madam, you impugn my honor."

Tami laughed. "You're doing pretty well. Haven't dropped anything on the floor. Yet."

With a shake of his head Jake quoted a line from an old Cary Grant movie: "Is there no end to the tortures that an oriental mind can think up?"

Changing the subject, Tami asked, "What's happening at the office?"

Jake's cheerful grin immediately disappeared. "McMasters's people want to bring back the ethanol subsidy."

"Really? I thought that was all settled—"

"So did we. But it's back."

Jake swiftly outlined the problem and its possible consequences.

"That's a pretty roundabout way to attack your space plan," Tami said.

"McMasters is a roundabout character," replied Jake.

"What are you going to do about it?"

"Meeting with the president tomorrow. Right after lunch."

Tami nodded and dropped the subject.

## ■ The Oval Office

Jake still felt more than a little awed to be in the Oval Office. He always detoured around the Great Seal of the United States that was the centerpiece of the room's carpeting; he couldn't bring himself to step on it.

He took a chair between Tomlinson and O'Donnell, the three of them lined up before the president's handsome dark mahogany desk. President Bradley Sebastian sat in the high-backed dark leather chair behind the desk, the expression on his thin, wan, lined face almost accusative.

He's aged, Jake thought. He's only been president for a little more than a year, but he looks a lot older than he did at the inauguration. The weight of his responsibilities? Jake asked himself. Of course, he's not wearing any makeup, he's not facing the public. Just a small bunch of decision makers.

At one side of the president's desk sat Adam Westerly, the president's personal aide: round, bald, his fleshy face set in an almost perfectly blank expression. But Jake knew the office buzz about Westerly; he was the president's strong right arm, his hatchet man. Behind his bland, innocent face was the kind of man who could slit your throat while shaking your hand.

President Sebastian asked, "So Frank, what's your take on McMasters?"

Tomlinson shifted uneasily in his chair, then replied, "It might be a ploy to sink the *Artemis* program."

"The space plan?" the president said. "I don't see the connection."

O'Donnell spoke up. "McMasters wants your job, Mr. President. If he can scuttle the space plan it'll be a big black eye for you."

"But how's this ethanol business connected with the space plan?"

Tomlinson said, "He drops his objection to the ethanol deal if we cut down on the *Artemis* program."

"We can't do that," Jake heard himself object. "The plan's already in motion. Investors are putting their money into it."

"As long as we guarantee that they can't lose their money," Westerly said. His voice was soft, his expression nonconfrontational. But he'd made his point.

The president shook his head woefully. "I never liked that part of the plan, guaranteeing investors that we'll cover their asses."

Tomlinson said, "It'll work. I'm sure of it."

The president stared at him. "How much of your own money have you put into it, Frank?"

"One million dollars," Tomlinson answered firmly.

Westerly's brows hiked up. "A million? Really?"

Jake thought that both Westerly and the president looked jealous. Then Westerly shrugged and said, "Of course, it's all guaranteed by Uncle Sam. You can't lose."

"But I'll have to wait fifty years to get it back."

O'Donnell quipped, "We'd better keep inflation down."

A minimal smile creased President Sebastian's pale countenance. "That's for sure."

Tomlinson returned to the subject. "So what do you want us to do about McMasters, Mr. President?"

Sebastian looked as if he'd prefer to forget the entire matter. But he said, "Have one of your guys talk with one of McMasters's guys. See what we can work out."

"Are you willing to reinstate the ethanol deal?" asked O'Donnell.

Nodding, the president replied, "If we have to. Might get us some votes out West."

And eviscerate the *Artemis* program, Jake added. Bitterly. Silently.

Jake sat glumly at his desk chair, staring at the box chart on his computer screen. The *Artemis* program. *His* space plan. He'd had plenty of help putting it together, experts from private industry, NASA, universities. But when push came to shove, it was Jake's plan—and he mightily wanted it to succeed.

But it was stalled at its very beginning. There had been one launch to the Moon: an unmanned mission carrying the components of a crew habitat to be erected on the Moon's surface. The package had been sitting in the middle of a crater called Scott, near the lunar South Pole, for almost a year. A human crew was supposed to land there and construct the habitat as the first step in building a permanent base on the Moon.

But the launch of the human team had been delayed—more than once. Jake stared at the map on his screen and wondered if his plan for the utilization of the Moon's resources was ever going to become reality.

His desk phone buzzed. Absently, his eyes still on the screen's display, Jake reached across his desk and picked up the receiver.

"It's eleven-thirty, Dr. Ross," his executive assistant announced. "You asked me to remind you."

"Yes," he said, his lunar trance broken. "Thanks, Nancy."

No more Moon gazing, he told himself as he replaced the phone's receiver. Time to meet McMasters's toady.

## ■ Phillips Seafood Restaurant

Jake took a taxi to Phillips Seafood Restaurant, on the Potomac River across the tidal basin from the Jefferson Memorial. It was a pretty location, and the restaurant was crowded, but not with the kind of Washington insiders who flocked to the K Street area eateries. Phillips was jammed with tourists, weary-looking families who had spent their morning toting bright-eyed young children through the capital's museums and galleries.

Jake had to push his way through a crowd of harried parents and yammering children clustered at the entrance to ask the receptionist for Mr. Donofrio's table.

The woman behind the reception counter gave him a slightly puzzled look, then hissed, "*Ms.* Donofrio." Before Jake could react, she grabbed an oversized menu and led him into the crowded, noisy restaurant.

*Ms.* Donofrio turned out to be a smart-looking young woman with stylishly short, tightly curled bright-red hair; somewhere in her twenties or early thirties, at most, Jake guessed as he slid into the booth where she was sitting.

She smiled prettily and said, "Dr. Ross," as she extended her hand to him.

"Jake," he said, taking her hand briefly.

"Jake," she repeated. Then, "I'm Jean."

Jake realized he had heard "Gene" when he'd made this luncheon arrangement with one of the executive assistants in Senator McMasters's office.

Feeling slightly flustered, Jake said, "Good to meet you."

"And you."

His initial embarrassment dissolved as he and Jean Donofrio exchanged pleasantries and ordered their lunches.

"I've never met a science advisor before," Jean said, smiling prettily. "I was expecting someone rather older, professorial."

Jake couldn't help smiling back at her. "I think I'm the first scientist Frank Tomlinson ever met." Before she could respond to that, he quickly added, "Of course, he's dealt with lots of them since coming to Washington."

"Of course," said Jean.

It was hard to judge her height while she was sitting down, Jake realized, but he guessed that she was at least a head taller than Tami. Good-looking, in a street-smart New Yorkish way. Stylishly dressed in an off-white blouse with a coral jacket over it. Pretty smile.

"What's your position in Senator McMasters's office?"

Still smiling, she answered, "I'm the senator's personal assistant."

"What do you know about the ethanol question?"

"The senator feels it was a mistake to cut the ethanol subsidy out of your energy bill. He thinks it should be reinstated."

It took a conscious effort to keep himself from frowning. "You know, we went through all this about ethanol when the energy bill was debated."

With a quick nod, Jean replied, "The senator feels the issue should be reexamined."

"Pressure from the energy corporations?"

"You have no idea."

All right, Jake said to himself. You know what comes next. But somehow he didn't want to take that step. Instead he asked, "What do you think we should do?"

Jean Donofrio's smile slowly faded. "I suppose you ought to reinstate the ethanol subsidy."

"Is that what McMasters wants?"

For a long, breath-holding moment the woman was silent, staring at Jake. Her eyes were grayish-green, he saw.

Intriguing.

"Can you keep a secret?" she asked.

Despite himself, Jake broke into a chuckle. "Nobody in this town can keep a secret, you must know that."

She nodded, ruefully. "Yes. It was a stupid question, wasn't it?"

"Kind of."

Jean reached across the table to touch Jake's hand. "It's just that ..."

"What?"

"The senator is worried about your space plan."

There! said a voice in Jake's head. It's out in the open now.

"The *Artemis* program?" He tried to look surprised. "I don't see the connection."

"That's because there isn't any. Not really."

"Then what—"

"Senator McMasters feels that your space plan is a waste of time and money. He thinks it should be cut back, or stopped altogether."

Jake heard himself reply, "It's a big vote-getter. Especially among younger voters."

Jean Donofrio said nothing.

"It's the wave of the future," Jake went on. "It's like Europe discovering the New World. New industries, new opportunities, new worlds ...."

"Senator McMasters doesn't see it that way."

"Then he's ..." Jake held himself back just in time. He took a breath, then finished, "Then he's behind the march of history. He's not fit to be president."

Strangely, Jean's smile returned. "I think you're right," she said. "But my boss doesn't agree."

# Jean Donofrio

For several moments Jake sat there, staring into those sexy gray-green eyes. She thinks I'm right? he asked himself. So where do we go from here?

Jean broke the silence. "I'm tired of working for Senator McMasters. He's a self-important little jerk. I would like to join Tomlinson's team. Your team."

Jake knew he should say something, speak up, reply to her request. But no words came out of his mouth.

Breaking into a sunny smile, Jean said, "You look surprised."

"That's because I am surprised," Jake admitted. "I had no idea ...."

With a shrug, Jean said, "I've been working with Eugene long enough to feel threatened."

"Threatened?"

"Eugene is after my body. Oh, he hasn't said it in so many words, but I understand the looks he gives me, the times in his office when the two of us are alone. He's hunting and I'm his target."

Jake heard himself squeak, "Target?"

"A couple of the older women in the office told me about him. He goes after the unattached females, and once he's had them, he finds a reason to get rid of them."

"McMasters does that?"

Jean nodded solemnly. "I'm in his crosshairs," she said. "And it's damned uncomfortable."

"So you want to get out of there."

"Indeed I do. Is there any way you could get Vice President Tomlinson to hire me?"

Jake blinked at her, perplexed by this wholly unexpected disclosure.

Her hopeful smile faded. "I've embarrassed you," she said. "I shouldn't have been so ... so open."

"No, no," Jake protested. "It's just ... well, this is something of a surprise."

She nodded minimally. "I should have realized that it would be."

He heard himself say, "I can talk to Frank about it."

"Would you?"

"Sure. Of course. Come to think of it, I'll be needing a full-time assistant as the *Artemis* program goes into high gear."

"You mean we could work together?"

"Let me ask Frank about it."

"Oh, thank you, Jake! Thank you so much."

"I can't promise anything."

"I know. Of course. But I appreciate your willingness to try to help me."

Jake nodded, while a voice in his head warned him that Jean Donofrio had manipulated him very neatly.

## ■ Vice President Tomlinson's Office

"She wants to work here, with us?" Franklin Tomlinson's face showed surprise mixed with suspicion.

Adam Westerly was sitting at one side of the vice president's desk; Tomlinson had asked the president's aide to hear what Jake had to report on his meeting with Senator McMasters's personal assistant.

To Jake, the oversized Westerly looked like a large roundish pile of rumpled clothes with a bald head atop it. As usual, his facial expression was almost perfectly blank.

Jake realized that he was biting his lip. With a conscious effort he opened his mouth and said, "I'm going to need a full-time assistant, you know ... as the *Artemis* program moves into high gear."

Tomlinson nodded and turned to Westerly. "What do you think, Adam?"

Westerly hiked his eyebrows instead of answering. The vice president said, "She could give us some valuable information about what's going on in McMasters's camp."

Nodding his multiple chins, Westerly said softly, "Or give McMasters valuable info on what's going on here."

Jake realized the implication. "You think she'd be a spy for McMasters?"

With a sighing shrug, Westerly answered, "Could be."

I don't think so," Jake said.

Tomlinson smiled at Jake. "Did she come on to you, Jake?"

"No! And if she had I wouldn't be here asking you to hire her."

Westerly broke into a grin. "Pure of heart, eh?"

"I'm a married man, Adam."

"So's McMasters."

Tomlinson leaned back in his desk chair and glanced out the window, at the view of the Capitol. "McMasters figures that if he could get us to cut back on the space plan it would hurt the president's stature in the voters' eyes."

"The boss's standing is forty-eight percent favorable, as of this morning. Not too shabby," said Westerly.

"Forty-eight?" Tomlinson asked.

"And sinking. It's a slow trend, but it's noticeable."

Jake said, "Then the *last* thing he should do is scuttle the *Artemis* program. It's got lots of support among the voters."

Westerly shook his head hard enough to make his cheeks wobble. "Jake, you're too close to the plan to see it in the larger context."

"What's that supposed to mean?"

Leaning in Jake's direction, the president's hatchet man explained, "The space plan has lots of support among the voters, true enough. But it's thin support. They see space as something ... how the hell should I put it?"

"Exciting," said Jake.

"Yeah, kind of," Westerly granted. "But not close to home. Not a bread-and-butter issue. Not as important as the employment figures, or the wars in Latin America, or crime in the streets."

"A pretty picture for the future," said Tomlinson. "Not a gut issue."

Jake stared at the vice president. "Frank, is that what you believe?"

Tomlinson glanced at Westerly before answering, "No. But it's what the voters believe."

"Pie in the sky," Westerly muttered.

"But it's important!" Jake insisted. "It's the most important goddamned thing this country can do."

With a slight frown and a shake of his head, Tomlinson said, "Jake, we're not going to scrap the space plan.

"We're going ahead with it."

Jake nodded, but he knew that the vice president's assurance was paper thin.

"It would help if the president was more enthusiastic about it," said Westerly.

Tomlinson agreed solemnly. "Amen to that."

For a long moment the three men sat in silence, each wrapped in his own thoughts.

Then Westerly said, "So what do you want to do about this Donofrio woman?"

The vice president blinked twice, then replied, "I suppose we should at least have a look at her."

"I could use a first-rate assistant," Jake said.

"She's probably going to be a spy for McMasters," Westerly warned.

"I don't think so," Jake objected.

With a thin smile, Tomlinson said to Westerly, "You don't want her in here, do you, Adam?"

"Hell no."

Jake started to say something, but thought better of it and kept his mouth shut.

"Let's take a look at her," said the vice president. "Adam, if you don't like what you see, then we won't take her on. Okay?"

"Deal," said Westerly. Jake nodded.

## ■ Spaceport America

Staring out the plane's window at the stark brown desert landscape, Jake realized that he felt good being out of Washington, even if it was only for a couple of days.

The land of the Navajo spread across his view, harsh and pitiless, but somehow beautiful. He always felt liberated, expansive in the limitless stark open desert lands of New Mexico.

We should move the capital here, he thought, out of Washington. Here, where water is really precious, where you realize every day how hard it is to survive. But the Navajo survive. So do the Zuni and the other tribes. They survive and even prosper, free, living in their own way.

The captain's voice came over the plane's loudspeaker: "We're starting our final approach to the Spaceport America landing field. Please make certain your seatbelts are securely fastened."

Jake tugged at his belt. It was tight enough to cut off the circulation in his legs—almost.

He leaned back in his seat as the plane completed its approach turn, lowered to the ground, and hit the concrete runway with a screech of tires.

Nicholas Piazza was standing at the doorway at the end of the access tunnel that connected Jake's plane to the Spaceport America reception building.

Piazza was the founder and CEO of Astra Corporation, one of the biggest private space firms and a major part of Jake's space plan. Well over six feet tall, he towered over Jake as he welcomed him to Spaceport America.

"Good to see you again, Jake. How are you?" he said as he engulfed Jake's hand in a strong grip.

With a grin, Jake said, "I'm fine. How're you?"

Releasing Jake's hand, Piazza made a "so-so" motion.

"Been better. Also been worse."

A young Native American man came up and silently took Jake's travel bag as Piazza led the way through the smallish airport reception area and out into the brilliant New Mexico sunshine.

A bright, new-looking sea-green Ferrari was parked just outside the main entrance.

"Looks new," said Jake.

"Two weeks old. She's a beauty, isn't she?"

Jake nodded.

Piazza grinned happily. He seemed quite young, with the kind of face that would look youthful when he was eighty: bright, inquisitive pale blue eyes, strong cheekbones, little stub of a nose. His hair was wispy, windblown, his skin a deep tan.

The young man popped the car's trunk and tossed Jake's travel bag into it, then slammed the lid and squeezed himself into the car's narrow rear seat. Piazza slid in behind the wheel while Jake climbed into the right-hand seat.

"So how's everything going, Nick?" Jake asked.

With a wide smile, Piazza answered—"Lousy." Then the car's engine started up with a deep-throated roar and they zoomed out of the parking slot.

Jake grabbed the seat belt angled across his chest in both hands as Piazza tooled through the parking lot and down an empty two-lane road.

"She'll do a hundred twenty easy," he yelled over the Ferrari's husky growl.

Jake nodded and glanced at the speedometer. The needle hovered around eighty.

Fortunately, the Astra Corporation's headquarters was less than five miles from the airport. Piazza pulled the car off the highway and screeched to a stop at a parking spot marked, RESERVED FOR THE BOSS.

Jake let out a puff of breath as Piazza turned off the car's engine. "You ought to be more careful, Nick. If anything should happen to you—"

Grinning, Piazza interrupted with, "Shakespeare said, 'We owe God a death … he that dies this year is quit for the next.' "

As he climbed out of the car Jake said, "I'd rather owe Him for as long as I can"

Piazza laughed. "Come on, Jake. Here we are, safe and sound."

Jake shook his head. "I'd rather ride a rocket to the Moon, Nick."

Piazza's smile faded as he got out of the car. "So would I, Jake. So would I."

## ■ Astra Corporation Headquarters

Jake followed Piazza into the glass-walled headquarters of Astra Corporation, and up a short flight of stairs to Piazza's office.

A sea of desks spread across the ground floor, but Jake saw that only about half were occupied.

"Kind of quiet," Jake said as Piazza ushered him into his private office.

Piazza strode to the impressive desk set in a corner of the office and plopped down into the high-backed swivel chair behind it.

"Quiet," he agreed. "Yeah."

Jake sat in one of the three dark-upholstered chairs in front of the desk. "I thought you were ready to launch a crewed mission to Scott Crater."

"I'm ready," Piazza snapped, his usually gentle voice hard-edged. "The rocket is ready. My people are ready. But the goddamned safety board back in Washington isn't ready. They won't let us move a frickin' inch."

Jake sank back in his chair. "What's the holdup?"

"They claim it's safety regulations. Everything's got to be inspected six ways from Sunday."

"Well, you do have a team of people riding your bird.

First launch of humans to the Moon since *Apollo 17*."

Piazza shook his head. "They're deliberately slowing us down, Jake. They don't want to see us go."

"That's—"

"You've got to do something, Jake," Piazza urged. "We can't have our whole schedule fucked up by some goddamned bureaucrats in Washington!"

"I'll … see what I can do," Jake replied, weakly.

Leveling an accusatory finger at Jake, Piazza said, "You do that."

Jake heard hot anger simmering behind the words. NASA held the power to delay Astra Corporation's Moon shot. Plenty of bureaucrats in Washington did not want to see a private company delivering the first humans to the Moon in nearly seventy years.

The two men stared at each other for several long, silent moments. Abruptly, Piazza pushed himself out of his chair.

"Come on," he said to Jake. "Let's go see the bird."

Somehow, everything seemed better once Jake and Piazza entered Astra Corporation's vehicle-assembly building. There was the gleaming white rocket that Piazza had dubbed *Lunar Express* stretched out before Jake's eyes. Even lying on its side like a beached whale it looked tremendously impressive.

Standing at one end of the giant bird, Jake craned his neck to look up at the five immense rocket nozzles, each one of them big enough for a man to stand up erect inside it.

"All dressed up and nowhere to go," Piazza said, mournfully.

"What's your launch window?" Jake asked.

"We've got another six days. After that, the next opportunity isn't until the end of next month."

Grimly, Jake said, "And you've got six astronauts set to go."

With a curt nod, Piazza replied, "And all they're doing is waiting, getting rusty, while those bastards in Washington sit on their goddamn hands."

"I'll see what I can do."

"You do that."

Jake spent the rest of the afternoon in Piazza's office, on the phone with the NASA bureaucracy in Washington. As he spoke with one pen pusher after another, a vague memory of a line from his high school Shakespeare classes threaded through his mind: "fat, sleek-headed men …."

One after another, they agreed and promised to do all they could to resolve the safety issues involved in the Astra Corporation's launch. And then passed Jake on to the next level of their bureaucracy.

It's like dealing with an octopus, Jake thought. You get past one arm and there's seven more waiting for you.

Finally he slammed Piazza's phone down on its receiver, with a heartfelt, "Damn!"

"See what we're up against?" Piazza asked, sitting in his desk chair with a forlorn expression souring his normally bright face.

Jake picked up the phone again. "Get me William T. Farthington, NASA Headquarters in Washington, DC."

Piazza sat up straighter in his swivel chair. "Bloviating Billy? Lotsa luck."

But within a few minutes William Farthington's round, bland face appeared on the desk phone's miniature screen.

"Jake!" said NASA's chief administrator. "How are you?"

"Frustrated," said Jake.

Immediately Farthington responded, "The Astra Corporation launch."

"Yep. Nick Piazza's people are being drowned in delays."

Farthington nodded unhappily. "I know."

"Can you do anything about it?"

For a long moment the NASA chief didn't reply. At last, "You know I'm leaving the agency."

Jake nodded. "So I heard."

"This job has aged me ten years."

Jake felt his lips curving into a hard smile. "How'd you like to go out in a blaze of glory?"

# Homeward Bound

Jake sat back and relaxed in his comfortable first-class seat, heading back home to Washington and Tami. He felt an inner glow of satisfaction. Bloviating Billy—William Farthington, the head of NASA—was throwing the fear of hell and damnation into the bureaucrats who worked for him.

Bloviating Billy was the nickname that William Farthington had acquired in Washington. Formerly a general in the army's Quartermaster Corps, Farthington had been appointed chief administrator of NASA on the strength of his talent for organization, not for any zeal in pushing harder and higher on the space frontier.

He was a master of elaborate speeches that essentially said nothing: *bloviating*, in Washington jargon. His job, as the Congress saw it, was to preside over NASA's gradual shrinkage. When he came into the agency's top job, no NASA-crewed mission had gone farther than the International Space Station—a few hundred miles above the Earth—for well more than several decades.

Then came B. Franklin Tomlinson with Jake Ross's ambitious space plan to return astronauts to the Moon; build a permanent base there; and begin to use the natural resources and the airless, low-gravity lunar environment to develop a base for new industries.

Not a government program. Jake's plan was based on using private industry, private investment. NASA would provide expertise and facilities, but not control, not direction.

When Bradley Sebastian was elected president of the United States, B. Franklin Tomlinson became his vice president, and Jake Ross's *Artemis* program became the United States' official path to the stars.

Except that NASA wanted to run the show. And if it couldn't run things, it would do its best to slow everything down to the point where the Congress grew tired of delays and outright failures and cancelled the entire operation.

The key to the problem was NASA's management. Would the agency work to get the space plan moving, or slow it down to the point of frustration and failure?

The agency's reaction was obvious. If NASA wasn't going to be in charge, then NASA certainly wouldn't strain itself to help the plan succeed.

Jake tried to get the agency's whole-hearted cooperation. The working stiffs—the engineers and technicians, the men and women who actually dealt with the hardware, who launched the rockets, who made everything *work*—they were eager to be a part of the exciting new space plan. But their managers and directors saw Jake's plan as a threat to their own security, their own ambitions, their own careers.

Thus NASA was officially a partner in the new space plan, but actually the agency was doing its best to slow down the program, to frustrate its ambitious goals, to sabotage the effort.

The big surprise in this administrative tangle was Bloviating Billy Farthington. Appointed chief administrator of NASA on his reputation as a paper shuffler who could quietly preside over the space agency's shrinkage, William T. Farthington had more guts and guile than almost anyone in Washington understood.

One of the people who recognized Farthington's hidden strengths was Jacob Ross, science advisor to the vice president of the United States.

Now Jake sat relaxed and smiling in his first-class seat aboard the Boeing 737 winging high above the green Midwest, heading for Washington.

Farthington was setting fires under his reluctant administrators, telling them in plain language to get Astra Corporation's bird off the ground or get themselves into the unemployment line.

It was the kind of move that seldom made headlines, but it would make Mike Piazza happy, and Jake felt good about that.

"I'll go out in a blaze of glory," Farthington had promised Jake. "That's more than I ever dared to hope for."

"Thanks, Mr. Farthington," Jake had said into his telephone. "Thanks a tremendous lot."

Even in his phone's minuscule screen, Jake could see Farthington's round, chubby face break into a pleased smile. "Thank *you*, Jake. And please call me Bill."

Jake leaned back in the plane's seat and closed his eyes. "Good work, soldier," he murmured.

He was just starting to ease into sleep when he felt a tap on his shoulder. Opening his eyes, he saw one of the flight attendants bending over him.

"Could you come up to the cockpit, please, Mr. Ross?" she half-whispered. "There's an urgent call for you."

Jake blinked. "A call?"

"High priority. From Washington."

Puzzled, Jake unclicked his safety belt and pushed himself to his feet. A call from Washington? he wondered. Why didn't they just call my cell—

Then a sudden fear gripped him. Tami! Something's happened to Tami!

He followed the flight attendant, who opened the door to the cockpit and gestured him into the flight compartment. It was a tight squeeze: Jake had to bend over slightly to keep his head from brushing the compartment's low ceiling. The copilot, on the right, turned in his seat.

"Jacob Ross?" he asked.

Jake nodded and said, "Yes."

The copilot handed him his own headset. Jake clamped the earphone to his head and adjusted the mike to his lips.

"Hello? This is Jake Ross."

It was Kevin O'Donnell's voice. "Jake?" "Yes!"

"It's the president. He's dying."

# Death

Jake stood slightly hunched over in the flight compartment for several long, breathless moments. O'Donnell's voice crackled in the earphone, urgent, tense: "Did you hear me? The president's had a stroke. A bad one. The medics only give him a couple of hours to live."

"I'm on my way into Washington," Jake said. As if that made any difference.

"When do you land?"

Jake asked the copilot, who gave him their expected time of arrival. He repeated the information to O'Donnell.

"I'll have a car waiting for you."

"Thanks, Kevin."

"Frank's back in Montana," said O'Donnell. "He's catching an air force jet to get back here."

Nodding, Jake began to ask, "How long does Sebastian have?"

"I told you," the chief of Tomlinson's staff said, with some irritation. "Two, three hours. Maybe less. We've got to circle the wagons damned fast."

"I'll be there in a couple of hours."

"Good. Come straight to the White House. And don't breathe a word of this to anybody. Not anybody!"

"Right."

The connection clicked off. Jake stood there, leaning against the compartment's closed door, his thoughts swirling.

The copilot reached up from his seat and took the headphone set from Jake's hands. "Bad news?" he asked.

Jake nodded wordlessly, turned, and opened the door to return to his seat—one thought burning through all the others spinning through his mind: Frank's going to become president of the United States. B. Franklin Tomlinson is going to be our president.

He sank back into his first-class seat, more bewildered than anything else, wondering what the future might bring.

A bulky, broad-shouldered Black man in a tight-fitting three-piece dark-blue suit was waiting for Jake as he stepped from the access tunnel into Washington National Airport's terminal.

"Jacob Ross?" he asked, in a deep, rumbling voice.

"Yes," Jake replied.

"Mr. O'Donnell sent me to pick you up."

The man didn't look like a chauffeur—more like one of the White House Secret Service guards. Without another word he took Jake's travel bag and led him through the crowded, noisy airport corridor and outside to a dark sedan parked under a No Parking sign. He opened the car's rear door, Jake climbed in. The driver tossed Jake's bag onto the right-hand seat, slid in behind the steering wheel, and merged into the heavy traffic.

Jake fished out his phone to call Tami. "No calls, sir," said the driver.

"I want to tell my wife I've arrived."

"No calls, sir."

"She'll get worried if I don't call."

For several moments they proceeded along the highway in silence.

"I won't tell her anything about the situation."

"I'm sorry, sir, but my orders are—"

"Fuck your orders!" Jake snapped. "If I don't tell her I've arrived safely she'll have the district police looking for me."

He could see the driver's red-rimmed eyes glaring at him. After a seemingly eternal moment the man finally said, "Okay, but no word about the president."

"I promise," Jake heard himself say. He felt ridiculous about it.

Tami picked up on the second ring. "Jake?"

"Landed safe and sound," he said, trying to make it light, happy.

"Good. Wonderful! I've got dinner—"

"I'm not coming straight home, honey. Something's come up at the White House and I've got to go there first."

"Oh?" Tami sounded only mildly disappointed.

"I'll get home as soon as I can," Jake promised. Then he added, "But it might be pretty late."

"Another dinner alone," Tami complained.

"Sorry, hon."

"That's the price I pay for marrying an important man."

"I love you."

"Ditto."

Jake tapped the End Call button and stuffed the phone back into his jacket pocket. Glancing at the car's rearview mirror, he saw his driver nod once, satisfied.

From the outside, the White House seemed normal. The marines at the gate checked Jake's ID as they always did, then waved the sedan through. The grounds looked as they usually did. Even the entrance to the presidential mansion appeared undisturbed.

But once he stepped through the entrance and into the house itself, Jake could feel the tension. The entryway crackled with electricity. Nearly a dozen aides, secretaries, even marine corps guards in their colorful uniforms were buzzing everywhere.

A plump middle-aged woman whom Jake recognized as one of Kevin O'Donnell's staff people hurried up to Jake.

"Dr. Ross! You're here," she gushed.

Jake suppressed an urge to ask where else could he be. Instead he said, "I got here as quickly as I could."

She gestured with one chubby hand. "Upstairs," she said, in a low voice. "Follow me."

Jake trailed behind her to the elevator that brought them up to the White House's top floor, the residence of the president and his family. The upper floor's central hallway was filled with people, some of them scurrying busily along, most sitting along the side walls, looking morose, worried, visibly depressed.

Before Jake had taken even half a dozen steps along the carpeted hallway, Kevin O'Donnell popped out of a doorway, rake thin, tight as a high-tension line.

O'Donnell bustled up to him. "Jake! You made it!"

"How is he?"

"Dying. The medics don't want a big crowd around him," O'Donnell said in a near whisper as he led Jake down the corridor. The vice president's chief of staff looked more flustered and nervous than usual—his wispy light-brown hair plastered every which way over his balding dome, beads of perspiration dotting his upper lip.

"Where's Frank?"

"He's on his way in. Riding in the back seat of an air force F-15, no less. Should be here in about a half hour."

Jake nodded.

O'Donnell cracked a door open and peered in. Pushing the door wider, he turned his head toward Jake and whispered, "There he is."

Surrounded by grim-faced doctors, President Bradley Sebastian lay in a double bed, his sunken face paler than the bedsheets, his eyes half closed. To Jake, he looked already dead. His wife was sitting in a corner, weeping softly into a dainty handkerchief.

Jake whispered, "How long ...?"

O'Donnell waggled his right hand. "Not long," he whispered back. Then he shrugged, "Helluva way to become the top dog."

Before Jake could figure out a response to that, he heard the throbbing roar of a helicopter outside. Must be Frank, he thought.

# Transition

O'Donnell gently closed the bedroom door. Jake realized that despite the crowd in the hallway, everyone was trying hard to be quiet. Tiptoes and whispers.

He followed O'Donnell down the crowded but deathly hushed hallway, back toward the elevator.

"We've got a lot to do," said O'Donnell, his voice low, "and a damned short time to get it done. Word's gotten out to the news reporters. They're gathering downstairs."

Jake nodded. "How can I help, Kevin?"

O'Donnell shrugged his bone-thin shoulders. "Don't know yet. But I'd appreciate it if you hung around."

"Sure. Can I tell Tami what's happening? She—"

"No! Not a word, not until we figure out what Frank wants to say, how he wants to put it."

Jake clamped his lips together and forced down the anger that surged within him. Tami can keep her mouth shut, he thought. But he didn't say it aloud.

The elevator doors slid open and out stepped B. Franklin Tomlinson, the next president of the United States.

"Where is he, Kevin?" Tomlinson asked. His face was more deeply serious than Jake had ever seen it before, his usual jaunty grin nowhere in sight.

"This way," said O'Donnell, gesturing toward the bedroom door up the corridor.

Jake followed the two men back to the bedroom where President Sebastian lay. He stopped at the doorway. Tomlinson strode through the medical people gathered around the dying man's bed, dropped to one knee at the bedside, and grasped Sebastian's frail hand in both his own. He bowed his head in prayer. Sebastian turned his head slightly toward Tomlinson, and Jake could see that the president's face was distorted, its left side pulled down hideously, obscenely.

Jake thought that the sight would make a dramatic tableau for the evening news broadcasts, but he kept his lips clamped tightly shut.

Once Tomlinson got to his feet and let go of the dying president's hand, O'Donnell grabbed him by the elbow and steered him back outside, into the hallway.

"The chief justice is on his way," O'Donnell told Tomlinson. "He'll administer the oath of office."

"We're going to wait until Sebastian is dead, aren't we?" Tomlinson asked, completely serious.

"Yeah, sure. Of course."

Jake followed the two men as they walked slowly down the crowded hallway. People made way for them without a word. The corridor felt strangely quiet to Jake: all these people bustling around, but no one speaking above a whisper.

The elevator doors slid open again and the chief justice of the Supreme Court stepped out into the crowded hallway, followed by Amy, Tomlinson's wife. The chief justice was wearing a slightly rumpled, dark, three-piece suit; Amy was impeccably outfitted in a black, knee-length dress, with a single string of pearls and pearl earrings her only adornment.

Jake felt himself tensing up. All dressed up and nowhere to go, he thought. Not until Sebastian gives up the ghost.

As if in answer, the president's personal physician stepped into the hallway, his face a mask of grief. Everyone turned toward him.

"He's gone," said the doctor. "Three forty-three P.M."

For a moment, the crowd stood frozen. Then Kevin O'Donnell turned to one of the uniformed marines and said, "Go downstairs and tell the reporters they can come up here now."

The ritual was brief, dignified. Tomlinson stood in the middle of the central hallway before the chief justice, his right hand raised, his left on a Bible that O'Donnell had somehow provided.

"I do solemnly swear that I will faithfully execute the office of president of the United States, and will to the best of my ability preserve, protect, and defend the Constitution of the United States."

Jake heard the words, the same words that Harry Truman had spoken. And Lyndon Johnson. And all the others.

The nation goes on. Despite death, despite wars and natural disasters, the nation goes on. The people elect their leaders and not even death can halt us.

Tomlinson turned to his wife and briefly embraced her. Then he raised his head and looked at the journalists gathered a little farther down the hallway.

"That's it for now," he said, his face tight, strained. "I'll have a statement for the public later this evening. Thank you."

Without a word, without a shouted question, the reporters and camera operators turned away and headed for the stairs that led down to the ground floor of the White House.

O'Donnell stepped up to the new president and stuck his hand out. "Congratulations, boss."

Tomlinson smiled weakly. "Maybe condolences would be more fitting."

"You're going to be a great president," O'Donnell countered.

Tomlinson's smile broadened a little. He quoted Hemingway: "Yes. Isn't it pretty to think so."

# President of the United States

Jake rode with President Tomlinson, his wife Amy, and Kevin O'Donnell from the White House to the official residence of the vice president, on the grounds of the Naval Observatory, a few minutes' drive from the White House.

The vice president's residence was a Queen Anne style three-story house from the Victorian era, rambling and elderly looking in Jake's eyes, with a steeply pitched roof and a couple of rounded turrets that would have looked better on a medieval castle. Tomlinson used it mainly for entertaining and housing some of his staff; he preferred to actually live in the house he and Amy had rented in the quiet residential neighborhood north of Georgetown.

"I ought to address the nation," Tomlinson said, as their limousine tooled up the winding driveway. The Sun had set, and shadows of night were creeping across the residence's gloomy structure.

"Sooner the better," O'Donnell agreed. "Kevin, can you get the speechwriters—"

"They're already cobbling something together for you," O'Donnell interrupted. "I've had them at it since earlier this afternoon."

Tomlinson nodded and murmured, "Good work, Kevin."

Even in the limo's darkened interior, Jake could see O'Donnell's pleased smile.

* * *

By nine that evening, Tomlinson was at the desk in the vice-presidential residence's spacious office, reviewing the speech that the writers had prepared, scratching away with his ballpoint pen, eliminating some phrases, strengthening others, adding a personal touch.

By ten o'clock, he was ready to face the cameras that the various news networks had trucked in. His office had been transformed into a television studio, with the new president seated behind the venerable cherrywood desk, facing a battery of cameras and lights.

His speech was displayed on the monitors set at either side of him and on a flat display screen on the desktop. The TV director—picked by lot from the dozen or so crowding the book-lined room—pointed a finger at Tomlinson.

He looked into the camera stationed in front of his desk and said, "Good evening, my fellow Americans. I am saddened to tell you that President Bradley Sebastian passed away earlier this evening, the victim of a cerebral hemorrhage.

As specified in our Constitution, I took the oath of office immediately after he was pronounced dead. I am now your president."

Glancing to his right, where his wife Amy was standing between Jake and Kevin O'Donnell, President Tomlinson continued, "This is a time for grieving for the past and working toward our future. As your president, I will strive to continue the programs that Bradley Sebastian championed, and work with both the political parties in the Congress to see that these programs move forward toward success.

"My goal is the same as yours—to see our democracy advance, to see that our people prosper, to see that the world becomes safer and stronger. We will face difficulties, problems of every description and complexity. But with your support, we cannot fail. America will continue to move forward, to lead the world into a new era of prosperity and peace. God bless the United States of America." And, following a solemn pause, "Thank you."

Tomlinson was staring straight into the camera in front of the desk as the TV lights winked out and the group gathered in the room exhaled audibly. No one applauded.

Jake felt the speech was too short, too abrupt. But it was what Tomlinson wanted to say, he said it, and that was that.

Now to see how the newspeople reacted to it.

That reaction—in the morning newspapers and TV commentaries—was generally positive. Tomlinson was credited with being brief and properly respectful to the late President Sebastian. Jake read the newspaper coverage off the computer screen at his desk in the White House, in the vice president's suite of offices, and watched snippets of TV commentaries for most of the morning.

Then O'Donnell's executive assistant called to tell him there was going to be a meeting with the president at eleven o'clock in the Oval Office.

Jake nodded at the young woman's image on his wall screen. Frank's not wasting any time, he thought. Good.

When Jake entered the Oval Office, Kevin O'Donnell was already seated at the right of the president's desk, deep in conversation with Tomlinson. Adam Westerly, the late President Sebastian's personal aide, was sitting in front of the desk. Nobody else was in the room.

President Tomlinson had taken off his suit jacket, as usual, and draped it across the back of his swivel chair. He sat there in his shirtsleeves and fire-engine red suspenders, nodding as O'Donnell yammered away about something.

Tomlinson looked up and smiled his megawatt smile as Jake entered the Oval Office. "Come on in, Jake. When is Piazza planning to launch his rocket?"

Jake blinked with surprise, then answered, "Next Wednesday, if everything goes right."

Tomlinson nodded. "I want to be there. I want to make a speech about our space policy."

Jake actually felt his knees go weak. He wants to make a speech about the *Artemis* program! At the launch center in New Mexico!

O'Donnell made a sour face. "And what if the launch doesn't go? What if the goddamned rocket blows up?"

"I'll make the speech anyway," said the president. "With a few changes, of course."

"It'll be a disaster," O'Donnell groaned.

"No it won't," Tomlinson countered. "It'll be a statement—a pledge—to carry on our program in spite of setbacks, in spite of problems."

Westerly—his round, chubby face set in a grim aspect—spoke up: "Mr. President, I think you should consider what your chief of staff is telling you."

Tomlinson closed his eyes and clasped his hands on the desk's edge. For about thirty seconds.

Then, opening his eyes, he said, "Okay, I've considered it. I'll make the speech at the launch site, no matter what happens to the damned rocket."

"That's crazy!" O'Donnell snapped.

"Maybe," the president conceded. "But I want to show the people that we're in this space program to stay. Despite setbacks. Despite delays. Despite competition from the Chinese or anybody else. We're going on. We're moving ahead. Period. End of discussion."

O'Donnell turned toward Westerly, who shrugged his heavy shoulders.

Jake thought, This could be the greatest boost our space effort has had since Kennedy's administration! But another voice in his head countered, *or the biggest fiasco.*

## ■ Spaceport America

It was eerily quiet in the predawn darkness of the New Mexico desert. Jake stood, Tami beside him, in the grandstand, which was packed with onlookers: government officials, curious tourists, families with little children.

But no one spoke above a whisper. Jake thought it was almost spooky. As if we're in a cathedral or a holy shrine.

Nearly two miles away from the crowded grandstand stood a towering, heavy-looking *Lunar Express* rocket booster, its white body catching the first rays of the Sun climbing above the distant mountains.

"The *Lunar Express* Space Launch Vehicle," an announcer's smooth voice came through the loudspeakers spotted around the grandstand, "or 'SLV' in the jargon of the launch team, was built by the United Launch Alliance, a consortium of Boeing and Lockheed Martin, two of the largest manufacturers in the world's space industries …."

Jake zoned the man's voice out of his attention and focused on the booster, standing tall and bright on its launchpad.

Artemis, he thought. The sister of Apollo. Somebody in Piazza's public relations department had looked up the ancient mythology to dig up that name for the new Moon-shot program.

A different voice broke into the announcer's spiel. "TWO MINUTES AND COUNTING. ALL SYSTEMS ARE GO."

The crowd in the grandstand seemed to take in a collective breath. All systems are go.

Isaiah Knowles nudged his way through the people standing next to Jake.

"Hello, Ike," said Jake. "How's it look?"

"No hitches," said Knowles. "Smooth and easy." But he wasn't smiling. To Jake, the former astronaut looked wired tight; his fingers were drumming against the seams of his trousers.

Prelaunch jitters, Jake knew. He felt them himself; his heart seemed to be bouncing around inside his chest.

The announcer was saying, "Six astronauts are set to return humankind's presence to the Moon. For the first time in more than sixty years, humans are going to the Moon!"

Jake had personally substituted "humankind" for "Americans." This was not the moment for nationalism, he felt.

The announcer's patter ended. The launch crew had come down from their positions in the gantry tower and ducked inside the blue and white Astra Corporation station wagons that surrounded the launchpad. Jake saw rooster tails of dust as the cars scooted away from the pad.

"ONE MINUTE AND COUNTING," came the launch controller's voice from the loudspeakers.

Tami clutched Jake's arm. He looked down at her and tried to smile. Nearly made it.

At T-minus thirty seconds, the umbilical cords that had been feeding electricity and oxygen to the *Lunar Express* dropped away. The spider work of the gantry tower slid back from the rocket, leaving it standing alone, waiting, waiting.

The loudspeakers blared out, "T-MINUS TWENTY-FIVE SECONDS."

Sunshine spilled across the desert floor. The stars of night had disappeared. The booster rocket stood proud against the clear blue sky.

"... fifteen ..." the waiting crowd took up the countdown chant. "... fourteen ... thirteen ...."

"ALL SYSTEMS ARE GO."

A cloud of steam billowed from beneath the launch structure. The crowd oohed.

"FIVE ... FOUR ... THREE ..."

The steam cloud flared red. From this distance Jake could not hear the roar of the rocket engines.

"... TWO ... ONE ... LAUNCH!"

For an instant nothing seemed to happen. Then slowly, majestically, the rocket rose out of the swirling cloud that surrounded the launchpad, up, up, straight into the clear blue sky, climbing higher and higher, spurting bright flaming exhaust from its tail. Jake let his binoculars dangle around his neck and craned his head to watch the SLV leaving the Earth.

The thunder of those rocket engines finally rolled over the grandstand, shaking everyone and everything there.

Jake felt his insides pulsating as he raised both his fists over his head and yelled, "Go, baby! Go!"

The loudspeakers blared, "For the first time since 1972 human beings are heading for the Moon. We are reopening the space frontier!" The announcer was speaking Jake's words.

The crowd cheered, laughed, stomped their feet so hard that Jake feared the grandstand might collapse. And the *Lunar Express* rocket, carrying six Americans, hurtled across the cloudless blue sky, dwindling until it was out of sight, heading for orbit and then on to the Moon.

Jake let his arms drop to his sides. The crowd around him stopped their cheering, but everyone was grinning, laughing, slapping hands with one another as if the launch was *their* doing.

And it was, in a way, Jake realized. They have a reason to feel satisfied. Those six astronauts heading to Scott Crater near the lunar South Pole are our representatives.

We've all had a part to play in this launch.

The crowd didn't budge from the grandstand until they saw the flash of light that marked the separation of the solid-state boosters from the SLV's main body.

The loudspeakers announced, "Booster separation on schedule. The main body of the *Lunar Express* is heading for orbit around the Earth."

People began to clamber down from the grandstand.

Reluctantly, Jake thought. The show's not over, he told himself. It's just begun, actually. But now we'll need the telescopes to show us the bird up there.

Jake and Tami, with Isaiah Knowles beside them, followed the crowd down to the ground and into the glass-walled headquarters of Astra Corporation. Giant TV screens had been mounted on the walls, all of them showing the gleaming white rocket streaking across the star-spattered black of space.

"They're on their way," Jake said happily.

"Yeah," said Knowles, wistfully. "Wish I was with them."

"Me too," said Jake.

Tami grinned at her husband. "Be patient, dear. You'll get your chance, sooner or later."

Jake looked down at her, realizing that she was right. By damn, he thought, sooner or later I *will* be able to ride to the Moon! "Not unless you go with me," he said to her.

"Try and stop me," Tami answered, grinning.

# The President's Speech

Facing more than a hundred journalists from around the world, President B. Franklin Tomlinson beamed his brilliant smile as he stood at the podium that had been set up on the main floor of the Astra Corporation's headquarters.

Behind him, row after row of bookshelves and souvenir sales counters were crowded with onlookers, ordinary people and families that had come to watch the launch. Now they were witnessing the new president's first speech to the nation, to the world.

"Hello, everyone," he said, grinning. "Quite a launch, wasn't it?"

The crowd cheered lustily.

Once they quieted, Tomlinson began his speech. "Today we've made a first step in our return to the space frontier. It was a breathtaking event—but it's only the beginning."

Looking straight into the camera directly in front of him, Tomlinson continued, "America has always been a frontier country, from the original Jamestown colony to our expansion across what was once known as the Wild West.

"Today we began our move into a new frontier, a frontier that begins just a hundred miles over our heads and spreads across the entire magnificent universe.

"It's a frontier that can provide new industries, new knowledge, new capabilities for the American people and the people of the world."

Jake felt almost breathless. He's saying it, a voice in his head exulted. He's actually saying the words I helped write for him.

"This is the beginning of a new American space program," Tomlinson went on, his face serious, his tone intense. "We're not returning to the Moon merely to plant our flag and a few footsteps. We're going back to the Moon to stay, to begin to build new industries, to develop new capabilities, to extend human knowledge and human resources across this exciting new frontier."

Jake shifted his gaze from the president standing at the podium to the crowd of onlookers behind him. He's got them, Jake said to himself. They're standing stock-still, eyes on their new president, drinking in the vision that he's presenting to them.

For nearly twenty minutes more, the president laid out the reasons for this new phase in the development of the space frontier.

"What we do in space affects every aspect of our lives here on Earth. New jobs, whole new industries, new discoveries and capabilities will expand and enlarge our lives and our livelihoods—and lead the way to new breakthroughs in our civilization. What we accomplish in space will affect employment, opportunity, and well-being for everyone here on Earth."

When Tomlinson finished, the crowd broke into hearty applause. Cheers and whistles rocked the Astra corporate headquarters building.

Grinning his megawatt smile, the president looked across the throng of news reporters standing before him. "I can take a few questions, if you like."

A forest of hands sprang up.

Nodding to one of the women standing in the front row of the reporters, Tomlinson said, "Katie?"

"Isn't your program going to be expensive? I mean, with urban decay and infrastructure problems, how can we afford to go off into the wild blue yonder?"

Tomlinson grinned at her. "Space isn't blue, Katie, it's black. And our program isn't being funded by taxpayers' dollars. It's based on voluntary investments by American citizens, ordinary people and corporate magnates … even news reporters."

Before the reporter could ask a backup question, Tomlinson went on, "Americans can buy shares in the new space program. Private funding is powering our return to the new frontier."

That prompted several more questions, most of them openly skeptical of the private funding idea.

"It's worked before," the president insisted. "That's how we built the big power dams in our western states. Private investment."

"Backed by the government's guarantee," snapped one of the reporters.

Tomlinson nodded. "Backed by the government, yes.

It's the safest investment a person can make."

From the rear of the assembled newspeople, a lean, cranky-looking man said, "I want to raise a different question."

Tomlinson nodded, smiling. "The Moon is airless. Waterless. It's just a dead ball of rock. What makes you think it can be of any use to anybody?"

Tomlinson's smile faded and he reached into his jacket pocket as he said, "I'm glad you asked that, Sam."

The reporters chuckled.

Pulling an index card from his pocket, the president said, "No, I'm really glad. Because it's a question that was asked before, nearly two centuries ago. Asked by one of our most famous members of the United States Senate."

Holding the card in front of himself, Tomlinson went on, "Here's what Senator Daniel Webster had to say, back in 1844, about our nation's expansion westward:

" 'What do we want of the vast worthless area? This region of savages and wild beasts, of deserts, of shifting sands and whirlwinds of dust, cactus, and prairie dogs? '... What use can we have for such a country?' "

Tomlinson looked up from the card. "Do you know what he was speaking about? California! Senator Daniel Webster was dead set against the United States admitting California to the Union."

His volume raised just a notch, "California, for god's sake! 'What use can we have for such a country?' The rocket you just saw launched toward the Moon this morning was built in California. The state has the sixth-highest gross domestic product in the world: two point seven trillion dollars! Trillion! Higher than France or Britain.

"'What use can we have for such a country?' We've made use of it. From Hollywood to the Mount Palomar telescope and the aerospace industry, California has contributed more to our national economy than all the prairie dogs in the world."

The crowd erupted in laughter. Even the reporters guffawed.

Tomlinson waited for them to quiet down, then continued, "There are valuable metals and minerals in the Moon's crust, plus the most important resource of them all: oxygen.

"And once we have a working base on the Moon we can reach out to the near-Earth asteroids, which contain even more natural resources.

"As a character in an old novel told his friends, 'It's raining soup! Grab yourself a bucket!' "

## ■ The Oval Office

Two days later, Kevin O'Donnell popped his head through the half-opened door to the president's office.

"They're in lunar orbit, right on schedule," he announced.

The president looked up from the reports spread across his desk and smiled broadly. "When do they land?"

O'Donnell answered, "In two hours, according to the schedule."

Tomlinson nodded. "I'll watch it from here, Kev."

"Right."

The anteroom door nearly closed. But Jake pushed through, followed by Jean Donofrio. She was wearing a light-green skirted suit, looking very chic and attractive.

Tomlinson rose from his desk chair. "Ms. Donofrio. Welcome aboard."

She strode confidently to the president's desk and extended her right hand.

"I'm thrilled to be on your team, Mr. President."

Tomlinson grinned as Jake maneuvered around the image on the carpet of the Great Seal of the United States, with the American Eagle clutching a sheaf of arrows in one claw and an olive branch in the other. As always, he couldn't bring himself to tread on the symbol of America.

The president said, "And I'm certain that Jake here is thrilled to have you aboard."

"I certainly am," he said, coming up beside Donofrio.

Tomlinson sat down on his desk chair; Jake and Donofrio settled into the armchairs in front of the desk.

"You know," the president began, looking at Donofrio, "there were a few people on my staff who worried about your coming over from Senator McMasters's team."

She blinked with apparent surprise. "Worried? Why?"

"They were troubled by the possibility that you were a snoop for McMasters."

"A snoop?" Donofrio asked. "You mean a spy?"

Tomlinson nodded, but with a disarming smile.

"Surely you don't believe that, Mr. President," Donofrio said.

His smile widening, Tomlinson said, "If I did, we wouldn't have taken you on."

"I would think not," she responded.

Despite their words, a chilly silence fell on the Oval Office.

Jake broke the uneasy hush. "We're all on the same team here. We don't have to worry about McMasters for the next three years."

Tomlinson cast a doubtful glance at him, then returned his focus to Donofrio. "Jake's not a politician."

"Not yet," she said, grinning.

Jake made himself grin back at them. "We have enough politicians around here."

"That's for sure," said the president.

For the next fifteen minutes, Jake, Donofrio, and the president went over the basics of the space effort: the funding arrangements, the goals, the ways in which it melded with other federal programs.

"It's going to be the central pillar of my administration's agenda," Tomlinson said, his face unsmiling, almost somber.

Jake mentally corrected, It *is* the central pillar of your administration's agenda. But he said nothing aloud.

At last the president rose from his chair. Jake and Donofrio took the unspoken hint and got to their feet also.

"Thanks for your time, Mr. President," Jake said.

Tomlinson grinned boyishly and said, "It was good to meet you, Ms. Donofrio."

She smiled prettily. "My friends call me Jean."

"Jean," echoed the president.

Once outside the Oval Office, amidst the desks and busy presidential aides, Jake said, "Let's go over to my office and watch the landing."

"Landing?" Jean Donofrio seemed puzzled for a moment, then she caught Jake's meaning. "Oh, you mean on the Moon."

"Right."

Jake led her through the quietly busy anteroom and out into the corridor beyond. Then halfway across the West Wing to his own office.

His administrative assistant was sitting at her desk, in front of his door. A thickset, middle-aged woman with gray hair, she looked up toward Jake as he asked, "Any calls, Nancy?"

Nancy shook her head. "Quiet as the dead of space. They're all watching the Moon landing."

Jake grinned at her. "Good." And he led Donofrio into his office.

"The *Artemis* mission will be landing at Scott Crater in a couple of hours," he told her as he gestured Donofrio to a chair in front of his desk.

Jake spent the time laying out the basics of the space program: its funding arrangements, its goals and objectives, its key personnel.

She sat before his desk, asking questions here and there, seemingly absorbing most of what Jake had to say.

He was interrupted by his intercom buzzing. "Yes, Nancy?"

"General Farthington is on the line, Dr. Ross."

Jake's heart thumped in his chest. The head of NASA calling? Something's gone wrong with the Moon launch!

He snatched up the telephone receiver. "Bill! What's happened?"

On the phone console's tiny screen General Farthington looked surprised. "Nothing's happened, Jake. Everything is boringly on the tick. I just need to talk with you; thought we could have a drink together over here at my office at the end of the day."

Jake's pulse rate slowed. "Today? With the launch and everything?"

"Relax. They'll be landing in less than two hours. Everything's on schedule. Can you come over here around six o'clock?"

With a glance at Jean Donofrio, Jake nodded slowly. "Okay. The hooting and hollering ought to be over by then, I guess."

"I'll leave word with the guards downstairs to expect you."

"Right. Six o'clock."

Jake hung up the phone, wondering what was so important to the head of NASA that he wanted to chat on the day that the space agency returned Americans to the Moon.

# Bloviating Billy

With tears misting his eyes, Jake watched the *Artemis* rocket's crew capsule settle onto the bare, stark, airless surface of crater Scott, near the Moon's South Pole. The landing was flawlessly dull.

The capsule settled onto its tail struts—the scene captured by the TV camera that had been brought to the Moon by an earlier uncrewed mission. Dust billowed for several long moments before the mission's commander, astronaut Mitchell Varmus, announced laconically, "We're down. Let's get to work."

Once they got out of the crew capsule and actually planted their boots on the Moon's dusty surface, each of the six astronauts made a little speech, each one a variation of "We're back, and this time there's going to be a human presence on the Moon *permanently*."

Stretching back in his desk chair, with Jean Donofrio and a half-dozen other staffers crowded around the TV screen on the wall, Jake felt a sense of—not disappointment, but impatience. Come on, you guys, he urged the astronauts silently. Stop congratulating yourselves and get to work.

Which the astronauts did soon enough, turning to the dome-shaped capsule that had been waiting for them on the Moon's surface for several months.

Ten minutes of watching the team beginning the task of assembling the Scott Crater base was about as interesting to Jake as watching a construction crew at work on Earth. Looking up from the TV screen he saw that most of the staffers looked equally bored.

Five men—and one woman—at work, Jake thought. They might be encased in space suits, but the work they were doing was far from fascinating—even on the Moon.

He glanced at his wristwatch: four thirty-two. Farthington is expecting me in an hour and a half. Wonder what he wants to see me about?

Jake walked out of the White House grounds and hailed a taxi to the NASA headquarters building. It was a short ride and traffic was light. The taxi driver—a skinny, swarthy man with two day's growth on his chin—had the scene from Scott Crater on the small TV screen mounted on his dashboard, and he seemed to be paying more attention to the broadcast from the Moon than to his driving.

Jake remembered that there are only two types of taxi drivers in the District: the ones who don't speak a word to you and the ones you couldn't shut up. This one was a talker.

"That's something, ain't it? Landin' on the Moon again."

"Yes, it is," Jake said.

"They gonna stay there how long?"

"A month. Then a new team will replace them."

"A whole month! They gonna hafta live in those suits for a whole month?"

"No," Jake explained. "They'll live in that domed shelter."

"Huh! Five guys and one girl. For a whole month. Could be interesting, dontcha think?"

Jake said nothing. But he realized that the male imagination wasn't restricted to the earthly environment.

General William T. Farthington, director of NASA, had a spacious corner office on the top floor of the agency's headquarters building. A pair of curtainless windows looked out onto the greenery and museums of the Mall, crowded with tourists.

Farthington rose from his desk chair as his administrative assistant showed Jake into the office and then closed the door behind him.

"Hello, Jake," said Farthington as he came around his desk, his right arm outstretched in greeting.

It always surprised Jake to realize that Farthington was several inches taller than he was himself. The man's roundish physique gave the impression that he was somewhat shorter.

But William T. Farthington—Bloviating Billy, as he was known throughout the halls of government—was actually a sizeable man.

Taking the NASA director's proffered hand, Jake said, "The mission's going very well, isn't it?"

"On schedule," Farthington said, a happy little smile on his round, jowly face. He gestured to the round conference table in a corner of the office. "Want something to drink? Coffee? Booze?"

Jake followed the NASA director to the table. "Are we celebrating?"

"Returning to the Moon? Hell yes!"

With a grin, Jake asked, "Do you have any Jack Daniel's?"

Grinning back, Farthington said, "Do bears sleep in the woods?"

Farthington dug out a bottle and two shot glasses from one of the cabinets lining the back wall of his office, carried them to the little conference table, and sank heavily into the chair next to Jake's.

As he poured a pair of healthy slugs of the Tennessee whiskey, he said, "It's been a good day."

"Amen to that," said Jake as he grasped his glass.

They both drank deeply, then put down their glasses with a pair of satisfied thumps.

Farthington sat in silence, staring at Jake.

"So what's up, Bill?" Jake asked. "What's on your mind?"

The NASA director said, "You know I'm scheduled to resign my position next month."

Jake nodded.

"I don't want to quit."

Jake felt his brows hike up.

"How would the president feel if I stayed on? At least for another year."

Jake blurted, "Surprised, I guess."

Farthington nodded and reached for his glass again.

He said, "I know what they call me around this town: Bloviating Billy. They picked me for this job of directing NASA because they thought I'd supervise the agency's shrinkage and then silently slink away."

Jake didn't know what to say, so he said nothing. "They didn't count on your *Artemis* program getting us back to the Moon. They didn't see what you saw, Jake—the importance of our space program."

"I guess the situation has changed," said Jake.

"Changed?" Farthington replied. "It's a totally different ball game! We're back on the Moon! We're going to use our space efforts to change things here on Earth! We're going to become a truly space-faring nation."

"A space-faring world," Jake corrected. "The Russians, the Chinese … they're not going to stand by and watch us forge ahead. They're going to compete with us."

"Or cooperate."

Jake blinked at the ex-general. "Cooperate?"

"If we play our diplomatic cards right, we can use our—I mean, *your*—space program to bring all the space-faring nations together in a worldwide program!"

Jake heard himself answer, "Maybe." Weakly.

"I want to be part of that," said Farthington. Spreading his arms wide, he went on, "I want to be part of transforming our world into a new era, where we use the resources and opportunities of space to make the world better, more prosperous, more peaceful."

Try telling that to the Taliban, Jake thought.

"We can do it!" Farthington insisted. "We've just taken the first step. And I don't want to quit now, not when we're finally starting to get rolling."

"I don't blame you."

Leaning eagerly toward Jake, Farthington asked, "Can you ask the president if he'll accept me staying on as head of NASA? Please?"

"If that's what you want, Bill."

"That's what I want. That's what I've waited my whole life for—a chance to help us do something that really can change the world. For the better."

"For the better," Jake echoed.

Farthington nodded hard enough to make his cheeks quiver. Then he held up a warning finger. "There's a lot of people in the

NASA bureaucracy who think I'm just a blustering old fool. Bloviating Billy. They won't like my staying on."

Jake looked at the NASA director's earnest eyes and heard himself say, "Fuck 'em. I'll talk to the president right away. This evening."

Farthington sank back in his chair. "Thanks, Jake. From the bottom of my heart, thank you."

Jake stuck out his hand and Farthington clasped it firmly.

"Ad astra," said Jake, with a grin.

"To the stars," Farthington agreed.

## ■ The Tomlinson Residence

Standing next to his wife at the room's makeshift bar, President Tomlinson asked, "So what's so important that you have to come here during cocktail hour?" Then, with a broad smile, he added, "Or are you just mooching a free drink?"

Jake hoisted his glass of ginger beer. "It isn't the drink."

Tomlinson crossed the book-lined library's floor and sat down in one of the room's comfortable leather armchairs, next to the sofa on which Jake was sitting.

"Then what is it?"

"General Farthington."

"Bloviating Billy? What's he want?"

"He wants to stay on at NASA."

Tomlinson's eyed widened. "He wants to stay on?"

Jake nodded. Tomlinson's wife, Amy, standing by the rolling cart that was covered with bottles, looked suddenly tense, apprehensive.

"Now that we've returned to the Moon, Farthington wants to be part of the new program. He wants to help us accomplish what we're trying to do."

"Bloviating Billy Farthington wants to get in on the glory," Amy said, from across the room.

"He wants to help," Jake corrected.

Tomlinson nodded and muttered, "Success has a thousand fathers."

Jake knew the rest of the adage: *Failure is an orphan.*

"I think he's sincere," Jake said. "Farthington wants to help us. He deserves a chance to help."

"And what about Yankovich?"

Lincoln Yankovich was Farthington's second in command, a bright, capable, younger leader who was due to ascend to the agency's top job once Farthington left.

Jake spread his hands. "He'll have to wait, I guess."

With a weary shake of his head, Tomlinson said, "This isn't going to go smoothly. We were all set to accept Billy's resignation and promote Yankovich to his spot."

As she crossed the room and sat on the arm of her husband's chair, Amy said, "Yankovich won't be happy about this. He'll squawk to the news reporters."

Tomlinson nodded agreement.

"He'll accuse you of keeping a political appointee in the top NASA job instead of a man of proven capabilities."

A flash of inspiration lit Jake's mind. "Wait a minute!" he snapped. "What if we put Yankovich in charge of the *Artemis* program? NASA's part of the program, that is."

Tomlinson stared at Jake for a long, wordless moment.

Then, "That's playing with fire, Jake. He'd be gunning for Billy's head every moment of every day."

"Maybe not," Jake argued. "Maybe the *Artemis* task will keep him busy. And then, when Farthington does retire, he'll be a natural to step up and take his place."

"Risky," said the president.

Jake lapsed into an ancient aphorism: "Behold the lowly turtle—"

Tomlinson completed the old saw: "He only makes progress when he sticks his neck out."

Amy said, "You'll be treading on dangerous ground, Frank."

The president looked up at his wife, smiled, and answered, "But I'll be making progress."

And Jake heard a voice in his head say, *Maybe.*

# The Deal

At a quarter to eleven the following morning, Jake's desktop phone buzzed. It was his assistant, Nancy, advising him that Lincoln Yankovich had arrived for his appointment with the president.

Jake glanced at the clock readout at the bottom of his phone's screen. Yankovich was fifteen minutes early.

Not a good sign, he thought. The NASA executive was expecting to be told that Farthington had tendered his resignation and that he, Yankovich, was being asked to take over the agency's top job.

Jake got up from his desk chair, sucked in a deep breath, and headed out to meet Yankovich.

The man was smaller than Jake expected. Lincoln Yankovich was a stylish welterweight in a trim-fitting, light-tan sports jacket over a checkered vest, slim and wiry, with wispy brown hair and a dapper little moustache. He had prominent cheekbones and pale, almost watery, soft-brown eyes. He smiled as Jake came into the anteroom where he was waiting for his appointment with the president.

"Mr. Yankovich," Jake said as he extended his right hand toward the man. "Glad you could come in this morning."

Yankovich stood up and smiled as he took Jake's hand in a firm grip. "When the president calls, you come," he said. His voice was a little high pitched, Jake thought. Nerves? Despite his air of nonchalant calm?

Jake sat next to him in the quietly busy anteroom. Executive assistants—male and female—strode briskly among the desks. Youthful aides made their way on various errands.

For lack of anything better to say, Jake asked, "How're things going at NASA?" It felt stupid.

Yankovich nodded, straight-faced. "Construction of the Scott Crater base is on schedule. The astronauts are sleeping inside its dome now, instead of in the ship."

"Good," said Jake.

"Yes," said Yankovich.

For a few more minutes they chatted about the work going on at the new lunar base, then Jake pushed himself to his feet. "Time to see the president."

Yankovich got up too. Jake could see the anticipation in his eyes.

They threaded their way through the desks and into the anteroom just outside the Oval Office. The executive assistant seated nearest the office's door—a lanky blonde in a no-nonsense gray business suit—got slowly to her feet. "Dr. Ross, Mr. Yankovich," she said, in a near whisper, "I'll tell the president you're here."

Jake glanced nervously at his wristwatch. One minute early.

The executive assistant leaned over her desk and spoke into the intercom. Then she straightened up, smiled automatically, and led the two men to the door.

President Tomlinson was buttoning his dark-blue jacket as Jake and Yankovich stepped into the Oval Office. From behind his desk he beamed a smile and said cheerily, "Hello, Mr. Yankovich. Good to see you."

Yankovich smiled back and said, "My friends call me Linc."

Gesturing to the upholstered chairs in front of his desk, Tomlinson said, "Have a seat, Linc."

Jake followed Yankovich to the president's desk—carefully stepping around the American Eagle design on the carpet—and sat down beside the NASA executive.

Leaning back nonchalantly in his swivel chair, President Tomlinson said, "Things seem to be going well at Scott Crater."

With a smile, Yankovich replied, "We're on schedule. The team will be ready to activate the main telescope before the day is out."

Tomlinson nodded, glanced at Jake, then turned his attention to Yankovich once more.

"Linc," he said, "I've got good news and bad news for you."

Yankovich's smile remained frozen on his face as he asked, "What's the bad news?"

"Farthington isn't resigning."

The NASA executive blinked once. Twice. "Isn't resigning?"

"He wants to stay on, now that we've returned to the Moon."

"But I thought—"

"So did I," said the president, almost sadly. "So did we all. But he wants to stay on. At least for another year."

"Another year?" Yankovich's voice was hollow, like a child who's just had a new toy yanked out of his hands.

For an endless moment the Oval Office was utterly silent.

Then the president broke into his warmest smile and said, "Now the good news. We need you to take charge of NASA's part of the *Artemis* program."

Before Yankovich could respond, the president went on, "You know that *Artemis* is the most important program on NASA's docket. Directing the agency's work on *Artemis* is the most significant job since the old *Apollo* program was terminated."

Yankovich muttered, "Head up the *Artemis* program."

"NASA's portion of the *Artemis* program," Jake corrected.

"It's a big responsibility," Tomlinson said. "The biggest thing NASA has going for it. We need a man of your experience and your capabilities to take charge of it."

"It will revitalize NASA," said Jake.

"And you'll be in charge of it," Tomlinson added. "Billy Farthington can keep his job for the next year or so, but you'll be the one actually running the agency."

"The most important part of the agency," Jake amended.

"Will you accept the responsibility?" the president asked.

Yankovich sat there staring at the president for a long, silent, breathless moment. Jake thought he could sense the conflict raging in the man's mind. His expectations dashed, yet this new opportunity raised before his eyes.

The president repeated, "Will you accept the responsibility, Linc?"

Yankovich sat up straighter in his chair. "If that's what you want, Mr. President … if that's what you need … certainly, I'll accept the responsibility."

Tomlinson broke into his megawatt smile and rose from his chair as he stuck out his right hand across the desk.

"Thank you, Linc! And I wish you every success at your new position."

Yankovich rose too and grasped the president's offered hand. But when he released it and turned toward Jake, Jake thought he saw a look of venomous bitterness burning in his light-brown eyes.

# Senator McMasters

Eugene McMasters (R-NY) leaned back in his commodious desk chair, his gray eyes narrowed, his thin lips a bloodless line.

"Farthington is staying on?" he asked, disbelieving.

The only other person in the wide, handsomely furnished office was Jean Donofrio. She nodded. "The president accepted Bloviating Billy's request this afternoon."

It was nearly seven o'clock. Despite the evening's encroaching darkness, the city outside McMasters's office window was blazing with lights.

"Lincoln Yankovich must be having convulsions," McMasters growled.

Donofrio, wearing a nubby, skirted suit of pearl gray, countered, "They've offered him the job of heading up the *Artemis* program."

"And he accepted it?"

"Of course. What else could he do? Cry foul?"

McMasters went silent for several long moments. But Donofrio thought she could hear the wheels spinning in her former boss's head.

At last he pronounced, "I'll block it in the committee hearing."

McMasters was chair of the Senate committee that oversaw the space program.

Softly, Donofrio contradicted, "I don't think it has to come before the committee, Senator. Farthington is just remaining in place."

"But Yankovich—"

"Is merely being given a new assignment. Tomlinson doesn't need the committee's approval for that."

"Are you sure?"

"I looked it up."

"Shit," McMasters hissed.

"It looks like a done deal, Gene."

McMasters glowered at her, then muttered, "We'll see what kind of deals get done when they come up for their appropriations hearing next year."

Donofrio thought that by next year the Scott Crater base would be a going concern, and opposition to it might not be as popular as the senator seemed to think. But she knew from experience that McMasters did not take kindly to disagreement, so she kept her mouth shut.

McMasters just sat behind his broad, gleaming desk for several long wordless moments, clearly unhappy. At last he let out a puff of air and started to get to his feet.

"Come on, let's go to dinner."

Donofrio remained seated and said, "I don't think that would be a good idea, Gene. We shouldn't be seen together. It was tricky enough getting here to your office without any snoops seeing me."

Standing behind his desk, glowering at her, McMasters said, "My staff people are loyal to me."

"Yes. Of course. But a public restaurant is different, isn't it." It wasn't a question.

"We could go to my apartment."

Donofrio made a sad face. "It's awfully risky, Gene."

"Then what?"

"We agreed that we'd have to stay apart while I'm on Tomlinson's staff."

He stared at her for a long, silent moment. Then, "Yeah, you're right. No sense upsetting the apple cart."

She rose to her feet. "Thanks for being so understanding, Gene."

"Understanding. Yeah," grumbled Eugene McMasters.

## ■ Moonbase One

Astronaut Mitch Varmus smiled pleasantly into the TV camera. He was a tall man, almost at the six-foot, four-inch height limitation for astronauts. But as he stood at the center of the newly erected Scott Crater habitation dome, he seemed completely at ease, totally at home.

*It's like he was born to be there*, Jake said to himself as he watched the television broadcast from the Moon.

"As you can see," Varmus was saying, "we're a little snug here inside the dome ... but we're not complaining. Outside this dome the temperature ranges from more than twice the boiling point of water to a couple hundred degrees below zero, depending on whether you're in sunlight or shadow."

Varmus and five other astronauts—including one woman, Victoria Haskell—were shoehorned into a circular space crowded with desks and viewscreens. Each of the five was seated at their workstation, focusing on the data flickering across their screens. All of them were wearing sky-blue NASA-issue coveralls. Varmus was on his feet, speaking to the millions of viewers back on Earth.

"Here inside the dome we have air and heat and everything we need to do our jobs," Varmus went on, smiling handsomely into the camera that automatically followed his movements. Edging between two of the desks, the astronaut went on, "We've erected the thirty-centimeter telescope outside our dome and we're checking it out. In a few weeks, a team of astronomers will land here and begin their search of the planets that have been discovered orbiting the triple-star system of Alpha Centauri, nearly five light-years away from our own solar system."

Varmus stopped at one of the desks, where a male astronaut was busily tapping away on his desktop computer's keyboard.

"But astronomy isn't the only scientific work we'll be doing here," he said. "We have automated little tractors outside, scooping up the topmost layers of the lunar regolith—that's the scientific term for the Moon's surface—and analyzing its contents. We've confirmed that the regolith contains a lot of carbon, aluminum, and other valuable resources—including oxygen, which comes in handy if you want to breathe."

Alone in his office, Jake leaned back in his desk chair as Varmus nattered away, thinking that the man could make a career for himself as a TV commentator when he retired from the astronaut corps.

It's all going well, he thought. Moonbase One is up and operating. We're back on the Moon, and this time we intend to stay.

Smiling to himself, Jake picked up the TV remote control and flicked from one news channel to another. Each station was showing the same broadcast from Moonbase One. Good, he thought. In a couple of weeks the astronomers will land at the base and the real scientific work will begin.

His desktop buzzer interrupted his happy reverie. Nancy's usually imperturbable face showed tension. "Dr. Ross, Ms. Donofrio is calling."

"Jean? Put her through, please."

Jean Donofrio's normally cool, self-confident expression was gone from her face. She looked upset, almost frightened.

"Jean, what's wrong?" Jake blurted.

"It's McMasters," she replied, almost breathlessly. "He's going to attack your space program, Jake."

"Now?" Jake squeaked. "Now when we're doing so well?"

"Yes! He intends to block NASA's appropriation for Project *Artemis*."

"That's stupid!"

"Maybe," Donofrio semi-agreed. "But he's going to put up a roadblock at the Senate Appropriations Committee's hearing next week."

For a wordless moment Jake stared at Donofrio's anxious face. Then he said, "Let him try it. They'll spit in his face."

Donofrio shook her head. "I don't think so, Jake. He can call in a lot of favors, you know. Obligations he's racked up over the years from other senators."

Grimly, Jake responded, "And we've got a working base on the Moon, Jean. And it isn't supported by government funding. McMasters is still thinking *Artemis* is a federal program. Well, it's not."

"But NASA's part of it is!"

"Screw NASA!" Jake snapped. "We can carry on the program without them."

Donofrio stayed silent for a breathless moment. Then she said, "Jake, do you realize what you're saying? You can't let NASA drop out of the *Artemis* program! The political repercussions—"

"Will fall on McMasters's head."

"No they won't! You'll be tearing the program apart."

"We'll see," Jake said. And he slammed a fist on the phone console, cutting off Donofrio.

"Cut NASA's appropriation?" President Tomlinson looked genuinely surprised. As usual, he was in his shirtsleeves and bright-red suspenders. His jacket was draped across the back of his black leather chair.

Standing in front of the president's desk, Jake said, "He can't do that. The committee won't go for it."

Kevin O'Donnell, sitting tensely on one of the sofas by the empty fireplace, grumbled, "You'd be surprised at what a congressional committee will vote for."

Motioning with both his hands, the president said, "Sit, Jake. And try to calm down."

Jake sank into one of the armchairs in front of the president's desk. But he said, "McMasters is trying to gut the program. He wants to kill it."

O'Donnell got up from the sofa and came over to sit down beside Jake. "He just might have enough support to pull it off."

"Then we'll go ahead without NASA," Jake insisted. "The program isn't funded by government money. It's all private funding."

"Except for NASA's participation," said O'Donnell.

"So we'll go ahead without NASA," Jake repeated. "Plenty of NASA guys will leave the agency and go to work directly on *Artemis*."

The president shook his head. "You don't want that, Jake. You don't want to drop NASA out of the program."

"Why not?" Jake snapped. "Why do we have to—" The president stopped him with a pointed finger.

"NASA is part of the program. Period. Dropping NASA from *Artemis* would be a terrible blow to our credibility."

O'Donnell chimed in, "You'll wind up spending more time in congressional hearings than anything else, Jake. You don't want that."

"The acrimony could destroy your space program," Tomlinson added, grimly.

*My* space program, Jake thought. Frank's already backing away from the controversy.

Feeling abandoned, Jake asked quietly, "So what should I do?"

President Tomlinson leaned back in his swivel chair. "Find out what McMasters wants. He's after something—"

"He wants to gut the program. *Your* program, Mr. President. He wants to give you a black eye."

Tomlinson nodded. "Maybe. That might be what he wants. We've got to find out what he'll settle for."

# Meeting McMasters

Jake felt jumpy as he sat in the quietly busy anteroom outside Senator McMasters's office. His fists were clenched on his lap. He was angry and he knew it, but beneath his anger was fear, an anxiety that somehow McMasters could scuttle the *Artemis* program.

Glancing around the anteroom's cluster of desks, Jake thought that the place looked like some Broadway show's impression of a Washington office: almost every desk was occupied by an attractive, smartly dressed young woman.

McMasters has a regular harem here, he thought. I wonder—

His musing was interrupted by one of the executive assistants calling his name in a softly appealing tone:

"Dr. Ross? The senator will see you now."

Jake got to his feet, consciously unclenching his hands. "Thank you," he said to the young woman, who had stepped to the door of the senator's office and opened it.

Senator McMasters was standing behind his desk, smiling enough to show teeth, as Jake entered his office. Jake remembered Kevin O'Donnell's advice: "After you shake hands with McMasters, count your fingers."

"Dr. Ross," said the senator, "we meet at last."

Jake countered with what he thought of as District of Columbia blarney. "It was good of you to invite me, sir."

McMasters gestured to the spindly little chair in front of his commodious desk. "Have a seat."

Jake sat.

The senator settled into his own plush swivel chair behind the desk. "So what can I do for you, Dr. Ross?"

"Jake."

"Jake," said the senator. "What's on your mind?"

"I thought I should give you a briefing about the *Artemis* program: its goals and objectives; its funding, where we're going and how we intend to get there."

"It's a very ambitious program, isn't it?"

Despite his inner tension, Jake grinned at the senator. "I think of it as a modern-day reenactment of our nation's expansion across the western frontier."

McMasters made a small nod. "You have a sense of history."

"America is a pioneering nation. Now we're starting to develop a base on the Moon, and—"

McMasters wagged a raised finger. "I don't see that as similar to our development of the West."

"But I do," said Jake. "And so do millions of American voters."

"We have lots of more important problems to deal with, Jake: the decay of our national infrastructure, crime in the streets, public health. How is exploring the Moon going to help solve those problems?"

"We're not exploring the Moon," Jake said firmly. "We're developing its resources. That can—"

Again McMasters interrupted. "Developing its resources? What resources? It's nothing but a dead ball of rock."

"That rock contains valuable resources, senator. With those resources we can build solar power satellites that could supply electrical power to us here on the ground cleanly, efficiently, cheaply."

"Pie in the sky."

"So were airplanes, once upon a time. So were antibiotic medicines. So were skyscrapers and automobiles and even electrical power itself."

Shaking his head, McMasters argued, "You're talking about things that'll take fifty years to develop. More! I'm dealing with problems that we have right here and now."

"And I'm talking about how we can help to solve those problems—not fifty years in the future but less than a decade from now."

"Pie in the sky," McMasters repeated.

Jake said, "If we had that attitude back in the nineteenth century, we'd still be arguing over whether we wanted to build Chicago or St. Louis!"

McMasters shook his head again. "You're a dreamer, son."

"So was Edison. And Ford. And the Wright brothers."

"We've got to devote our resources to solving the problems we're facing today," McMasters insisted. "Not chasing some fancy tooth-fairy fantasy."

Jake heard himself mutter, "There are none so blind as those who will not see."

"Bullshit," McMasters snapped.

Jake lifted his chin a couple of notches and took a deep breath. "I'm afraid I'm wasting your time, senator."

"You goddamned well are."

Getting to his feet, Jake said, "I'm sorry you feel that way."

"I'm going to cut NASA out of your pipe dream. We'll see how far you get without them."

"To the stars," Jake growled. Then he turned and walked out of Senator McMasters's office.

# Analysis

Jake felt like a schoolboy who had been sent to the principal's office for discipline.

He sat in front of President Tomlinson's desk in the Oval Office feeling miserable. Kevin O'Donnell sat at his right and Adam Westerly at his left. They all looked terribly unhappy.

"You let McMasters get under your skin, Jake," said the president, more in sorrow than in anger.

Jake nodded unhappily. "I guess I did."

O'Donnell almost smiled. "Remember Ev Dirksen's third law of politics—"

Westerly, sitting on Jake's other side like a massive pile of rumpled laundry, finished, "Don't get mad. Get even."

"Easier said than done," Jake grumbled.

The president did not smile. "We've got to be ready to counter McMasters at the committee hearing."

"Which is next Monday," Westerly pointed out.

The Oval Office went silent. Next Monday, Jake thought. There goes the weekend. I was going to go with Tami to watch her show at WETA, but that's in the trash bin now. She'll understand. She'll take it like the trouper she is.

"Earth to Jake Ross!"

Jake realized that Kevin O'Donnell was speaking to him.

"Yes, what?"

O'Donnell was grinning crookedly at him. "You drifted away there for a minute, pal."

With a small shrug, Jake replied, "I was watching my weekend sail away."

"You and me both," said O'Donnell. Turning back to the president, he said, "We've got to find something that we can use to counter McMasters."

"That won't be easy," said Westerly. "He's been in the Senate for nearly fifteen years and I've never heard a whisper about him. Oh, he stocks his staff with good-looking women, but none of them are complaining. He's got a straight-arrow reputation."

"He wants my job," said President Tomlinson.

"And he's willing to gut the space program to get it," Jake pointed out.

Tomlinson's normally cheerful expression was nowhere in sight. Quietly, the president said, "We can't let him do that."

"Who knows him well enough to maybe have something on him?" Westerly asked. "Something we can use."

O'Donnell's face brightened. "What about that woman who used to work for him? What's her name?"

"Jean Donofrio," Jake answered.

"Yeah," said O'Donnell. "Let's talk to her, see if she knows anything we can use."

"Good thinking," said Westerly.

Jean Donofrio sat on the front three inches of the chair in front of Jake's desk. It was late afternoon; the street outside was already clogging with homeward-bound traffic.

As usual, Donofrio was smartly dressed, in a sea-green skirted suit that brought out her gray-green eyes. But she seemed terribly tense, as uptight as a perp being questioned by a police sergeant.

"The senator has always been very proper with me," she was saying, her voice small, low enough so that Jake found himself leaning forward from behind his desk to hear her.

With an impatient shake of his head, Jake said, "I'm not looking for scandal fodder, Jean. I need to know what makes him tick. What's he really after?"

"The White House," she blurted.

Jake sank back in his desk chair. "That much I could figure out for myself. But how does he intend to get there? What are his priorities?"

Donofrio seemed to relax a little. Her rigid posture eased somewhat. "Well … he wanted to run for the presidency the last time around. But he stepped aside for Senator Sebastian."

"And the Sebastian-Tomlinson ticket won the election."

"Yes. And Senator McMasters became the most powerful figure in the Senate."

"He and Sebastian got along well."

"On the surface," Donofrio replied. "The senator was sort of … well, I guess *envious* would be the best word to describe how he felt."

"And now Sebastian is dead and Tomlinson is in the Oval Office."

"And Senator McMasters feels …" she hesitated. "How can I put it? He feels he's been tricked out of being president. He was hoping to be Sebastian's running mate, you know. And he would have been, if it hadn't been for Senator Tomlinson and his 'Back to the Moon' program."

Jake nodded. He suddenly understood. McMasters must hate my guts, he told himself. He must want to destroy anything and everything I stand for. That's why he's trying to destroy the *Artemis* program.

"He doesn't like you, Jake," said Donofrio, confirming his suspicion. "He thinks you and your Moon program kept him from being Sebastian's running mate. Kept him from becoming president when Sebastian died."

"So there's no dealing with him," Jake surmised. "No way to work out our differences."

In a small voice, Donofrio answered, "I don't see how."

"Not even if Tomlinson offered him the vice presidency?"

With a shake of her head, Donofrio half-whispered, "I don't think so."

"I wonder," Jake said.

# A Proposition

Once he'd buttoned his suit jacket (navy blue with barely visible white pinstripes) President Tomlinson extended his right hand to the visitor.

"Senator McMasters!" the president said, beaming his best smile. "It's good of you to come and visit me."

McMasters smiled back as he took the president's hand in a firm grip. "It was good of you to invite me, Mr. President."

Kevin O'Donnell, Adam Westerly, and Jake were also on their feet, at the twin sofas in front of the Oval Office's empty fireplace.

The president gestured to the plush leather chair in front of his desk. "Have a seat, senator."

"Thanks," said McMasters, keeping his smile in place as he sat and eased back in the comfortable chair.

"You know Wes, of course," said the president, nodding toward Westerly. "And Kevin."

"Certainly. And I've even met Dr. Ross recently."

Jake felt his body tense. This isn't going to be a friendly meeting, he knew.

But President Tomlinson kept smiling as he said, "I understand you're unhappy with Jake's space program."

*My* program, thought Jake. When Varmus and his crew landed safely at Scott Crater it was *his* program. This morning it's mine.

McMasters's smile faded a little. "Mr. President, I think we have much more important problems to deal with than flying to the Moon."

"The *Artemis* program is a private effort, privately funded. It's not spending a penny of government money."

"Your so-called private investment is guaranteed by government backing. When your Moon program collapses, the Treasury Department will have to pay the bills."

His own grin dimming just the slightest bit, Tomlinson said, "Then we'll have to make certain it doesn't collapse."

"I don't believe that's possible," said McMasters.

"I do."

McMasters shrugged his shoulders. "Then we have two opposite views, don't we?"

Tomlinson leaned back in his swivel chair. "President Sebastian believed in the *Artemis* program. He backed it one hundred percent."

Frowning—almost scowling—McMasters countered, "Sebastian backed your Moon program to get you on his ticket and win the youth vote with their space-nut fringe."

All trace of his smile vanished as Tomlinson said, "Those space nuts helped us get to the Moon in the first place. Space technology has made tremendous contributions to our electronics industry, to medical technology, to our defense capability."

McMasters jabbed a finger at the president. "We would have made those advances anyway, without throwing away a hundred billion dollars to land a half-dozen astronauts on the Moon!"

Tomlinson shook his head. "You just don't see it, do you? You don't understand that we're opening up a new frontier."

"Poppycock!"

"Fact."

"We'll just have to wait and see which view is the correct one," McMasters said, as he started to push himself to his feet.

"Hang on a minute, senator. We're not finished yet"

"Oh?" McMasters sank back into his chair.

"There's the committee meeting coming up on Monday. I understand you're going to recommend that NASA's participation in the *Artemis* program be cut out entirely."

"I certainly am," said McMasters, with some heat. "I don't believe that the taxpayers should spend a cent on this Moondoggle program of yours."

Strangely, Tomlinson broke into a chuckle. "Moondoggle. That phrase hasn't been used since the old *Apollo* program, more than sixty years ago."

"It has a certain ring to it," said McMasters. "I think it's utterly appropriate today."

Tomlinson glanced at Jake and the two other men sitting tensely on the sofas by the empty fireplace. Jake thought the president's glimpse lingered a moment longer on Adam Westerly than on O'Donnell or himself.

"You know," the president said, "I've got to nominate a person for the empty vice president's chair."

McMasters smiled bitterly. "Now you're trying to bribe me?"

"I'm offering you the position."

"No thanks," said McMasters firmly. "I don't want any part of your administration."

Tomlinson nodded. "I thought not. But I also thought I should give you the opportunity to turn it down."

"I … uh … I appreciate that."

The president got to his feet. The other men in the Oval Office rose to theirs, too.

"It was good of you to come and meet with me, senator."

Coldly, McMasters replied, "It was good of you to invite me, Mr. President."

From where he stood by the fireplace, Jake heard O'Donnell whisper, "Like Caesar and Brutus."

# Senate Subcommittee on Space

Eugene McMasters was not the chair of the Senate subcommittee on Space, Science, and Competition. But when he took his seat in the hearing room it seemed to Jake that all eyes—witnesses, spectators, and the other committee members—focused on the Republican from New York.

The subcommittee chair, a Republican from Louisiana, rapped his gavel once and declared, "Meetin' will come t'order."

Almost half of the banc of seats for the subcommittee's members were empty. Lots of absentees, Jake said to himself. Glancing at the press corps's section, he saw that it too was sparsely populated. Nobody's expecting fireworks this morning, he realized.

He'd told Tami of his worries about this meeting. Sure enough, he saw his wife working her way past the half-empty rows of seats and placing herself in among the other news reporters. He smiled at her and she smiled back.

The subcommittee made its way through a boring agenda with no problems, no objections. Until the chair finally pronounced, "That completes this morning's schedule, unless there's some new business to discuss."

Senator McMasters raised his hand as he leaned toward the microphone before him and said, "I have an item of new business, Mr. Chair."

Frowning slightly, the chair said, "Reco'nize the senatah from New Yawk."

"As you know," McMasters began, "we have embarked on a new and very expensive space program."

One senator interrupted, "We've got Americans working on the Moon right now."

"Yes, we do," said McMasters. "Gobbling up the taxpayers' hard-earned dollars on a program of dubious value to this nation."

"Dubious value?" The woman looked surprised, almost shocked.

McMasters smiled tightly at her. "While a handful of astronauts are cavorting on the Moon, American citizens here on Earth are trying to deal with a crumbling national infrastructure, with crime on our streets, with problems of health and education."

The woman nodded silently, and Jake realized that she was a stooge for McMasters, planted there to act as a straight man for his spiel.

But the subcommittee chair said, "As I unnerstand it, this new space program is funded by private investment, not tax dollahs."

"Some of it," McMasters agreed. "But a substantial part of the program is supported by the National Air and Space Agency—NASA."

Dead silence in the hearing room. Jake could hear the clock on the wall behind the senators ticking slowly.

McMasters went on, "I don't believe we should be spending taxpayers' dollars on what is essentially a private program. I move that we strike NASA's part of this new Moondoggle completely out of the program."

The chair blinked several times before replying, "Completely out of it? You mean totally?"

"Totally. Completely. Not one cent of taxpayers' money should be spent on this ridiculous adventure on the Moon."

The hearing chamber erupted. The few reporters covering the meeting all pulled out their cell phones and started yammering into them. Every one of the spectators seemed to have something to say. Except Jake. He sat on the bench in total silence, listening to his dream being torn apart.

Then from the rear of the hearing chamber a powerful voice cut through the noise.

"Mr. Chair! May I address the committee?"

Turning, Jake was startled to see that it was William T. Farthington.

Banging his gavel for silence, the chair nodded at Bloviating Billy. "Th' chair recognizes Mr. Farthington, the chief administrator of NASA."

His paunchy figure dressed in tan jacket and darker slacks, Farthington made his way through the half-empty rows of spectator benches and sat in the witness chair, facing the senators.

"Please pardon my late arrival," he began, as he pulled a handkerchief from his jacket pocket and mopped his bald dome. "I wasn't informed that the subcommittee would be discussing NASA's contribution to the *Artemis* program until a few minutes ago."

"We welcome your participation," said the chair, graciously.

Hunching forward and clutching the microphone before him with both his hands, Farthington said, "I want to make a single point. A single point that's very important to me, to the space agency, and to the American people and the people of the world."

He paused. Like everyone else in the hearing chamber, Jake focused on the NASA chair. He might be known throughout the government as Bloviating Billy, a man who could talk endlessly without really saying anything, but at this moment, William T. Farthington looked more like a man on a vitally important mission.

"NASA is an integral part of the *Artemis* program. The agency has a vital role in what I consider to be the most important program this nation is undertaking today. We are opening up the space frontier. After more than half a century of diddling around and letting our hard-earned capability for human space missions slowly die away, we have a team of people on the Moon, with more to come.

"To remove NASA from the *Artemis* program will be to kill it." Turning his portly form squarely toward Senator McMasters, Farthington said firmly, "We have a choice: do we want to develop the space frontier and all that it promises for the American people and the people of the world, or do we want to throw away this opportunity to build a better, safer, richer future for ourselves and our children's children?"

For a long breathless moment there was absolute silence in the hearing chamber.

Then somebody in the audience started clapping and within an eyeblink almost everyone was on their feet, applauding and cheering. Jake saw that even the subcommittee chair was grinning broadly. Everyone seemed overjoyed. Except Senator McMasters, who sat in glowering silence, his eyes focused on Jake like a pair of red-hot branding irons.

# Adjournment

The subcommittee chair whacked his gavel one more time and, over the chatter of the standing audience, announced, "Meetin' adjourned!"

As the senators began to file toward the assembly room behind their banc of seats, Jake slid past the bench he'd been sitting on and stepped up to the witness chair, where Farthington was getting to his feet.

Smiling faintly, the NASA chief grabbed at Jake's extended hand and muttered, "Shortest speech I ever made."

"And the best," said Jake, pumping away.

Glancing up at McMasters's departing back, Farthington said, "We haven't heard the last of him."

"No, I guess not."

Turning, Jake saw that the hearing chamber was nearly empty now, except for a couple of news reporters speaking intently into their phones. He didn't see Tami, though. Where had she gone?

Farthington seemed pleased. Jake wondered, "You sure saved the day, Bill. How'd you know to come here? How'd you know what McMasters was up to?"

"Your wife phoned me."

"Tami?"

"Yep. Good thing, too."

"It sure was." But where is she? Jake wondered.

Then he saw her elfin form reentering the nearly emptied hearing chamber. She came straight to where Jake and Farthington were standing.

"Good going, Mr. Farthington!" Tami exclaimed.

General Farthington, Jake thought. But he didn't correct his wife.

Farthington smiled, looking almost embarrassed. "Glad you called me, Mrs. Ross."

"Let's get some lunch," Jake said, as the three of them headed toward the door that opened onto the hallway outside.

With a shake of his head, Farthington said, "I've got to get back to my office. I left a dozen or so people standing there with their mouths open. They never saw me move so fast!"

Jake laughed.

One of the two reporters still in the chamber came out from behind the news desk as he called, "General Farthington—sir—can I have a moment?"

"Not now. I've got to get back to my office." He added, "You want to share a cab ride with me?"

"Great!" exclaimed the reporter.

The two of them hustled out into the hallway, but not before Farthington turned his head and gave Jake a high-five sign.

"He sure saved the day," Jake said. Then he amended as he and Tami stepped into the hallway, "No, *you* saved the day. You're a hero, Tami."

"Heroine," she corrected.

Jake grabbed her shoulders and kissed her, right there in the middle of the busy hallway. One of the passersby whistled appreciatively.

"Come on," Jake said, sliding his arm around Tami's waist. "I owe you a lunch, at least."

It wasn't until they were in a taxicab riding toward Phillips Seafood Restaurant that Jake remembered, "Where'd you disappear to when the meeting broke up?"

Tami hesitated, then admitted, "Even heroines have to pee now and then."

"All you've done is pour gasoline on the fire," said Kevin O'Donnell, sourly.

The president's aide was sitting disconsolately in front of Jake's desk.

"I didn't want McMasters to—"

"I know. I know. But getting Bloviating Billy to shoot him down in the middle of the subcommittee hearing ... he won't forget that. Or forgive it."

Jake could feel his entire body tensing. Leaning forward in his desk chair, he asked O'Donnell, "What would you have done, Kevin?"

For several moments O'Donnell was silent. Jake thought he could hear the gears grinding away inside the man's head.

At last O'Donnell broke into a sheepish grin. "Probably the same damned thing," he admitted. "Bloviating Billy to the rescue."

Jake grinned back at O'Donnell. "He's not bloviating anymore. William Farthington just might be a real asset for us."

"Who'd have thought it?"

"The Lord moveth in mysterious ways," said Jake.

O'Donnell nodded once, then said, "McMasters must be sore as hell. He'll move heaven and earth to kill your program now."

With a courage he did not truly feel, Jake replied, "Let him try."

"Don't worry about it. He will, pal. He will."

# Augmented Reality

Two days later Jean Donofrio marched into Jake's office and announced, "I've cleared your afternoon's schedule."

Startled, Jake snapped, "You what?"

"You have a date, sir," she said, smiling brightly. "At NASA's Greenbelt center."

Jake got up from behind his desk. "A date? What date?

It's almost lunchtime."

"There's a car waiting for you downstairs. With a couple of sandwiches and some sodas packed in it."

Jean was still smiling happily as she led Jake through the seemingly endless corridors of the NASA research center in Greenbelt, Maryland.

Jake kept stride with her, barely. He felt a tightness in his chest, a shortness of breath: signs that his old case of asthma still lingered in his lungs, ready as always to keep him grounded.

"Jean …" he panted, "slow down a little. Where are we going, anyway?"

She turned her head toward him, and he saw the smile on her lips. "To the Moon, Jake."

Before Jake could figure out a reply, he spotted Lincoln Yankovich, NASA's number-two executive and head of the *Artemis* program, standing by an open doorway a dozen yards ahead of him.

Yankovich put out his hand as Jake approached. "Dr. Ross," he said, with a smile, "good to see you again."

Taking Yankovich's proffered hand in his own, Jake puffed, "Hello, Linc."

Gesturing to the open doorway, Yankovich said, "They're all set up for you."

"What's this all about?" Jake demanded. "What's going on?"

"You're about to take a trip to Scott Base," replied Yankovich, "through the marvel of Augmented Reality." He pronounced the capital letters.

Jake looked around the room they had stepped into. It was a large, open area, mostly empty. Jake saw steel beams supporting the ceiling. Some electronics consoles stood in one corner, with a trio of denim-clad technicians in front of them.

Turning to Donofrio, Jake grumbled, "What's this all about, Jean? I don't have time—"

Looking guilty, Donofrio said, "I took the liberty of clearing your calendar for this afternoon."

"And you whisked me out here to Greenbelt. Why?" Yankovich answered, "To send you to the Moon."

Jake looked from the NASA executive to Donofrio and back again. They both had Christmas-surprise smiles on their faces.

As they approached the trio of technicians by the electronics consoles, one of them—tall, lanky, his light-brown hair hanging almost to his shoulders—stepped up to them and stuck out a lean, long-fingered hand.

"Hi. I'm Dave Quill."

"I'm Jake Ross."

"Yeah. Ms. Donofrio told me she'd be bringing you in this afternoon."

Somewhat annoyed, Jake said, "Could you tell me what we're doing here."

"Augmented reality," said Quill, as if that explained everything.

His annoyance growing, Jake asked, "And just what is augmented reality?"

Quill broke into a pleased grin. "It's like virtual reality—only better."

Jake saw that one of the other technicians was bringing a set of nubby-looking gloves and a pair of goggles over to them.

"Virtual reality?" he asked.

"Only better," Quill repeated.

Donofrio interjected, "You're going to the Moon, Jake. Astronaut Mitch Varmus is waiting for you."

As Jake reached for the gloves that the technician held out for him, Quill explained, "Augmented reality gives you a full, three-dimensional audio-visual simulation. You'll see yourself on the Moon, experience what it's like to be there."

The technician who was helping Jake worm his hands into the gloves added, "But you won't experience the Moon's lower gravity. We're still working on that problem." Jake nodded as he flexed his fingers inside the gloves.

They felt slightly scratchy, as if they were lined with Brillo pads.

Quill was saying, "We've done away with those big, cumbersome helmets that the old VR sets use. Everything they did is in the goggles now."

Jake accepted the goggles from the technician and slipped them on. They were heavily tinted; he could barely make out Jean Donofrio and Lincoln Yankovich standing a few feet away from him.

The technician stepped behind him and Jake felt him tighten the goggles' strap until it fit snugly around his head.

He stood there, feeling like a customer in a men's clothing store trying on a new, slightly ill-fitting suit.

"Okay," he said. "Now what?"

Quill's voice answered, "Close your eyes and count to ten, backwards."

Feeling silly, Jake squeezed his eyes shut and started counting. He heard a voice—probably an automated timer—counting down with him: "… six … five … four …"

He reached zero and opened his eyes.

He was standing on the Moon! The ground beneath his feet was a pitted, uneven expanse of gray. In the distance were mountains that looked old, aged, slumped smooth and tired. The horizon was much closer than he had ever seen it before; the sky was black and ablaze with stars. Jake's breath caught in his throat. Before he could say anything, he saw a figure in an astronaut's space suit stepping up in front of him.

"Hi," the astronaut said, extending a gloved hand. "I'm Mitch Varmus."

Jake reached for the man's hand. It felt solid, completely real. He saw that his own hand was encased in a thick glove, just like Varmus's.

"Welcome to Scott Base," said Varmus.

A voice in Jake's head marveled, *I'm on the Moon! I'm standing on the Moon!*

Varmus explained, "There are miniaturized microphones in the straps of your goggles. But there's about a three-second pause between what I say and when you hear it. We're really a quarter-million miles apart, you know."

Jake nodded and immediately felt idiotic. "I understand," he acknowledged. And saw that his head was inside a glasslike bubble helmet and his hand, his arms, his entire body was clad in a bright orange space suit.

For a little more than three seconds Varmus made no reply. At last he asked, "Want to take a little stroll?" He sounded almost jovial.

"Sure!" Jake answered.

Behind Varmus's standing figure Jake could see the dome of the base the astronauts had erected. Several other space-suited figures were working on some piece of equipment just outside the pressurized dome's air lock entrance.

Varmus pointed away from the dome, then reached out to grasp Jake's shoulder. Jake felt the weight of his grip: strong and certain.

"Come on; this way."

## ■ Scott Base

The tour of Scott Crater was fantastic. Jake felt as if he really was on the Moon, standing out on the floor of the crater, encased in the bright-orange pressure suit.

He quickly became accustomed to the slight delay in his exchanges with Varmus. Three seconds to bridge the distance between Greenbelt and Scott Crater, Jake thought. That's not so bad.

Varmus led him across the pitted ground and Jake saw clouds of dust where they stepped. He noticed his and the astronaut's boot prints on the dusty ground. Nobody's ever been here before, Jake marveled. I'm stepping where no one has gone before!

Varmus bent down—slowly, in the slightly stiff protective suit—and picked up a fist-sized rock from the many strewn on the crater's floor. He handed it to Jake, and Jake felt the solidity of the rock, its weight in his gloved hand.

Jake couldn't make out Varmus's face behind the curve of his helmet's visor, but he could hear the satisfaction in his voice.

"We're very happy that you could find the time to visit with us, sir."

Breaking into a big grin, Jake replied, "I wouldn't have missed this for the world." Then he realized they weren't on the world, really, and his cheeks flushed.

"This AR system is going to make Quinn a very rich SOB," Varmus said.

"Quinn?" Jake blurted. "You mean the kid who—"

"That kid has already turned down million-dollar offers from RCA and Generous Electric for this AR technology."

"Really?" Jake thought he might invest in augmented reality technology himself. Every kid in the world is going to want one of these sets, he realized.

Varmus led Jake to the entrance of the dome that the astronauts had erected.

"Home, sweet home," he said as he gestured Jake into the pressure lock.

Jake stepped inside, followed by the astronaut, and saw the outer hatch swing shut, closing off his view of the moonscape outside. The air-lock chamber was small, barely big enough for the two of them, and dimly lit in lurid red light. Then he heard the hiss of air as the air lock was automatically pressurized.

Varmus pressed a stud on the tiny control panel set on the wall next to the inner hatch, and the door slid open. "Welcome to Scott Base," said Varmus, with a stiff little bow.

Jake—still encased in the pressure suit that the AR system had drawn around him—stepped over the coaming of the hatch. Varmus followed close behind him.

"It's a bit cramped in here," Varmus said as he unfastened his bubble helmet and lifted it off his head. Jake realized his space suit had disappeared; he was in his office clothes again.

Looking around, Jake saw that the interior of the dome was packed with desks and consoles. "Where are the living quarters?" he asked.

Varmus pointed across the circular space. "Back behind those privacy screens." Moving his hand, he added, "And that little claustrophobic space over there is our dining area. Seats six. If you're not overweight."

Jake grinned at the astronaut. Varmus stepped over to a bench that ran in front of a row of open lockers. Easing himself down on the bench, he said, "Now comes the tricky part: getting myself out of this suit and its backpack."

"Can I help?"

Varmus shook his head. "You're a quarter-million miles away, Dr. Ross. You can handle simple objects, like that rock I gave you while we were outside. But you can't unlatch the straps holding my backpack."

Jake said a disappointed, "Oh."

"Not to worry," said the astronaut. "We've got it all under control." He wormed first one arm, then the other, out of the shoulder straps that held his life-support pack on his back. It settled on the bench behind him with a gentle thump.

"The designers made it easy," Varmus said, as he started to unzip the top of his suit. "Of course, the lower gravity helps."

One-sixth of an Earthly *gee*, Jake remembered.

Once he was down to his skivvies, free of his pressure suit, boots, and the undergarment of thin tubes that circulated cooling water over his body, Varmus got to his feet and reached into the locker behind him for a pair of blue coveralls.

"I want to show you what our telescope outside is looking at," he said as he pulled on the coveralls, then slipped his feet into soft-looking slippers.

Jake followed him to one of the consoles and, at Varmus's gesture, sat down in front of what looked like a television screen. It showed an image of a grayish sphere, with a dull reddish sphere glowing in the background.

"That's Proxima b," Varmus explained. "The planet orbiting around Alpha Centauri's smallest star."

Jake nodded. Alpha Centauri was a three-star system, he knew. The smallest star was a red dwarf dubbed Proxima, because it was nearer to Earth than any other star in the universe—just a tad more than four light-years away.

"That's what the astronomers back Earthside are studying," Jake said.

"Among other things. Almost looks close enough to touch, doesn't it?"

"Almost." Jake knew that the international astronomer's organization was looking for funding to send an unmanned probe to Proxima b. Trip time: slightly more than fifty years, one-way.

Jabbing a finger at the image on the screen, Varmus said, "I hear the astronomers are proposing a probe to that sucker."

"Nothing formal, as yet," said Jake.

A faraway look in his eyes as he stared at the screen, the astronaut murmured, "It sure would be something … going out to another star."

With a slight smile, Jake said, "Not for a while, Mitch. Not for a long while."

Varmus sighed. "Yeah. But it sure would be something, wouldn't it?" The look on Varmus's face somehow made Jake think of Leif Erikson, crossing the stormy Atlantic Ocean in an open Viking longboat to reach America several hundred years before Columbus.

For nearly an hour Varmus led Jake through the domed base. "The guys outside are scooping up the top layer of regolith. It's full of good stuff: aluminum, carbon, magnesium, calcium … there's even a little iron and titanium. And that's just the topmost layer."

Jake nodded. The raw materials for building solar power satellites were in the Moon's surface layers, he knew. Varmus's team was confirming what the old *Apollo* astronauts had discovered.

"The Moon can become a resource base," he said.

Varmus agreed with a grin and a nod. "Pittsburgh in space."

The other astronauts began reentering the dome, one and two at a time. Jake squeezed in at their dining table and watched them wolf down sandwiches and colas as they chattered about the work they were doing outside.

A voice wormed into Jake's ear. "Time's up, Dr. Ross." It was Dave Quill's voice. "We're ending the visit."

And suddenly Jake was sitting alone on an upright wooden chair in the middle of the spacious, mostly empty AR chamber. He felt a pang of grief, like a child who's had his favorite toy yanked out of his arms.

Quill was leaning over him, grinning expectantly. "How'd you like it?"

Jake rose slowly from the chair, his legs trembling. "Fine!" he exclaimed. "Terrific. It was wonderful!"

Jean Donofrio strode up to him, beaming. "Isn't it great?"

"It's tremendous," said Jake. "How can I buy into this?"

Quill's grin got even wider. "I've got a couple of financial guys working on that."

## ■ The Oval Office

"You've got to try it, Frank," Jake insisted.

Sitting beside Jake in front of the president's desk, Kevin O'Donnell shook his head. Minimally.

"The president of the United States doesn't have time to play astronaut."

But Tomlinson cocked a brow at his chief of staff. "Now wait a minute, Kevin. This might be a good public relations gimmick."

O'Donnell started to counter, "You don't need—"

"It'd be terrific," Jake enthused. "The president of the United States talking to the voters from the Moon!"

"They won't see him on the Moon," O'Donnell said. "Just sitting in a goddamned chair with some fancy electronics rig on his head."

Tomlinson's bright smile dimmed considerably. "Yes, that's right."

Jean Donofrio, the third person sitting in front of the president's desk, said, "Could Quill arrange it so that the people watching on TV could see what the president was seeing?"

"Maybe," said Jake. "I'll ask him."

O'Donnell's face was set in his usual tight little scowl. "Maybe we oughta get back to what's important, huh?"

Still grinning, President Tomlinson asked, "What's important, Kev?"

"McMasters."

The president's grin disappeared. Jake felt his insides go taut. The real world, he said to himself.

"What's his next move?" O'Donnell asked. Turning to Donofrio, he asked, "Jean, any thoughts?"

She shrugged minimally and lied, "I don't know."

Jake said, "He's chair of the Senate Committee on Commerce, Science, and Transportation."

"Tell us something we don't know," O'Donnell groused.

"He wants to cut NASA out of the *Artemis* program," said the president.

"We can't let him do that," O'Donnell said. "It would gut the program."

Jake countered, "Would it? Or would it make a bunch of NASA people leave the agency and join *Artemis*?"

Tomlinson murmured, "A wholesale move from the government to the private program."

Shaking his head, O'Donnell argued, "That'd shake up NASA *and Artemis*. It'd set the program back by a year, at least."

"I don't know about that, Kevin," said Jake.

"Well I do. You can't get a hundred or more people to quit the space agency and sign up in your private program in the blink of an eye. Your *Artemis* program isn't organized for that kind of a transfer. It'd take months to get them all settled in *Artemis*. Even if most of the NASA geeks want to move to the private program, which a lot of them won't want to do, in the first place."

The president, who had been following the exchange between the two men with his eyes, asked softly, "Kev, are you saying that it can't be done?"

Looking more uncomfortable than usual, O'Donnell answered slowly, "No … not really. But it would take some time to get it all straightened out. It would louse up the *Artemis* schedule but good."

"But it could be done."

Jake jumped in with, "For god's sake, we've got half a dozen people working on the Moon! Of course it could be done! We can do anything we set our minds to!"

O'Donnell cast his eyes to the ceiling, as if seeking heavenly assistance.

President Tomlinson said, "Let's get General Farthington in here and see what he thinks about this. Maybe we could work out a kind of loan, send the NASA people involved with *Artemis* to work with the program without quitting NASA."

"That could work," Jake said.

"Sure," O'Donnell moaned. "Easy as walking on water."

With a grin, Jake said, "Jesus did."

O'Donnell's expression could have curdled milk. "You ain't Jesus, kid."

"Jesus didn't walk on the Moon," Jake countered. "I have."

O'Donnell crossed himself.

## ■ Jean Donofrio's Apartment

It was a pleasant, spacious penthouse apartment in a twelve-story building off Connecticut Avenue, tucked in among the embassies and residences of the ambassadors and other diplomats who lived in Washington.

Jean Donofrio opened her front door, stepped into the apartment's foyer, and tossed her handbag onto the delicate side table in the entryway. It hit the edge of the table, teetered there for a moment, then thunked to the carpeted floor.

Jean stared at it, anger rising within her at the general cussedness of inanimate objects, then slammed the door shut and left the handbag there as she strode into her living room.

She stopped in front of the wide window that looked out onto Connecticut Avenue. The capital of the United States spread out beyond the window. The capital of the world, really.

And where do I fit in? she asked herself. She had thought Gene McMasters was a good catch for a country girl from Jackson,

Tennessee. He doesn't really care for me, I'm just one of his office harem, she knew. And he's not much in bed. But I could make him care. I could make him divorce his stupid wife and marry me, if I wanted to.

But do I want to?

Turning away from the window, Jean stepped to the sofa and sank into its overly yielding cushions. That's me, she thought: overly yielding.

She leaned back and stared at the ceiling. In her mind's eye she saw B. Franklin Tomlinson, the president of the United States.

He's already married, Jean told herself. And Mrs. Tomlinson won't let go of him. Why should she? But Frank is susceptible. I can see the way he looks at me. He's wondering if I'm available. Yes, sir, Mr. President, she said to herself. I'm available. Ready, willing, and able.

How would Gene react? The heartless bastard would cheer me on. He doesn't care for me, he's just *Wham, bam, thank you ma'am.* Without the "thank you."

But Frank Tomlinson. The president of the United States. He'd be different. He'd be kinder, more sensitive.

Jean rose from the sofa and headed into her bedroom, thinking, I can make it with the president. And McMasters would thank me for it.

She laughed aloud. It's a win-win situation. I win both ways.

# Reorganization

With a sour expression on his face, President Tomlinson said, "I've got a group of bankers coming in here in fifteen minutes to tell me what I'm doing wrong to the financial industry."

Kevin O'Donnell grimaced. "They're never happy, are they?"

Sitting next to O'Donnell in front of the president's desk, Adam Westerly cautioned, "You should try to make them happy, Mr. President."

Tomlinson nodded, but said, "Yes, but how? The economy's in good shape, but they act as if Black Tuesday was hanging over their heads."

Jake was the third person sitting before the president's desk, at O'Donnell's left. He glanced at his wristwatch, then said, "We'd better make up our minds about *Artemis*'s organization, then."

Tomlinson nodded.

Almost in a growl, O'Donnell said, "McMasters has placed NASA's budget request on the agenda for his committee's meeting next Thursday."

With a slight frown, Westerly rumbled, "He'll recommend cutting NASA's work on *Artemis* out of the agency's budget." The man actually had no official position in the president's staff, but Tomlinson had kept him on as a special advisor. His viewpoint was important, valuable, the president believed.

"We should never have outlawed dueling," Tomlinson muttered.

The three men sitting before his desk gaped at him.

"I could meet McMasters on the field of honor and blow his stupid brains out."

Jake blinked at the president. "That's illegal."

"Too bad."

O'Donnell sat up straighter in his chair. "Uh, Frank, we need some reality here."

Tomlinson grinned at him and nodded. "I know Kev. I know."

Westerly suggested, "Suppose we preempt McMasters."

"Preempt him?"

"We show the committee that we're already reorganizing NASA to handle the *Artemis* program without disturbing its other, ongoing efforts."

O'Donnell broke into a rare grin. "That's right! Show the committee we're not allowing *Artemis* to get in the way of the agency's other programs."

Tomlinson shook his head. "I don't know …."

Westerly smiled. "We could get Bloviating Billy to testify, explain the reorganization to the committee."

"And put them all to sleep," Jake said.

O'Donnell half-turned in his chair and tapped Jake's knee. "When they're asleep they can't vote."

The president laughed and said to Westerly, "Adam, I think you've got something here."

William T. Farthington fixed Jake with a hard stare as he said, "You want to segregate everyone working on *Artemis*? Put 'em in a separate organization altogether?"

The two men were sitting in a booth toward the back end of the Old Ebbitt Grill. It was the lunch hour. The place was bulging with DC bureaucrats and the men and women who worked for and with them. The buzz of their many conversations filled the restaurant and its jam-packed bar with a constant high-intensity hum, punctuated here and there by a sudden burst of laughter.

"We've got to get ahead of McMasters," Jake urged. "Otherwise he'll scuttle *Artemis*."

"I don't think he could do that, even if he tried," Farthington said, leaning across the table separating him from Jake so he could be heard over the background chatter.

"I'd like to make sure that he can't."

Farthington sank back and stared at Jake for a long silent moment. "Put all my people working on *Artemis* into one group," he murmured.

"Headed by Yankovich," said Jake, nodding.

"You want to move 'em to New Mexico? Put 'em in with Piazza's gang?"

Jake's nod morphed into a shake of his head. "I don't think that's necessary, Bill. Or desirable. Just separate them from your other programs, give them a location they can call their own."

Farthington said nothing for a moment, then, "Okay. Can do. I'm supposed to appear at the committee meeting next week. I'll tell McMasters and the others about it then."

"Good," said Jake. "It'll show that the agency is actively engaged in *Artemis*."

"Maybe I should bring Yankovich along with me. Let him tell the committee what we're involved with on *Artemis*."

Jake felt his brows hike up. "Good thinking, Bill."

With a grin, Farthington said, "Beats bloviating."

# Committee Meeting

The Senate Committee on Commerce, Science, and Transportation, chaired by Eugene McMasters, convened in one of the Senate's rococo-adorned meeting chambers.

Sitting a few rows behind the witness chair, Jake glanced out the two-story-high window on the left side of the room. It was a beautiful day in late spring out there, trees breaking into leaf, bright sunshine lighting the busy streets.

McMasters tapped his fingernails on the desktop in front of him and the hearing chamber instantly fell silent.

That's power, Jake said to himself.

"The meeting will come to order," McMasters said.

His voice was only a little above a whisper, but all the room's attention focused on him.

McMasters offered a motion to suspend reading the minutes of the previous meeting. The motion passed unanimously. The other senators didn't even have to raise their hands; they simply nodded their acceptance.

As the committee worked its way through the agenda, Jake looked over his shoulder. William T. Farthington was nowhere in sight. He's not going to skip this meeting! Jake said to himself, alarmed.

"Next item on our agenda concerns NASA's participation in the private space endeavor known as Project *Artemis*," said McMasters, in a cold, almost frigid tone. "We were expecting the director of NASA, General William—"

"Present and accounted for," came Farthington's voice from the rear of the hearing chamber. Jake twisted around on his seat and saw the NASA director striding down the chamber's central aisle, with his second in command, Lincoln Yankovich, a step behind him.

Jake couldn't help grinning. Farthington knows how to make an entrance, he thought. The NASA director was large, roundish, his unbuttoned suit jacket flapping as he hustled down the aisle. Following right on his heels, Yankovich was slim, stylish, and obviously in a bit of distress as he struggled to keep up with his boss.

"Sorry to be a li'l bit late, Senator McMasters," Farthington said, as he plumped himself down on the witness chair, his voice rich with a hint of a mellifluous Deep South accent. "We got sorta stuck in traffic."

With a crooked little smile, McMasters replied, "Glad you could get here."

Ignoring the jibe, Farthington said, "I'm very glad to have this opportunity to address your committee, senator. Big things are happening in our nation's expansion into the space frontier, and I'm proud to explain the work that NASA is doing to help that development."

And for the next half hour Farthington painted a verbal picture of how Project *Artemis* was establishing a *permanent* human presence on the Moon, and how NASA was a key partner in this exciting new endeavor.

Even Jake felt thrilled at the future Farthington was outlining. The senators seated on McMasters's either side were smiling and nodding as the NASA chief's words flowed over them.

"And now, to give you the details of this cooperative effort between NASA and private enterprise, may I introduce my second in command, Dr. Lincoln Yankovich, who is in charge of our agency's contribution to the *Artemis* program."

In a frosty tone, McMasters said, "The chair recognizes Dr. Yankovich."

Farthington got up from the witness chair and stood by it as Yankovich seated himself.

"Senator McMasters," Yankovich began, his voice thin and reedy, "and members of this distinguished committee, I have the high honor of directing the National Aeronautics and Space Administration's participation in the *Artemis* program, which—even as we speak at this moment—has a team of astronauts working on the Moon to prepare a permanent habitat for our astronauts, scientists, and industrial personnel.

"The first slide, please."

For the next half hour and slightly more, Yankovich presented a smooth review of NASA's work at Scott Crater, complete with individual photographs of the team working on the Moon and artists' renderings of what the Scott Base would look like when' completed.

As his final slide faded from the screen set up at the right of the committee's banc of seats, Yankovich said calmly, reasonably, "And this is merely the beginning of the *Artemis* program's objectives. One of our major goals is to build a solar power satellite and place it in orbit around the Earth at slightly higher than twenty-two thousand miles above the equator. From that position it will beam some fifty thousand megawatts of electrical energy to Earth, enough to meet the energy requirements of several states, cleanly and efficiently, with no damaging pollution to the air or water of those states."

Jake studied the senators' faces as they focused on Yankovich's presentation. He's got them! Jake said to himself. He's showing them a future that they all want to see. And take credit for.

# Postgame Analysis

It almost felt like a victory celebration. Jake sat in the Oval Office with President Tomlinson, Kevin O'Donnell, William Farthington, Lincoln Yankovich, and Adam Westerly reviewing the results of McMasters's committee meeting.

"Did you see the look on McMasters's face when he gaveled the meeting closed?" O'Donnell asked, his face wreathed in a rare smile.

Tomlinson, leaning back, relaxed in his desk chair, was grinning.

Westerly crowed, "Looked like he was eating broccoli."

"He wasn't happy," said Jake.

Farthington broke their mood. "He was certainly pissed off. We've made an enemy of him."

O'Donnell nodded reluctantly. "He was already our enemy, General."

"But we upset his apple cart. In public. He's not going to forget that. Or forgive it."

President Tomlinson asked, "So what do we do about it, Bill?"

With the barest shrug of his shoulders, Farthington answered, "We complete the base at Scott Crater and get some working scientists up there as soon as we can. Before McMasters finds a way to stop us."

"He can't stop us now," Jake countered. "We're working on the Moon, for god's sake."

"It would be good if those astronauts found something useful, something that the man in the street—the average Joe—could get excited about."

"Like diamonds, maybe?" O'Donnell asked, in a small voice.

"Or an oil deposit," said Westerly.

With a shake of his head, Jake groused, "Get real! We have a team working on the Moon, for god's sake. Isn't that enough?"

Farthington shook his head. "What was miraculous yesterday becomes an ordinary part of the background noise very quickly."

The president nodded agreement as he murmured, "Bread and circuses."

"Keep the peasants excited," said Farthington. "We don't have peasants in this country," Jake snapped.

"True," said the president. "But we do have voters."

By the time Jake got home that evening, all the excitement of the committee meeting had evaporated out of him.

As he opened the door to the apartment, Tami jumped up from the sofa where she'd been sitting, and rushed to him.

Jake tossed his slim briefcase on the table by the door and slid his other arm around her waist. They kissed.

"Good show!" Tami said enthusiastically. "I watched it at the studio. You pulled the rug out from under Senator McMasters's feet."

"And made him into an implacable enemy," Jake said wearily.

With a shake of her head Tami replied, "He was already an implacable enemy. You want to develop the space frontier; he wants the White House and he's willing to scrap everything you stand for to get there."

"So how do we stop him?"

Leading Jake toward their kitchen, she said, "Develop Scott Base. Build that solar power satellite.

He smiled at his wife. "That's going to take time, honey. More than a year, at least. And all that time, McMasters will be working to stop us."

Tami recognized Jake's dour mood. She turned to the kitchen cabinet that held their liquor supply.

"You need a little Jack Daniel's," she said brightly.

"I need an idea that'll get McMasters off our backs," he grumbled.

The Jack Daniel's didn't help Jake's mood. Tami remained bright and cheerful all through dinner and even suggested that they go down to their favorite ice cream parlor for dessert, but Jake merely shook his head morosely.

"Tami, you don't understand!" he barked at her as they were clearing the dinner dishes off the foldout table. "This is a serious problem! We can't have McMasters carrying an axe, ready to chop us down at the first opportunity he gets!"

He stalked out of the kitchen and threw himself onto their living room sofa. Tami followed him a step behind.

"Jake," she said, "you'll find a way. You'll figure it out, I know you will."

He looked up and smiled at her. "Yeah. Too bad we can't stuff McMasters into a rocket and shoot him off to Alpha Centauri."

Tami dropped down onto the sofa beside him, her deep-brown eyes suddenly flashing wide. "That's it!" she exclaimed.

# The Space Lottery

"What's it?" Jake asked.

"Send people to Scott Base!" said Tami, grinning hugely. "Ordinary people. Regular folks. It'd be terrific!"

Jake stared at her. "We can't do that. Suppose one of them gets hurt on the Moon? Or dies? It'd kill the whole program."

"You're a gloomy cuss tonight."

"I can't turn Scott Base into a tourist hotel."

Undeterred, Tami enthused, "All right, how about this? Offer a visit to Scott Base to a reputable scientist who has an experiment that needs to be done on the Moon."

Jake started to reply, caught himself before he could utter a word.

"Make it an international program," Tami went on. "Open it up to scientists from anywhere on Earth."

"NASA had a program sort of like that years ago," Jake remembered. "Carried small experiments that students built in the old Space Shuttle."

Nodding vigorously, Tami agreed, "You could bring the scientists and their experiments to the Scott Base. It'd be terrific publicity!"

"Until somebody gets hurt."

"Don't be such a sourpuss!"

A small smile inching across his lips, Jake said, "It would be terrific publicity for *Artemis*." But then he added, "Until somebody gets killed."

"A martyr to science," Tami said.

"That's not how McMasters would describe it."

She stared at him for a wordless moment. Then, "What's that thing you always say about the turtle? He only makes progress when he sticks his neck out?"

Despite his misgivings, Jake grinned at his wife. "I know another story."

"Oh?"

"It's about the first completely automated airliner flight. From New York to Los Angeles."

Tami arched a questioning brow.

"The passengers all get strapped down in their seats and as the plane starts taxiing to the runway the intercom comes on. A mechanical voice says, 'Welcome aboard our first completely automated flight. There is no human crew aboard, only robots.' "

Tami interrupted, "Only robots?"

"Yeah," said Jake. "The robot captain goes on, 'We will fly in complete safety. With our robot crew, nothing can go wrong … can go wrong … can go wrong ….' "

Tami did not laugh.

Lincoln Yankovich leaned back in his black leather desk chair and touched a fingertip to his pencil-thin moustache.

He asked, "Invite scientists from all around the world to bring experiments to Scott Base?"

Jake nodded. "It would create international support for the *Artemis* program."

With a wary little nod, Yankovich murmured, "We need support here at home, Jake."

"Here too, of course."

"You realize that it would be risky. Very risky. If anything went wrong …." Yankovich let the thought dangle, unspoken.

Sitting in front of the NASA executive's desk, Jake argued, "NASA's done this kind of thing before. You took a United States senator up on a shuttle flight, years ago."

With the barest of nods Yankovich retorted, "And he set an interplanetary record for upchucking."

Suppressing a grin, Jake pointed out, "But he supported NASA faithfully as long as he was in the Senate."

"True enough."

"A guest investigator program will generate tremendous interest among the people. And the world's scientists."

Yankovich murmured, "Give scientists the opportunity to do an experiment on the Moon."

"Broaden support for the *Artemis* program."

"We'd have to put together a team of people to evaluate the proposals that the scientists send to us."

Jake agreed. "Retired astronauts. University professors."

Nodding more vigorously, Yankovich added, "Politicians, too. You ought to be on the evaluation board, Jake."

"Me? I'm no politician."

Yankovich broke into a rare grin. "The hell you're not."

## Counterpoint

"A lottery?" Senator McMasters exclaimed.

Sitting in front of the senator's desk, his staff chief, a pasty-faced old-timer, wise in the ways of Washington maneuvers, nodded slowly.

"It's a genius move, senator. It'll generate interest in the *Artemis* program from everybody—teenaged kids to Nobel laureate scientists."

McMasters frowned at the man and turned to his public relations director, a stylishly dressed woman whose sculpted, high-cheekboned face was a monument to cosmetic surgery.

"What do you think, Mavis?"

Carefully arching a brow at the senator, she replied, "I agree with Harold. It's a stroke of genius."

"Every geek kid in America will send in an idea," Harold foretold. "And every scientist."

"It's a winning idea," said the PR director.

"And it doesn't need to go through your committee or any other part of the government," the staff chief added. "*Artemis* is a private program. If anything goes wrong, it'll be on their head, not ours."

"It won't even have to go through the safety people?" McMasters demanded. "Flying to the Moon can be dangerous, can't it?"

Mavis nodded. With a shrug Harold answered, "Maybe. Maybe not."

McMasters growled a heartfelt, "Shit!"

Nicholas Piazza leaned his lanky body back in his desk chair and brought his long-fingered hands up to his chin in a prayerful gesture.

"Carry scientists up to Scott Base?"

Sitting in front of Piazza's desk, Jake nodded vigorously. "Scientists who have an experiment to do on the Moon."

"Don't we have enough scientists going to the Moon?"

Patiently, Jake explained the reasoning behind the guest investigator idea, finishing with, "It'll generate tremendous interest in the *Artemis* program."

Piazza's youthful face looked intrigued. But he asked, "And what do we do when one of them croaks at Scott Base? Invite his folks to the funeral?"

"We make damned certain that they don't get themselves killed."

"Easier said than done, Jake."

Hunching forward in his chair, Jake coaxed, "There are risks, of course. But there are advantages, too.

Tremendous advantages. This could create worldwide interest in *Artemis*."

"I can see that. But the interest would turn to condemnation if anything went wrong."

Jake nodded agreement. But he said, "Nick, if we get five or six guest investigators to Scott Base and then back home safely, I think we could weather even a fatal accident."

For a breathlessly long moment Piazza simply stared at Jake, saying nothing, his pale blue eyes locked on Jake's dark brown ones.

At last he said, "It's a risk, Jake. A risk we don't really need to take."

"I think it could help the program tremendously," Jake countered.

"Maybe," Piazza said. Then, sitting up straighter in his handsome leather chair, he asked, "Is it a risk you're willing to take?"

"Me?" Jake blurted.

Pointing a long finger at him, Piazza replied, "Yeah, you. Are you so sure that it's all safe and reliable that you're willing to take a jaunt out to Scott Base?"

Jake blinked once, then answered, "Yes, I guess I am."

"You guess?"

Jake realized it was *put up or shut up* time. "I'm willing," he said firmly. "I'll go to Scott Base. I'll go to the bottom of the goddamned ocean if it'll help the *Artemis* program."

Piazza smiled at him. "Good. I'll set up the arrangements."

Jake grinned back, just a little bit weakly.

# Book Two: Summer

## ■ Spaceport America

"T-minus ten minutes."

Jake heard the launch controller's voice in his helmet earphones. He was lying on one of the acceleration couches of the *Lunar Express II*'s crew capsule, together with six other men and women on their way to Scott Base.

It had been a hectic six weeks for Jake. He had lost count of the number of times he'd flitted from Washington to the headquarters of Astra Corporation in New Mexico, where he trained for his flight to Scott Base, on the Moon.

Jake felt tired, almost exhausted. His training for this Moon flight had been intensive: physical tests, learning how to get into a protective space suit, augmented reality sessions to prepare him for living at Scott Base. If it hadn't been for Jean Donofrio's unstinting help in running his office he could never have undertaken this mission to the Moon, he knew.

"T-minus five minutes," the launch controller said in a flat, unemotional tone. "All systems are *go*."

Jake realized he was biting his lip. I ought to feel excited, he told himself. Exhilarated. But all he felt was a bone-deep weariness.

Turning his head inside his bubble helmet, Jake saw two of the scientists heading Moonward lying beside him. They looked calm, assured. No butterflies in their stomachs.

Jake's guts felt as if a horde of winged antelopes were flitting around inside him.

"You can still back out of this," Tami had told him, the night before he left for the launch.

"No I can't," Jake had answered. "I can't back out. Not now. Not ever."

She slid her arms around his neck and whispered, "I'll be waiting for you, darling."

Lying on the acceleration couch, Jake realized there was a fair chance that he'd return to her in a pine casket.

But he clenched his gloved fists—and his teeth—and waited for the countdown to reach its climax.

The launch controller's voice was replaced by the automatic countdown sequencer's flat, emotionless: "Ten seconds … nine … eight …."

Jake sucked in a deep breath and consciously yawned widely. *This is it*, he told himself. *You're flying to the Moon.*

He could hear gurgling noises and the clicks and slams of equipment awakening.

"… four … three … two …."

*Here we go!* Jake had to urinate. Glad that he was connected to the waste collector system, he let go just as the rocket's mighty engines lit off.

The roar was the most tremendous howl of power Jake had ever heard. The capsule began to vibrate, shaking Jake violently, like a rat caught in a cat's steely jaws.

He felt a gigantic invisible hand pressing down on his chest, squeezing him into the contoured couch on which he lay. It was hard to breathe; the force of the rocket's acceleration was squeezing the air out of his lungs.

"Goddamned asthma," he muttered to himself. He hadn't told the medics about it and now he wondered if it was going to kill him.

Pressing his eyes shut, Jake lay there while the rocket tried to shake the life out of him. He clenched his fists, but he couldn't lift his arms up from where they lay at his sides, they seemed to weigh four hundred pounds apiece. His vision blurred. He couldn't breathe.

And suddenly it all stopped.

The noise and rattling stopped, as if someone had turned them off. Opening his eyes, Jake saw his arms floating off the couch on either side of him.

"Woo-ee!" A man's voice shrilled in his helmet earphones. "That was some ride!"

"We're in zero gravity," a woman's voice said.

Jake turned his head enough to see the small window on his right. Nothing but blackness. *We're in space! We've left Earth.*

Then the big blue ball of Earth slid across his view. Deep-blue ocean decked with clouds of the purest white. Wrinkled brown mountains and stretches of land. More clouds curving in from the sea. No sign of cities. No trace of human habitation.

There! A thin white line, straight as if drawn with a ruler. *That's a jet airliner,* Jake realized. He was looking at his home, the home of the human race, the people who had risen from cave dwellers to the makers of jet airliners and rockets that could fly you to the Moon.

His eyes filled with tears.

## ■ Scott Base

It took slightly more than twenty-four hours to reach the Moon. Jake and his fellow travelers ate, slept, and evacuated their wastes without getting up from their acceleration couches. All the comforts of home, Jake thought, although he knew they would all smell pretty bad by the time they landed at Scott Crater.

There was one professional astronaut together with the six scientists crowded into the *Lunar Express* capsule. Jake started to correct himself, murmuring, "Five scientists and one political—" But then he stopped. Hey, I'm an astronomer, he told himself. I can do useful work up there. Maybe.

"You can crank up your seats now," said the astronaut in charge of this flight—a boyish-looking air force retiree from Texas named Ray Carstairs. One by one, the passengers did that and then slid open the visors of their helmets. After nearly an hour of oohing and aahing at the view of Earth as they orbited the planet, Carstairs told them it was mealtime.

It was a little clumsy trying to eat while still encased in their space suits. The gloves made it tricky to grasp the little plastic spoons that came with the prepackaged meals. Jake took it slowly, easing small spoonfuls of the nearly tasteless food past the collar ring of his helmet and carefully into his mouth.

Didn't drop anything, he told himself proudly. Some of the others were not as neat; gobbets of food and tiny globules of liquids hovered weightlessly among the passengers.

The hours passed slowly, with nothing to do. After two orbits around the Earth, Carstairs announced, "Okay, we're go for the lunar insertion burn."

The rockets roared again, but only briefly. Jake hardly felt any push. But he thought, *We're off to the Moon!*

A couple of the passengers dozed off, but Jake couldn't sleep, despite cranking his couch down to the reclining position and squeezing his eyes shut. After giving up on sleeping, he pulled up to the sitting position again and looked out the compartment's small window. Nothing but the blackness of space out there. No Earth, no Moon—just empty darkness. Jake turned back to the displays of the instruments arrayed in the front of the compartment, where Carstairs sat. Their dials clicked away slowly.

At last Carstairs announced, "Okay, we're ready for our deorbit burn and landing at Scott. Visors down and locked, please."

Glad to have at last something to do, Jake reached for his helmet's visor. His gloves made his fingers a little clumsy, but he got his visor locked in place.

"Confirm you're locked and loaded, please," Carstairs commanded.

One by one, the passengers confirmed.

Jake was last. "Locked and loaded," he said. It felt a bit silly, but he said it.

Carstairs nodded inside his bubble helmet. Then he announced, "Deorbit burn in fifteen seconds."

Jake silently counted off the seconds. Precisely at fifteen he felt a gentle push, more like someone nudging him playfully than the chest-squeezing pressure he'd felt at liftoff.

In his helmet's earphones, Jake could hear the chatter between their astronaut and the controller at Scott Base.

"Confirm deorbit burn," said the woman's voice. "You're on the curve, Ray."

"Comin' to see you, honey," Carstairs said jovially.

"I'm right here, waiting for you," the woman replied.

Jake turned his head to peer out the tiny window again. Nothing but blackness. Then, abruptly, the gray surface of the Moon came into view, utterly bare rock, lifeless, riddled with meteor craters.

Dead as a doornail, Jake said to himself. But then the memory of an old poem rang in his mind:

> "... to the land vaguely realizing westward,
> But still unstoried, artless, unenhanced.
> Such as she was, such as she would become.

Robert Frost, he remembered: *The Gift Outright*. And he looked at the barren lunar landscape again. *Such as she was, such as she would become.*

As the spacecraft hurtled toward the empty, naked surface of the Moon, Jake told himself, We're going to build cities there, new nations, new civilizations, new worlds.

A sudden surge of rocket power jolted Jake against the restraining straps holding him down against the couch.

Then the capsule's descent started again, and again he was thumped by a squirt of the descent rockets.

Then the noise of the rockets abruptly shut down and all the vibrations ceased.

Before Jake could pull in a ragged breath, he heard Carstairs announce happily, "That's it. We're down.

Welcome to Scott Base."

Jake felt like singing. He was in Scott Base's lone shower, scrubbing away nearly two days of accumulated grime as the hot water poured over his naked body. Each of the new arrivals took a turn in the shower. Jake was the last, and he marveled that the hot water lasted so long.

Then, freshly scrubbed and decked in a regulation sky-blue set of coveralls, he stepped out into the crowded, busy living/working area of Scott Base.

The circular area was jammed full of desks and computer screens, shoehorned together so tightly there seemed to be hardly enough room to squeeze between them. Jake remembered from his AR tours of the base that the partitions on the other side of the area from where he stood marked off the privacy cubicles where the staff slept. Turning slightly, he saw the single longish table where meals were taken. But most of the floor space was devoted to the working area, the places where the scientists would do their jobs.

"Well, you cleaned up pretty well," said Mitchell Varmus, grinning warmly as he extended his hand toward Jake.

The astronaut was already wearing a pressure suit—minus its helmet and gloves.

Jake grinned back at Varmus. "Looks like you're all dressed up for an outing."

"My team and I are returning to home sweet home," Varmus said. "We leave the base to you. Everything's in working order."

"I appreciated the hot water."

"Hey, what's a nuclear reactor good for if it can't heat some shower water?"

As Jake walked Varmus toward the base's entry hatch, the astronaut said, in a lowered voice, "We really appreciate your coming up here, Dr. Ross. It—"

"Jake," corrected Jake.

Varmus's smile broadened. "Jake. We all appreciate your coming up here. It means a lot to us."

Jake grinned back at the astronaut. "Means a lot to me, Mitch. A helluva lot."

Scott Base ran on Greenwich Mean Time, which meant that dinner was due shortly after Varmus and his team departed. The scientists who sat with Jake were quiet; the reality of where they were and what they had to do was just starting to become real to them.

That evening Jake called Tami. He had to wait his turn, as each of the newcomers had a specified time for a call back to Earth. At last, in the questionable privacy of his narrow, screened-in sleeping area, Jake saw his wife's face on the TV monitor at the foot of his bunk.

"I'm here, Tami," he said. "Safe and sound."

Some three seconds later Tami added, smiling happily, "On the Moon."

"Yeah."

Again the three-second wait. Then, "How's it feel?" she asked.

"Fine. Snug as a bug in a rug."

"Really?"

"Really." Lowering his voice, Jake added, "I only wish you were here with me."

"Me too."

"What time is it in Washington?"

Tami glanced away from the screen, then answered, "Quarter to three."

"You've been waiting all night for me to call?"

"Jake, darling, it's the middle of the afternoon."

They both broke into laughter. Jake talked with Tami until an operator's voice broke in with, "You've used up your allotted time, Dr. Ross."

Jake said his goodnight to his wife, then clicked off the tiny light over his cot and closed his eyes to sleep.

If he had any dreams, he didn't remember them when he awoke the next morning.

# Discovery

The days and nights settled into a routine that wasn't quite dull, but pretty close to it. Teams of two and three people left the base, plodding in their pressure suits slowly, carefully, obviously wary of walking in the Moon's one-sixth of Earth's familiar gravity.

He talked with Jean Donofrio every day; she cheerfully assured him that the office was running smoothly without him. Jake didn't know whether he should be pleased or apprehensive. News reporters interviewed him, but after the first few "live from the Moon" chats, their calls became less frequent.

Jake went outside twice, goggling at the vistas spreading around him. Scott Crater was just a tad over one hundred kilometers wide, ringed by slumped and weary-looking mountains that had been sandpapered smooth by eons of meteoric infall. The dome of the artificial base looked out of place, almost bizarre, as if sited in the middle of the lunar desolation by an alien visitor.

And Jake realized that he and his fellow humans were the aliens. But we're not visitors, he told himself. We're here to stay, to grow, to expand our knowledge and our capabilities.

Turning away from the dome of their base, Jake looked up to see the Earth, riding low on the black horizon.

Blue and vibrant, decked with purest white clouds, the home of the human race.

But we're leaving home, he thought. We're expanding humankind's territory. What was it that the Russian rocket scientist, Tsiolkovsky, said?

And he remembered, "Earth is the cradle of humanity, but one cannot live in a cradle forever."

Standing on the pockmarked floor of Scott Crater, staring through his bubble helmet at the blue and white beauty of the Earth, Jake murmured, "We're leaving the cradle. We're growing up."

A sharp buzz in his helmet's earphones shattered his mood. "Dr. Ross? This is Charlene Martinson."

Jake instinctively blurted, "What's wrong?"

"Nothing!" Martinson answered. "But Dr. Zarek wants to show you something."

Zarek was the leader of the three-person astronomy team, Jake knew.

"Right now?"

"He's pretty spooled up about it." Charlene Martinson's voice was trembling with excitement.

Nodding inside his bubble helmet, Jake said, "Okay. I'm coming in."

It took more than half an hour for Jake to squirm out of his protective pressure suit and vacuum the accumulated gray lunar dust off its boots and leggings. Charlene Martinson—almost Jake's own height, brown-haired, gawky as a teenager—stood beside him, obviously impatient.

At last Jake was free and standing in his sky-blue coveralls again. Feeling relieved, he said to Martinson, "Okay, where's Dr. Zarek?"

She led him through the welter of closely spaced desks to one that was placed next to the base's sloping, circular wall. A short, stubby man with a dark buzz cut and the scraggly beginnings of a beard was standing behind the desk, staring at the big viewscreen mounted on the base's encircling dome.

"Dr. Zarek?" Martinson said, almost in a whisper.

William Zarek wheeled around, as if startled. Jake saw that despite the attempted beard, the astronomer was youngish, at least five years younger than himself. Maybe more.

"Dr. Ross!" Zarek exclaimed as he put out his hand.

Clasping Zarek's hand in his own, Jake said, "Jake. Please call me Jake."

"Good," said Zarek. Turning toward the display screen, he said, "There it is."

Jake saw a graph. Nothing but sharply angled lines parading across a cross-hatched grid.

"What is it?" he asked.

Zarek blinked once, then said, "That's a plot of the orbit of Sirius B."

Jake knew that Sirius—the brightest star in Earth's heavens—was a binary, with a blazing blue-white major star and a tiny white dwarf companion orbiting around it. Known since antiquity as the Dog Star, Sirius's companion had been quickly dubbed "the Pup."

Before Jake could ask a question, Zarek picked up a laser pointer from his desk and highlighted a particular blip in the orbital path.

"You see?" he asked, his light tenor voice shaking with excitement. "See the dips here, and here? The star has a planet orbiting around it!"

Jake nodded.

"A planet about the mass of Earth!" Zarek crowed.

Jake could feel the man's excitement. "Do you have a visual?"

"Not yet. I've sent a request to the Astronomical Association for some time on Big Eye, but they haven't replied yet."

"An Earth-sized planet orbiting Sirius B. Less than ten light-years from us." Jake reached out and patted Zarek's shoulder. "That's quite a discovery, Dr. Zarek."

Nodding happily, Zarek said, "I was hoping that you might add your weight to my request ... Jake."

"Certainly," Jake replied. "I'd be glad to."

Zarek broke into a happy grin. But he didn't give Jake one single word of thanks.

## ■ New Earth

Bureaucracies are not noted for their speed of action, but having the president of the United States' science advisor pushing them made the Astronomical Association hierarchy move with unusual speed.

In less than four days the Big Eye telescope in orbit around the Sun was turned to look at Sirius B, as the dwarf star was designated.

Jake stood with Dr. Zarek and his two cohorts as the imagery from Big Eye appeared on the display screen above Zarek's desk. Jake saw in one corner of the screen the blinding white sphere of the dwarf star Sirius B. And in the exact center of the screen hung a bluish ball, suspended in the darkness of space. Jake's breath gushed out of him.

"It's a planet, all right," Zarek said, in a near whisper. "Almost exactly the size of Earth."

Standing on Jake's other side, Charlene Martinson pointed to the screen. "Is that glint an ocean?"

Zarek nodded. "Or a big lake."

"Look at the spectrographic analysis!" yelped the male astronomer standing with them.

"Oxygen in the atmosphere."

"A lot of nitrogen, too."

"Look!" Zarek shouted. "Chlorophyll!" "It's like Earth," Jake said.

Martinson pushed past Jake and threw her arms around Zarek's neck. "We've found a new Earth!"

Despite his assistant's clinch, Zarek could not take his eyes from the screen's imagery. "A new Earth," he breathed.

For the next two hours—as much of Big Eye's time that the Astronomical Association could grant them—Zarek and his team pored over the data the giant orbiting telescope was revealing to them.

Jake summed it up in his mind: The planet was close to the Earth's size and mass. It had an oxygen-rich atmosphere. It had glittering blue oceans. There were chlorophyll-bearing organisms on the land surfaces. A new Earth, less than ten light-years distant.

Zarek and his two associates had a party that evening. Jake, the two geologists who had ridden to Scott Base with him, and astronaut Ray Carstairs joined the celebration.

"Wait 'til the Astronomical Association breaks this to the news outfits," Carstairs crowed, waving a glass of lemonade over his head. "You guys are goin' t'be famous!"

Jake gulped down a slug of tomato juice and agreed with the astronaut.

ASTRONOMERS ON MOON
DISCOVER EARTH-LIKE PLANET

*New York Times*

NEW EARTH FOUND BY LUNAR TEAM

*Chicago Tribune*

ARE ALIENS LIVING ON NEW EARTH?

*National Enquirer*

Senator Eugene McMasters sat at his desk in red-faced fury.

"So what do we do about this?" he demanded of the trio sitting in front of the desk, facing him.

His chief of staff shrugged minimally. Harold Newby was a gray-haired veteran of Washington politics, calm in the worst of storms. "Not much we can do, Chief. The news media's nuts about the story."

"But is it true? Not something Tomlinson's people have cooked up?"

His public relations director shook her carefully coiffed head. "The Astronomical Association released the story," Mavis Johnstone said softly, gently. "They wouldn't do that if it wasn't true."

The third person facing McMasters was Oscar Edelman, the senator's science advisor, a rail-thin man with lank, dirty-blond hair. He nodded his agreement. "They've found a planet that's very similar to Earth. Whether it's populated or not is not known."

"How soon before that is known?" McMasters demanded.

Edelman shrugged his frail shoulders. "They're programming several radio telescopes to listen for possible radio transmissions. And there's talk of sending one or more unmanned spacecraft to study the planet close-up."

McMasters seemed to vent steam.

Edelman explained quickly, "It'll take fifty years for a spacecraft to reach Sirius. Possibly more."

"So we won't know if there's people on that planet or not for at least fifty years," the senator growled.

"Not unless the radio telescopes pick up something."

"If they don't, that means the planet's dead?"

"Nosir. It just means that if there's intelligent life on the planet, it hasn't reached the level where it's developed radio technology."

"And we won't know that for fifty years, at least."

Squirming uncomfortably, Edelman replied. "Unless we pick up some radio signals."

McMasters glared at him.

Edelman stopped squirming and pulled himself up straighter in his chair. "There's something pretty doggone odd about this so-called New Earth," he said.

"Odd?"

"It shouldn't be there."

Leaning forward in his sizeable desk chair, McMasters demanded, "What the hell do you mean by that?"

"Sirius B is a white dwarf star," Edelman began to explain, like a teacher drumming facts into a slow pupil. "Ages ago it was a normal star, but it collapsed and exploded. Like a supernova."

"A super what?" McMasters demanded.

Ignoring the senator's question, Edelman went on, "The star's explosion would've probably destroyed any planets orbiting around it. Or at least scoured them clean, boiled off their atmospheres and oceans."

"So?"

"So here's this planet orbiting Sirius B. With an oxygen-rich atmosphere and large bodies of liquid water. By all we understand of stellar dynamics, it shouldn't be there. It *can't* be there."

"But there it is," said Charlene Martinson, in a near whisper.

Edelman nodded. "There it is," he echoed.

Senator McMasters was not impressed. "So your highbrow theories are all wrong. The planet is sitting there, you can't deny it."

"No," Edelman replied, his voice a little shaky. "I can't deny it."

And the third man sitting before the senator's desk, Newby, quoted, "Another beautiful theoretical bubble burst on the sharp edge of an observed fact."

# Conundrum(s)

The "impossibility" of New Earth's existence did not perturb the news media. Headlines proclaimed the planet's existence and demanded the government send probes to study it close-up.

By the time Jake returned to Washington, though, the initial furor of the planet's discovery had abated considerably.

The morning that Jake slid behind his new desk in the White House, a summary of what the astronomers had learned about Sirius B was on his desk.

"You've had your fifteen minutes of fame," Jake muttered as he looked over the pages of text and pictures.

He didn't feel sad, exactly, merely … curious. "We've got a first-class mystery here," he said to himself. "How do we solve it?"

Jean Donofrio tapped on his half-open office door.

Looking up, Jake saw that she was wearing a smart-looking red dress and carrying an armload of papers.

"No rest for the weary," she said brightly, as Jake beckoned her into his office. Jake recalled that the phrase was originally, No rest for the *wicked.*

"Is that all for me?" he asked, as she sat down in front of his desk.

Smiling as she deposited the pile of papers on his desk, Donofrio replied, "Most of it is just routine. I can sign off on them if you like."

Jake nodded his approval.

Lifting a legal-looking envelope from the stack, Donofrio handed it across the desk. "This one you'll have to take care of personally."

Puzzled, Jake took the envelope from her. It had already been slit open. He pulled out the stiff single sheet inside it and read it. Twice.

"I've been gifted with one thousand shares of ART, Limited? What the hell is ART, Limited? Some museum?"

Donofrio shook her head. "It's Dave Quill's new corporation: Augmented Reality Technology."

"Quill? The AR guy?"

"Yes. Apparently he's gifted you with a thousand shares of his new company."

"Me? Why?"

"I've asked him about that," said Donofrio. "He thinks you helped him get established and he wants to thank you."

"I didn't do anything."

"He thinks otherwise. We talked it over at dinner a few nights ago, and he's very determined to have you on his board of directors."

"I can't be on anybody's board of directors," Jake groused. "I even had to give up my university position when I came here to Washington with Frank."

Donofrio shrugged her slim shoulders. "Tell that to Dave. He's quite determined."

Jake huffed impatiently, then said, "Okay, set me up with a meal with Quill."

Donofrio nodded and tried to keep from smiling.

The weeks flew past. Although the astronomical community was abuzz with the "problem" of Sirius B-1's existence, the news media soon dropped the story. Except for science buffs, the New Earth faded from the headlines.

Jake had other problems to deal with.

An outbreak of Ebola virus in Central Africa led to accusations from the European Union that the United States was not doing enough to curb the malady. Jake wrote a speech for President Tomlinson, but the criticism—especially from overseas—kept up its drumbeat.

Astronomers worldwide were demanding that one or more probes be sent to the Sirius system to investigate the recently discovered "New Earth," but that story was confined mainly to science columns and the odd guest editorial.

Then a royal donnybrook broke out between women's groups and deeply conservative organizations over the news that several types of birth defects could be discovered in utero. Discovered, but not cured. Only by terminating the pregnancy could the problem be eliminated.

"Murder of the innocents!" proclaimed conservative spokespersons.

"Eliminating dangerous defects," countered the medical media.

In the Oval Office, President Tomlinson told his closest aides, "We're walking on land mines here."

Adam Westerly nodded hard enough to make his fleshy cheeks wobble. "Keep out of it as much as you can. Whatever you say, you're going to lose a lot of voters."

Kevin O'Donnell agreed. "Midterms coming up in November."

"I can't just ignore this," the president said.

Jake, the third man sitting in front of the president's desk, agreed, "No, you can't. We're talking about human lives here."

They argued the question for more than a half hour. At last the president sighed tiredly and said, "All right. The three of you come up with a position for me and write some standard answers for me to give to the newshounds."

The three men rose from their chairs and headed for Westerly's office—the biggest of their three. Two hours later they were no closer to agreement than they had been when they'd left the Oval Office.

# Questions

"I'm very grateful that you've taken the time to see me, Dr. Ross," said Zack Bronstein.

Jake smiled easily as he leaned back in his desk chair. "I'm happy to make time for the *Wall Street Journal*, Mr. Bronstein."

Bronstein didn't look much like a news reporter to Jake. He was a little over six feet tall, with broad shoulders and the burly physique of a football player. Which he had been, at Yale.

"Please call me Zack."

"Is that short for Zachary?"

Zack Bernstein nodded. He had a pleasant face, squarish, with carefully combed light-brown hair and piercing hazel eyes.

"Okay, Zack. And I'm Jake."

"For Jacob? Are you Jewish?"

Jake smiled as he shook his head. "No. Midwestern Protestant. Religious parents."

"I see."

"What do you do at the *Journal*?" Jake asked.

"Science reporting, mostly."

Jake nodded. He didn't remember seeing Bernstein's byline in the newspaper. He must be a lower-echelon reporter, Jake told himself, or maybe a new hire.

"I'm fascinated with this discovery of an Earth-like planet," Bernstein said.

"Most of the news media have pretty much dropped the story."

"They're mostly idiots," said Bernstein, with a pleasant smile. "They think that if it's not bleeding or burning, it's not news."

"And you think otherwise?"

"Hell yes." Leaning forward slightly in his upright chair, Bernstein said, "I think it's the most exciting story since Moses led his people across the Red Sea!"

Chuckling, Jake said, "So do I."

"So where do we go from here? What plans do you have for exploring New Earth?"

Jake shrugged his shoulders. "Nothing solid. Not yet.

It would be a major undertaking to send even robotic spacecraft to study New Earth."

"Have you started the ball rolling?"

Jake hesitated. Be careful, he told himself. Whatever you answer, it could be distorted, misrepresented in the story he writes.

Picking his words carefully, Jake replied, "I've had several conversations with our members of the Astronomical Association. They'll bring the matter up at the Association's next international meeting."

"That won't be until October. In Buenos Aires."

"That's right."

"Nothing sooner than that?"

Forcing a smile, Jake said, "The planet isn't going away, Zack."

"But it's an Earth-like planet! And Sirius is less than ten light-years away from us!"

Jake countered, "It would take fifty years or more to get there, with our best rocket technology."

"So let's start now!"

Jake started to contradict the reporter, but hesitated. Why argue with him? he asked himself. He's on the same side that I am.

"I agree with you, Zack. We should start now. I'm going to do everything in my power to get us started."

Bronstein was practically quivering in his chair. "And I'll get the *Journal* to support you. We'll back you one hundred percent."

Jake smiled patiently. "That's a big commitment for a reporter to make about the *Journal*."

Bronstein broke into a crooked grin. "My uncle's on the board of directors. How do you think I got this job?"

Grinning back at the reporter, Jake remembered that one of the great motivators in the nation's democracy was the old American know-who.

The weeks flew by. The discovery of New Earth was pushed off the headlines, replaced by the controversy of the "birth defects" argument. Fetuses were being aborted—*murdered*, the Far Right news sources insisted—in the effort to eliminate birth defects. Increasingly bitter, angry speeches were made on the floors of the Senate and House of Representatives.

Adam Westerly shook his head sadly as he sat on one of the Oval Office's delicate striped sofas. "This could tear the party apart," he moaned.

From his desk, President Tomlinson agreed. "It's really bitter. What the hell can we do about it?"

"Not much," Westerly said glumly. "Let them fight it out at the polls."

"And hand the midterms to the Democrats?"

"Whatever you say, Mr. President, is going to turn half the party against you. Keep quiet. Ride out the storm."

"But this is turning into a fundamental Constitutional crisis, Adam," President Tomlinson insisted. "When does a person have the full rights of a citizen?"

Westerly growled, "Not before he's born, for god's sake."

Jake, sitting on the sofa facing Westerly, kept silent.

He knew that this controversy had pushed New Earth out of the headlines.

All to the good, he thought as Tomlinson and Westerly continued to debate the fetal rights issue. The Astronomical Association is arguing over sending an unmanned probe to New Earth. The planet hasn't shown any signs of intelligent life, but that could be because any life forms that might be living there haven't reached the level where they can communicate with us.

"Jake!" The president's voice snapped him back to reality. "Are you listening?"

Sitting up straighter on the delicate little sofa, Jake said, "Sorry. I was thinking about New Earth."

"Off in the wild blue yonder," Westerly said, with a thick-lipped grin.

The president asked, "What's going on with the Astronomical Association?"

"Their annual meeting will be in Buenos Aires, two weeks from now."

"And what are they going to do about New Earth?" Westerly asked.

"They'll vote to send an uncrewed probe to Sirius B-1."

"So they'll be asking for money to fund that," said the president.

Jake nodded.

"How much?" asked Westerly.

Jake hesitated, then replied, "They'll need a couple billion, I imagine."

"Billion?" Westerly emphasized the *B*.

"Billion," Jake agreed. "Over ten years, I would think."

"Billion," repeated the president.

"It's an investment in the future," Jake said.

"It's a rathole," Westerly growled.

The president said nothing, but Tomlinson's face looked pained.

# Answer

The controversy about treating birth defects by aborting the fetus grew like a swelling tidal wave, engulfing all other problems facing the White House.

Jake tried to devote at least a little of his attention to the New Earth question, but he was pressured to deal with the birth-defect issue instead.

"No matter what the president says on this issue, it's going to cost him votes," Adam Westerly intoned gloomily.

Kevin O'Donnell agreed, but insisted, "He can't sit on the sidelines, Adam. He's got to show some leadership!"

"He'll be leading us all into the unemployment line," Westerly grumbled.

Jake tried to find a scientific rationale behind the issue, but he couldn't. A woman either believed that aborting the baby she was carrying was her choice, or she didn't. Scientific evidence one way or the other seemed to make no difference.

Now, as they sat before the president's desk in the Oval Office, Jake thought he understood the matter clearly.

"It's not a science issue," he told the president and his advisors. "It's an emotional one."

O'Donnell gave him a sour look. "You're no goddamned help at all, Jake."

Westerly insisted, "The president's got to say *something*, for god's sake. He can't duck this issue forever."

"Midterms coming up in six weeks," O'Donnell reminded.

The three of them looked to the president, sitting behind his desk, Westerly determined to get a position statement from the president, O'Donnell just as convinced that anything the president might say would cost the party a ton of votes.

For more than twenty minutes they hashed out the issue with the president, without coming to any agreement.

"But I've got to say something," the president insisted. "I've got be a leader."

Jake said, "You could tell it like it is, Mr. President."

"Like it is?"

"This is a matter of individual conscience. A woman has the right to choose her own path on this issue. It isn't something the government can dictate."

Tomlinson stared at Jake.

"This is the United States of America," Jake went on. "Not some tin-pot dictatorship where the government decides what the people will have to do. The government can't settle every issue."

Westerly objected, "But the people look to the president for leadership."

"Tell it like it is," Jake insisted. "This is a moral issue that has to be decided by the individual citizens themselves."

O'Donnell made a sour face.

But Westerly mused, "Tell the people that *they* have to make their own decisions."

And toss the idea of leadership into the ashcan," O'Donnell groused.

Strangely, a thin smile creased President Tomlinson's lips. "Tell it like it is," he murmured.

"Tell the people the decision is up to them," said Westerly.

"Which it is," Jake said. O'Donnell just shook his head.

"Jake," the president asked, "could you write me a speech about this?"

Jake felt a flash of alarm. "Me? I'm no speechwriter!"

His smile widening, Tomlinson said, "I'll get my writers to work with you. But you've hit on the right idea: in America, the people decide. They tell the government what to do, not the other way around."

O'Donnell turned to Jake, his expression somewhere between surprise and disbelief. "You're turning into a real politician, kiddo."

Jake gaped at him. "Me? Never!"

But the president said, "Yes, you are Jake. Yes you are."

# Book Three: Autumn

## Buenos Aires

The sky was bright and blue and virtually cloudless. The city bustled with cars and busses thronging the broad avenues. Jake stared at the skyscrapers and office buildings as he sat beneath the open roof in the rear seat of the taxicab that was threading through the traffic from the airport to the huge, sprawling hotel where the Astronomical Association was holding its annual meeting.

It's springtime down here, Jake realized. Back in Washington the trees were losing the last of their leaves and people were digging out their windbreakers and overcoats. But here it's spring: the birds are singing and the trees are greening.

The hotel where the astronomical meeting was headquartered had been built in the grand old colonial style, opulent and a bit overbearing in Jake's estimation. But the horde of astronomers and their families seemed quite awed by its stolid, massive grandeur.

After the usual grind of registering and being shown to his room, Jake offered the bellman a tip—which the elderly man refused with quiet dignity—then closed the door, kicked off his shoes, and flopped onto the luxuriously soft bed.

He reached for the ornate telephone on the bedside table and dialed the operator. Fortunately, the woman spoke impeccable English. He asked her to call Tami for him, in Washington. The woman said, "Of course," quite cheerfully, then added, "Señor Medvedev has asked that you call him as soon as you can."

Medvedev, Jake remembered. The Russian foreign office man who—together with Bill Farthington and U.S. Air Force General Harold Harmon—had quietly put an end to the undeclared but deadly dangerous war that had been taking place in orbital space. Thanks to their united efforts, Russia and the United States were no longer incapacitating each other's reconnaissance satellites.

With a weary sigh, Jake told the operator to put him through to Medvedev's phone.

Even in the phone's minuscule screen, Grigor Medvedev's squarish face, with its lump of a nose, piercing gray eyes, and high forehead, spoke of a man accustomed to giving orders—and having them obeyed.

"Grigor," Jake said cheerfully, "I didn't know you'd be attending this meeting."

Medvedev smiled disarmingly. "Russia is just as interested in New Earth as you Yankees are, Jake. We want to help investigate the planet."

"That's good! Wonderful!"

They quickly agreed to meet at the hotel's bar, down in the lobby level.

Jake hung up, then called the hotel operator again and asked her to cancel his call to his wife. I'll call Tami when I'm finished with Grigor, he told himself. Argentina's two hours ahead of Washington; she won't be asleep until much later. It'll be okay.

Medvedev was already ensconced in one of the booths that lined the lobby bar. The place was half empty and quiet, but the booths on either side of the one where the Russian sat alone were each occupied by a pair of burly, lumpy men in gray suits. Grigor's security team, Jake guessed.

Medvedev smiled warmly as he half rose from his bench when Jake slid into the booth on the other side of the table. They reached out and clasped hands.

"This is a pleasant surprise," Jake said, smiling broadly.

Medvedev grinned back at him. "You weren't briefed by your people that I would be here?"

With a shake of his head, Jake replied, "Nope. Not a word."

"Good," said Medvedev. "I am still a man of mystery."

Jake laughed.

A waiter appeared and asked for Jake's order. Glancing at the Russian, Jake asked, "What are you drinking, Grigor?"

"Vodka," said Medvedev. Then he added, with a sour grimace, "Argentine vodka."

Guessing that the Argentines wouldn't have ginger beer, Jake ordered a Jack Daniel's on the rocks.

"So," Medvedev said as the waiter left their booth, "we have an astronomical puzzle on our hands, eh?"

And for the next hour they discussed the conundrum that New Earth presented.

With a shake of his head, Jake admitted, "I can't figure it out. By all we know of astrophysics, that planet can't be there. Yet there it is."

"Obviously," Medvedev replied, "we don't know enough about astrophysics."

"I guess not."

"So New Earth gives us an opportunity to learn! That's good, don't you think?"

Jake nodded, reluctantly.

His expression suddenly turning harder, Medvedev said firmly, "Russia must be part of the exploration of New Earth."

"Of course."

"Jacob, my friend, I mean that Russia must be a full partner in whatever program the Astronomical Association decided to undertake."

Jake started to reply, but hesitated. He asked, "What can Russia contribute to such a program?"

With a weary smile, Medvedev admitted, "Not as much as we could have back in the old days. We have allowed our space facilities at Baikonur, Plesetsk, and elsewhere to deteriorate badly. But they are still formidable space centers! We can still launch the world's most reliable rockets."

Jake realized that by "most reliable" Medvedev actually meant that the Russians still relied on rocket boosters that had been designed almost half a century earlier.

Hunching across the table that separated them, Medvedev clutched at Jake's arm. "We can be a strong partner!" he hissed. "Don't try to push us out of the picture."

Jake stared at the Russian. "We have no intention of pushing you out of the picture, Grigor. As far as I'm concerned, Russia is an important factor in whatever the Association decides to do."

Medvedev made a tiny grin. "Good, friend Jake. Now all I have to worry about is the military and the know-nothings in the Kremlin."

# Plenary Session

The Astronomical Association's meeting lumbered on ponderously for three days. Jake watched and listened to the speeches, and attended the smaller, more intimate gatherings of the select subcommittee that had been appointed to determine the association's response to the problem of New Earth.

Jake was surprised that even the astronomers referred to the planet as New Earth. But then he realized that it was easier to call it that instead of Sirius B-1, or some other piece of astronomical jargon.

Medvedev did not attend any of the subcommittee meetings, as far as Jake could see, although there was always a trio of Russian astronomers present. They were strangely silent, though; it was if they had been instructed to watch and listen, but not to offer any of their own views.

Evenings were quite different. The Russian astronomers behaved like any other tourists, taking in the city's night spots. Entertainment was what they sought, not science. Buenos Aires had plenty of clubs and bars and bordellos to entertain them.

The final scheduled day of the conference was devoted to a plenary session of the Association. Nearly a thousand astronomers, from Iceland to Patagonia, from Vladivostok to Canberra, filled the hotel's capacious ballroom, which had been transformed into a meeting hall. The association's leaders—mostly elderly men, but with several "youngsters" in their fifties and even a few women—gave speeches to the assembled multitude.

No one mentioned New Earth, though, until the very last speech, given by the association's venerable president.

Leaning on a dead-black cane, the old man walked slowly to the podium. The huge hall fell absolutely silent.

With a thin-lipped smile, he began, "Now we must consider the problem of New Earth. This discovery of a seemingly Earth-like planet orbiting the dwarf star Sirius B presents a conundrum. By all we know of astrophysics and planetary astronomy the object cannot exist. And yet there it is."

Jake realized that the auditorium was so quiet he could hear the whisper of the air-conditioning fans set high in the ceiling. He saw Medvedev sitting amidst the Russian delegation of astronomers, off to one side of his own seat with the much larger American group.

The association's president went on, "Therefore your governing board has unanimously decided to request that our member nations' various governments fund a program to send at least three uncrewed probes to Sirius B-1 …."

The rest of his sentence was drowned out by thunderous applause. All the astronomers shot to their feet, cheering like football fans. Jake saw Medvedev turn his head and look squarely at him. The Russian grinned and nodded. It was done.

But Jake realized it was merely begun. Now he had to get back to Washington and make sure that the Congress approved the money needed to send the probes to New Earth.

# Roland T. Jackson

Jake slept through most of the long flight back to Washington. Sure enough, autumn had arrived in all its many-colored splendor. The air felt crisp, sharp. The capital's streets were bright with red and gold and amber leaves that had fallen from the now nearly bare trees.

Tami wasn't at the airport to meet him. Jake phoned her at WETA-TV, only to find that she was out on an interview with a pair of congresswomen. But she'd left a recorded message:

"Welcome home, darling! I'll see you tonight at dinner." She sounded bright and cheerful. But Jake found himself wishing that she'd been at the airport.

He went straight to the White House, where a few of the staff people greeted his return. As he made his way past the desks of the staffers, Kevin O'Donnell intercepted Jake. With a sour grin on his tight, humorless face he grabbed Jake's hand and shook it as he said, "Coming back to work, at last."

With a grin, Jake reached into his briefcase and pulled out the colorfully wrapped gift he'd bought in Buenos Aires. "Brought you a little something, Kev," he said, handing the smallish package to the president's chief of staff.

O'Donnell looked genuinely surprised. "For me?"

"From the Argentine pampas."

Almost like a child at Christmas, O'Donnell tore away the wrapping, opened the small box, and pulled out a beautifully modeled miniature wooden statue of an Argentine bull.

"The minute I saw it," Jake explained, "I thought of you."

O'Donnell's expression morphed from surprise to suspicion. "A bull?"

"Leader of the pack."

"Huh!" With an obvious effort, O'Donnell put on a smile. "Well ... thanks, Jake."

Jake grinned at him. "Hope you like it."

Cocking a suspicious brow, O'Donnell asked, "Does this mean you think I'm a bullshitter?"

Despite himself, Jake broke into a hearty laugh. "Now whatever would give you that idea, Kev?"

O'Donnell laughed too.

Almost the moment Jake sat down at his desk, President Tomlinson's administrative aide summoned him to the Oval Office.

Taking a chair before the president's desk, Jake quickly summarized the highlights of the Astronomical Association's meeting.

"So they expect us to fund a probe to New Earth," Tomlinson said, clearly unhappy with the idea.

"Three probes," Jake corrected. "And not us alone. Every member nation is going to contribute."

"But they expect us to put in the major amount."

Jake hesitated a moment, then admitted, "Yes."

The president leaned back in his desk chair and stared silently at the ceiling.

"It's an Earth-like planet!" Jake exclaimed. "We can't just let it sit there. It may be inhabited, for god's sake!"

"I know," Tomlinson said softly. "But there's a lot of sentiment against poking into it."

"Yahoos," Jake snapped. "Know nothings. The same kind of people who want to keep Darwin out of schoolrooms."

"They vote, Jake."

"Let 'em vote. They're only a small minority of the electorate."

"I'd rather have them with me than against me."

Jake did some rapid arithmetic in his head. "Okay, look at it this way. Midterm elections are next month. We keep quiet about New Earth until after the elections. Then we ask Congress to put up our contribution for the exploration of New Earth."

Tomlinson didn't reply for several agonizing moments.

At last he nodded and said, "That might work."

Jake breathed a sigh of relief.

The midterm elections came and went without making much of a change in the composition of the Congress. Republicans voted for Republicans, pretty much, and Democrats for Democrats. Tomlinson's supporters gained one Senate seat, and lost six in the House of Representatives.

"No great shake-up," announced the dean of Washington's news reporters. Tomlinson seemed mildly disappointed with the results; Jake was glad there'd been no groundswell of opposition to the president's programs.

Nearly two weeks after the election, the Astronomical Association's delegation of leaders met with the president in the Oval Office. No big news occasion: the astronomers asked for America's help in sending a trio of uncrewed probes to New Earth; Tomlinson smiled and promised to do his best.

Jake was surprised, though, to see Roland T. Jackson among the astronomers. Rollie was a retired engineer, revered by the aerospace professionals who marveled at the long series of breakthrough aircraft he had designed over the years.

Why is Rollie here? Jake asked himself as he sat in the Oval Office through the president's meeting with the astronomers. How did he get in among the astronomers? He's not one of them.

As the meeting ended and the astronomers—plus Jackson—were taking their leave of the president, Jake walked up to Jackson and shook hands with him.

Rollie Jackson reminded Jake of a lemur. He was a small, slight man, his face bony with prominent cheekbones, his eyes large and dark, his hair thinning and silver gray.

"I'm surprised to see you here," Jake said.

Jackson smiled, almost shyly. "Actually, I came to see you."

Surprised, Jake said, "But Rollie, you can call me any time!"

His smile turning self-deprecating, Jackson replied, "Tell your staff. I couldn't get through to you."

"Couldn't get ..." Jake felt anger flare inside him. "I'll have some heads chopped!"

With a quiet laugh, Jackson tapped Jake's chest. "Don't get into a huff. I'm here now. Got a few minutes?"

"For you, Rollie? Certainly!"

As Jake led the diminutive engineer back to his own office, he asked, "How'd you get in with the astronomers?"

"Oh, the chair's a former student of mine. He and I codesigned an improved version of the old Maksutov type telescope. I spend some of my nights hunting for comets, you know. Got my name on three of them. The air force uses our Maksutovs to track Chinese missile tests."

Jake stared at Jackson. Was there no end to the man's quiet accomplishments? As they reached the desk of Jake's administrative assistant, Jake stopped and introduced Jackson to the woman. She got up from her chair, her cheeks flushing.

"Nancy, I want you to let me know whenever Roland T. Jackson calls. Wherever I am, find me."

Nancy nodded. "Yessir."

Jake led Jackson into his private office with a, "Come on in, Rollie. You're always welcome here."

Nancy stood at her desk, holding back tears.

# Missile Defense

Instead of going to his desk, Jake showed Rollie Jackson to the small round table in the far corner of his office.

"Would you like something?" Jake asked as he pulled out the chair beside Jackson's. "Coffee? Tea? Booze?"

Jackson's lean face broke into a tight smile. With a slight shake of his head he replied, "Nothing, thanks. I'm fine."

"So what brings you here, Rollie?"

Fishing into his jacket pocket, Jackson pulled out a small DVD. "I think you ought to see this."

Somewhat puzzled, Jake asked, "What's this?" as he accepted the cassette.

"A piece of film from a research lab up in Massachusetts. I think you should take a look at it."

Jake went to the bookshelf across the room and slipped the DVD into the diskette projector resting there. Then he carried the remote control back to the table where Jackson sat quietly waiting.

As Jake pressed the control that lowered the window shades and the projection screen, Jackson began to explain, "The lab's been working on high-power lasers for several years. What you're going to see is one of their latest tests."

The screen on the other side of the office showed an old air force fighter plane, rusted and sagging with age, sitting in the middle of a green country field. A line of trees was visible in the distance. The sky was bright blue, dotted with puffy white clouds.

So far away that Jake could barely make out their figures, a cluster of men in lab coats and overalls was gathered around a sizeable boxlike construction.

"That's a carbon dioxide laser," Jackson said. "Ten megawatts output power."

Jake asked, "Megawatts?"

"Yep. A lot of power in a small package."

The men stepped away from the laser. For several seconds nothing seemed to happen.

Then the fuselage of the fighter plane was sawed in half, just behind its cockpit. Jake stared as the plane was neatly severed by an invisible force that raked down its rusted body. In an eyeblink the plane was sliced in two.

The projection screen went blank. Automatically, Jake pressed the control that raised the window blinds again. As he did so, he asked Jackson, "How far was the laser from the plane?"

"Quarter mile," Jackson answered. "We've done the math: a laser of that power in a satellite in low Earth orbit could take out a half-dozen ballistic missiles in less than three minutes."

"Less than three minutes?"

"Up in LEO. At that altitude there's not much air to absorb the laser beam's power."

It all clicked in Jake's mind. "It could be developed into a defense against missile attack!"

Jackson nodded solemnly. "That's right."

"We could protect America against a nuclear strike!"

"Protect the world, Jake. The entire world."

Bureaucracies are not noted for the swiftness of their reactions, but within ten days Jake found himself sitting in a conference room in the basement of the Pentagon with General Harold Harmon—chief of the Air Force Space Command—nearly a dozen other air force officers and civilian scientists, plus Roland T. Jackson. They watched the video of the laser test in Massachusetts, then sat in silence as the overhead lights came back on.

Without waiting to be asked to speak, Jackson said—in a surprisingly powerful voice—"Lasers like that, up in orbit, could shoot down ballistic missiles while they're still in boost phase."

General Harmon fixed Jackson with a hard stare. "How many would be needed to protect the United States against a full-out missile attack?"

Jackson's face eased into a tentative smile. "I've done some back-of-the-envelope calculations. A minimum of fifty would do the job: around the world, around the clock."

One of the officers sitting next to the general shook his head. "The Russians would simply build more missiles and overload the system."

"Not if they were partners with us." "Partners?"

"The Russians, the Chinese ... everybody. A network of ABM satellites could protect the whole world against any missile attack. Especially if the whole world was part of the network."

"That's impossible."

"Couldn't be done."

"You're daydreaming, Jackson."

Jake spoke up. "I remember when sending people to the Moon was daydreaming."

Harmon leaned forward in his chair. "What does the president think of this idea?"

Massaging the truth a bit, Jake replied, "He wants to know if you think such a program is feasible."

The conference room went absolutely silent.

# The Decision

President B. Franklin Tomlinson fixed Jake with a hard stare. "You're saying we could shoot down a full-scale missile attack?"

Fighting back a sudden urge to cross his fingers, Jake said, "Yessir. General Harmon and his people say it's possible."

"From anywhere? Russia? China? Iran?"

"If we put up enough antimissile satellites," Jake answered.

Adam Westerly, sitting beside Jake in front of the president's Oval Office desk, made a derisive snort. "And what would the Russians and the Chinese be doing while we're putting up your ABM birds?"

"Putting up their own," said Jake.

"Do they have this technology, too?"

"No," said Jake. "We share it with them."

"Share ...?"

The president stared at Jake. "You mean we give them the information, let them build antimissile satellites of their own?"

"Yessir."

"That's nonsense!" Westerly snapped.

The fourth man in the Oval Office, Kevin O'Donnell, said, "Why in the hell would we give those bastards this technology?"

"Because that's the only way this idea will work," Jake said firmly.

"The only way ...?"

President Tomlinson pointed a finger, pistol-like, at Jake. "Explain that, please."

Jake pulled in a breath, thinking, I wish Rollie were here. He'd be much better at this.

But he went ahead with, "If we start putting ABM satellites into orbit all by ourselves, without letting the Russians or anybody else in on the program, what are they going to think?"

"That we're protecting ourselves against their missiles," said O'Donnell.

"And preparing to attack them," Jake added.

The president nodded vigorously. "That's right. They'd think that once we got our defensive network in orbit, we could attack them whenever we choose to and blunt their counter-attack."

"Worse," said Westerly. "They'd think that we'd attack them as soon as we had our ABM shield in place."

"We'd have a war in space," Jake said. "Like the one we were having over reconnaissance satellites. Only worse."

Westerly mused, "A war that could trigger the kind of all-out missile attack that we're trying to prevent."

"Armageddon," said Jake.

O'Donnell muttered, "Jesus Christ."

Leaning forward in his chair, toward the president, Jake went on, "This is a *global* situation. It won't work on a national basis. That would just lead to the war we're trying to prevent. We either share this technology with the Chinese, the Russians, the Europeans, and anybody else who wants to join us, or we forget about it."

President Tomlinson muttered, "And I'm going to have to sell this idea to the Congress."

"To Senator McMasters," said Westerly. "And all the other yahoos," O'Donnell added.

The president decided to invite Senator McMasters and his science advisor to the Oval Office.

"If we can get McMasters behind this idea, the rest of the Democrats will follow his lead."

"That's a big *if*," said Kevin O'Donnell. Gloomily.

Breaking into a cheerful grin, President Tomlinson said, "We'll let McMasters know that a good part of the work on this program will take place in New York State."

O'Donnell grinned back. "Sweeten the pot for him, eh?"

Jake tried to suppress a frown. This is too big for party politics, he thought. But then he found himself wondering, Isn't it?

McMasters and his science advisor—a biologist from Cornell University—sat in the Oval Office with the president, Jake, and Adam Westerly and watched the film clip from the Massachusetts laboratory.

Sitting beside the senator on one of the office's delicate little sofas, President Tomlinson said, "General Harmon and his people want to put lasers like that in satellites. They could shoot down ballistic missiles like *that*." And the president snapped his fingers.

McMasters's science advisor said, "The other side would just build more missiles, enough to overwhelm your system."

Tomlinson smiled like a man who had just watched a feral animal step into his trap. "Not if the other side was building antimissile satellites, too."

McMasters started to say, "But they—" then he stopped.

Softly, President Tomlinson said, "We share the technology."

"With the *Russians*?"

Nodding, the president answered, "And the Chinese, and anyone else who wants to make the world safer."

"That's crazy!" McMasters snapped.

"It could end the hostility between us and the Russians. And the Chinese. Even the Iranians."

McMasters didn't reply for long, tense moments. At last he said, "So you want to play peacemaker, huh?"

"Yes," said Tomlinson. "Don't you?"

# The Speech

The weeks blurred past. Jake lost track of how many times he had traveled to England, to NATO headquarters in Brussels, to Poland and France, and even to Moscow.

Grigor Medvedev hosted a meeting in a hotel near the Kremlin where Jake met top scientists and military leaders from Russia and China. Suspicious, even hostile at first, the men slowly came to agree that a network of antimissile satellites in orbit around the globe could protect the entire world against nuclear holocaust.

In the midst of one of their long, intense meetings, one of the Chinese representatives asked the key question: "And who will control this network of antimissile satellites? The United States?"

Dead silence descended upon the conference room until Jake answered, "No. The network must be controlled by an international organization, which will include representatives of all nations, including China, of course."

A ghost of a smile flickered across the Chinese representative's face. "And Taiwan, as well?"

"Taiwan, also," said Jake. Then he added, "Even Luxembourg."

Several of the hard-bitten men around the massive conference table broke into audible chuckles.

The Chinese representative nodded and smiled more widely. "Yes, we must not leave out Luxembourg."

President Tomlinson chose March 23 as the date for his speech. Tension at the White House ratcheted up to a fever pitch. News reporters understood that the president's speech was to reveal a major change in American foreign policy. The White House was swamped with journalists, including a strong contingent from overseas.

When Jake arrived that evening with Tami, he saw that the usual security team had been reinforced by U.S. Marines in full dress uniform, carrying sidearms.

As they headed for the West Wing, Tami whispered to Jake, "Looks like the marines are ready for the shootout at the OK Corral."

Jake smiled bitterly. "The fireworks will come after Frank finishes his speech."

The State Dining Room had been cleared of its usual furniture, except for a small desk in a corner from which the president would deliver his speech. A phalanx of TV cameras and lights was grouped in front of the desk.

The room, jammed with guests, crackled with tension. Everyone knew that the president was going to make a major policy speech. Hardly anyone knew what it would be about.

Senator McMasters was already in the room when Jake and Tami were ushered in.

"He looks as if he's had a few drinks already," Tami whispered to Jake as they made their way through the gathering crowd.

"Wish I'd had," Jake whispered back.

Jake noticed Rollie Jackson's diminutive form in the crowd, standing with a small huddle of what Jake assumed were scientists from the laser lab in Massachusetts.

Grasping Tami's wrist, he started off in Rollie's direction.

But then a stentorian voice announced, "The president of the United States!"

All conversations stopped. Everyone turned toward the door where B. Franklin Tomlinson was striding into the room, tall, looking confident, beaming his megawatt smile. His wife, Amy, was beside him, wearing a short-skirted light-blue cocktail dress, her cheerleader's smile fixed on her pretty face.

As he sat before a bank of microphones, Tomlinson's confident grin disappeared. He looked as tense as Jake had ever seen him.

The president began:

"Good evening, my fellow Americans. And citizens of all the world's nations.

"On this night, forty-seven years ago, President Ronald Reagan announced the start of a program to end the mutual terror that had gripped the world since Hiroshima was destroyed by a nuclear bomb.

"Tonight, I want to explain to you that our technological progress has finally reached the point where we can indeed make nuclear missiles—to use President Reagan's words— 'impotent and obsolete.' "

The crowd gathered in the State Dining Room was absolutely silent. Jake thought he could have heard the proverbial pin drop.

Calmly, with deliberate care, Tomlinson explained that American technology had reached the point where satellites armed with powerful lasers could shoot down ballistic missiles within minutes of their launch. "We have the means to end the nuclear terror that has gripped the world for the past four generations. We can put an end to the threat of nuclear devastation."

The president hesitated, then went on, "But this is a goal that the United States cannot achieve alone. This is a historical moment, where we must enlarge our vision from a national to a global perspective.

"I therefore call upon the nations of the world—all of them—to join us in an effort to build missile defenses in orbital space that are capable of stopping a nuclear missile attack launched from anywhere on the globe. We are all children of Mother Earth. It's time that we acted like brothers and sisters, time to put an end to the threat of nuclear devastation.

"As President Reagan said nearly fifty years ago, 'Would it not be better to save lives than to avenge them?' We now have the technological means to make that vision into reality. Do we have the moral strength to work together—all across the world—to make our world safe from nuclear holocaust?"

Unbidden, the people crowding the State Dining Room burst into applause. Tomlinson looked surprised for a moment, then broke into a big grin and nodded his acknowledgement of the audience's appreciation.

# The Aftermath

The following morning Jake drove to his office in the White House even earlier than usual. The night before had been hectic, with everyone—from news reporters to politicians and scientists—wanting to ask the president about his proposed program.

Tomlinson answered them all with, "It's time to end the mutual terror of nuclear war. It's time to use our smarts to help bring a lasting peace to the world."

Jake saw that some guests believed what the president was saying, but many were doubtful.

"A multinational program?"

"Share this technology with the Russians? The Chinese?"

A guest from the Chinese embassy pointed out, "Whoever controls these defensive satellites will have the lives of all nations in their hands."

Tomlinson nodded agreement as he replied, "That's why the controllers must be international, from many nations."

"You're going to encourage the Russians to attack us before you can get your network into orbit!"

"And have us counterattack them? The Russians are more sensible than that. We can remove the threat of nuclear war, for god's sake! That's something everyone on Earth should be happy to see."

"Not the terrorists."

"Pulling their fangs is a good thing, don't you think?"

And on, far into the night. By the time Jake and Tami got home they were both emotionally exhausted.

Strangely, Jake awoke at dawn feeling strong, refreshed. He left a note for his sleeping wife and drove to the White House.

His email inbox was choked with messages. Sifting through them, Jake saw that most of the comments were favorable, especially those from ordinary citizens across the nation.

Frank's done it, he said to himself. He's sold the idea to the voters. Now to get it through the Congress.

As he waded through the many messages, Jake began to wonder how this antimissile effort was going to affect the *Artemis* program. We have Scott Base scooping up minerals from the Moon's regolith. Could some of those minerals be used to build antimissile satellites?

I ought to look into that, Jake said to himself. But another voice in his head cautioned, Scott Base should be restricted to peaceful, nonmilitary programs. You don't want to risk starting a war on the Moon, for god's sake!

Still, he thought that the raw materials for the antimissile satellites could be dug up from the Moon's surface and then sent down to low Earth orbit, where they'd be manufactured into the satellites. That could work. Couldn't it?

He leaned back in his chair and realized that the antimissile program was going to have effects reaching much further than he had originally imagined.

The antimissile program was dubbed *Athena*, after the ancient Greek goddess of wisdom—and intelligent, life defending war.

President Tomlinson's program passed through the House of Representatives by a comfortable margin of 237–198, after nearly a week of sometimes blistering debate.

"That was the easy part," Kevin O'Donnell said to Jake.

O'Donnell was sitting with Jake at the little round table in the corner of Jake's office, his jacket hanging on the back of his chair, his tie pulled loose, looking as if he were hiding from his responsibilities.

It was the end of a long, tense day, and O'Donnell seemed to be wilting before Jake's eyes.

Jake asked, "It wasn't that easy, Kev, was it?"

Trying to make a smile, O'Donnell replied, "Oh, I figured we'd get through okay. The ultraconservatives don't like the idea of letting the Russians and everybody else in on the technology, but—like the literary types say—reason prevailed."

"Narrowly," said Jake.

"Enough."

"You did a good job, Kev."

Managing a small smile, O'Donnell replied, "You helped, pal."

"So did the president."

O'Donnell nodded, then said, "Now we've got to get the program through the Senate."

"That won't be easy, will it?"

O'Donnell's smile grew wider. "Oh, about as easy as walking across the Atlantic Ocean."

Jake laughed.

"McMasters is putting together a bloc of votes to shoot the whole thing down," said O'Donnell.

With a nod, Jake asked, "Will he have enough votes to do that?"

O'Donnell shrugged his frail shoulders. "We'll soon find out."

Jake said nothing. But looking at O'Donnell's wan, weary face, he wondered if they'd have enough strength to get the *Athena* program through the Senate.

# Eugene McMasters

Jake followed the debate in the Senate on C-SPAN, sitting tensely at his desk in the White House, watching the senators arguing back and forth. It all comes down to trust, he told himself. Can we trust the Russians, the Chinese, and all the other nations to cooperate with us? Can we actually build a defensive net of satellites capable of shooting down any ballistic missiles launched from anywhere on the globe? We have the technology, Jake knew. But do we have the intelligence to *use* the technology wisely, properly?

His desk phone's buzz startled Jake out of his musings.

It was the president's administrative aide. "The president would like to see you in the Oval Office, Jake."

"When?" he asked.

"Now."

Without turning his TV off, Jake got up from his desk and hurried toward the Oval Office. He noticed a trio of men sitting in the anteroom: Senator McMasters's aides, he realized. Nodding a curt greeting to them, Jake went past them, to where a presidential aide was holding open the door to the Oval Office.

Jake stepped in and saw that the president was sitting on one of the delicate little striped couches in front of the empty fireplace. And sitting on the opposite couch, facing him, was Senator Eugene McMasters. Both men looked tense, wary.

Adam Westerly was ensconced on an armchair to one side of the sofas, overweight and rumpled as usual, his face a rigid mask. Kevin O'Donnell sat farther back, near the president's empty desk, looking more puzzled than pleased.

President Tomlinson shot to his feet as Jake entered the office. All three of the other men rose too, more slowly.

"Jake," said the president, "you know Senator McMasters, of course."

Jake mumbled agreement, and stepped between the couches to shake McMasters's outstretched hand.

"Gene's come here to offer his help to us," the president said.

Jake couldn't help blurting, "Help?"

Tomlinson looked edgy, but he was making a tight smile. McMasters was stone-faced.

"I've come to the conclusion," the senator said as he sat back down on the sofa, "that this missile-defense idea is something that the Senate should pass. We have a historic opportunity here; it would be wrong to reject it for reasons of partisan politics."

"I'm glad you see it that way," said the president, his handsome face taut, guarded.

"And if the offer is still open," McMasters went on, "I'm willing to accept the vice-presidential job."

Tomlinson blinked with surprise, but quickly broke into a grin. "It's yours, Gene."

Jake sat slowly on the couch beside the president. Glancing at Westerly and O'Donnell, he saw that neither of them looked happy. McMasters nodded once, like a man who had just completed an unpleasant chore, and slowly got to his feet. All the others rose too.

"This is a historic moment," Tomlinson said, breaking into a genuine smile. He extended his hand to McMasters, who gripped it in his own.

Jake didn't know whether he should feel happy or worried.

# A Tangled Web

"I, Eugene Douglas McMasters, do solemnly swear that I will support and defend the Constitution of the United States against all enemies, foreign and domestic; that I will bear true faith and allegiance to the same; that I take this obligation freely, without any mental reservation or purpose of evasion; and that I will well and faithfully discharge the duties of the office on which I am about to enter. So help me God."

A sizeable group of guests clustered around McMasters, the president, and the chief justice of the Supreme Court as they stood gravely on the South Portico of the White House. It was a brilliant afternoon, pleasantly warm, with a soft breeze wafting across the cloudless blue sky.

Jake watched as McMasters lowered his raised hand and grasped the extended hand of the chief justice, then turned slightly and shook hands with the president.

The witnesses to the brief ceremony were dwarfed by the swarm of news reporters and photographers crowded around them. Everyone seemed to breathe a sigh of relief, Jake thought. The deed was done. Gene McMasters was now the vice president of the United States.

The visitors—minus the newspeople—moved inside to the East Room for a cocktail reception. The president was at his smiling best, shaking hands and chatting with the invited guests. Jake realized again how tall Tomlinson was. Except for a couple of the Secret Service agents standing on the edge of the crowd, he was easily the tallest man in the room. McMasters looked almost frail standing beside the president. The new vice president also pressed the guests' flesh, but the look on his face was stony, almost grim.

He's not happy with this, Jake realized, as he studied McMasters's expression from halfway across the largish room. McMasters's wife was beaming joyfully as she shook hands with the guests, but the man himself looked deadly serious. Why did he accept the veep's position if he's not happy with it?

Mrs. McMasters seemed pleased enough, Jake thought. Radiant. Her snow-white hair made her look somewhat older than McMasters himself, but she was dressed prettily in a rose-pink cocktail sheath, exchanging pleasantries with the line of guests filtering past her and her husband.

After a successful event, the reception broke up at last. Slowly the guests bade their farewells and left the White House. President Tomlinson draped an arm across the shoulders of his new vice president and walked him back outside to the entrance where a gleaming black limousine waited.

Shaking McMasters's hand, Tomlinson smiled happily as he told his vice president, "We're going to accomplish some great things, Gene. Together, you and I, we're going to make history."

No smile broke out on McMasters's face, but he said, "I guess we will, Frank. I guess we will."

Jake watched the new vice president and his wife duck into the limo. The car drove away. Jake couldn't shake the feeling that something was very wrong.

In the departing limousine, Eugene McMasters turned toward his wife and said, "Well, that's done."

"Vice president of the United States," breathed his wife. "Oh, Gene, I'm so proud of you."

He almost smiled at her. "Only one more step to the top."

"You'll get there, dear. I know you will."

McMasters nodded brusquely. "Damned right I will."

* * *

Jean Donofrio was one of the last guests to leave the East Room. All through the long afternoon and evening she had hovered at the president's side, smiling at the guests, smiling at *him*, waiting for Tomlinson to notice her.

He did grin at her a couple of times, but it was the same smile he made for all the other guests. Nothing special, nothing specifically for her. Of course, his wife was at his side every minute; it was impossibly difficult to pry her loose from him.

Then, as the last of the guests was leaving, Mrs. Tomlinson stood on tiptoes to give her husband a peck on the cheek, then walked toward the East Room's doors, with a pair of Secret Service agents trailing behind her. The president smiled at her briefly, then returned his attention to the last of the departing guests.

Jean seized her opportunity.

"It all went very well, didn't it?" she asked the president.

He looked at her as if he hadn't really noticed her before. "Yes," he agreed, with a warm smile. "I think it did."

"I was surprised that Gene accepted your offer," she said.

His smile waning, the president responded, "To tell the truth, so was I."

"But you handled it beautifully."

"Thank you, Ms. Donofrio."

"My friends call me Jean."

Tomlinson dipped his chin in acknowledgement. "I'm glad that you count me as one of your friends."

"Oh, yes. Of course."

"Good. Jake speaks very highly of you."

He's been talking about me! Jean tried to keep the surge of joy she felt from showing on her face. She almost succeeded.

Looking around at the aides and staff people who were still in the room, Tomlinson said, "You ought to brief me on what Jake's doing with his *Artemis* program."

"I'd be happy to," said Jean Donofrio. "Any time."

"How about tomorrow, after the working day is finished. I'll give you a call."

"That would be fine!"

# The Senate Debate

With the newly appointed vice president in the chair's seat, the Senate debate over the *Athena* missile-defense plan plowed ahead.

The senators listened to speeches from Grigor Medvedev, from a Chinese physicist, and from half a dozen other representatives of foreign nations—not to mention testimony from a phalanx of American scientists, some of them bitterly opposed to the idea of sharing the system with other nations.

Then the debate went into closed session. No news reporters or TV cameras allowed. Jake sat in the nearly empty visitors' gallery and listened to the back and forth.

"Why should we give this hypersensitive technology to the rest of the world?" demanded the senior senator from Wyoming. "American brains and hands created this new technology. American minds should direct it!"

A senator from California reached back into history. "Nearly three hundred years ago a great American patriot said, 'Millions for defense, not one cent for tribute.' What was true then is equally true today," she said.

But the junior senator from Florida, tanned and golden-haired, countered, "We are on the threshold of a new era. We can end the mutual terror that has gripped international relations since Hiroshima. We can make the world safe. The whole world!"

"Give control of this antinuclear shield to a gaggle of foreigners? Never!"

"The missile shield will protect the entire world. It's only logical that it should be controlled not by any single nation, but by an international organization."

For more than a week the debate surged back and forth.

Returning to the White House after another wearying day of listening to the deliberation, Jake went straight to the Oval Office. "It's going to be close," he said to the president as he sank wearily into one of the commodious leather chairs arrayed in front of the president's desk.

Tomlinson shook his head. "Not if McMasters can deliver his bloc."

Jake hesitated a moment, then plunged ahead. "Can we trust him to do that?"

The president did not look surprised by the question. He replied, "He's promised to."

Jake repeated, "Can we trust him?"

Tightly, the president answered, "We'll find out soon enough."

At last the time for voting arrived. Jake sat in the Senate's visitors' gallery—now crowded with onlookers—with a small pad and pencil in his hands as he ticked off the votes, one by one.

By the time a couple of dozen votes had been registered, Jake realized that McMasters was indeed delivering his people. Thirty aye votes. Forty. We need fifty-one, Jake told himself as he scratched lines on his note pad.

By the time he recorded forty-nine ayes, Jake was perspiring as if he'd run a hundred-meter dash.

Fifty.

Fifty-one!

The jam-packed gallery erupted. Some booing, but most applauding and smiling with relief, as Jake was.

The final count was sixty-seven in favor, thirty-one against, and two abstentions.

We've done it! Jake said to himself, while most of the onlookers in the gallery stood up and cheered.

Most of them.

Jake was only mildly surprised to see Jean Donofrio sitting in front of the president's desk. Everyone else had left the Oval Office. The exhilaration of their victory in the Senate had quietly faded into a relaxed sort of mutual satisfaction. The debate was over. The votes had been counted. The *Athena* program—international in scope, global in range—was now officially approved.

The president was leaning back in his desk chair, his jacket draped across the chair's back, his tie pulled loose. Donofrio looked startled when Jake opened the door and took a step in.

With a big grin, the president said, "We did it, Jake."

"We sure did," Jake agreed, smiling back at him.

"Come on in and have a drink."

With a shake of his head, Jake replied, "If it's all the same to you, Mr. President, I'm bushed. I'm heading home."

Tomlinson nodded. "Okay. Give my regards to Tami."

"Will do."

"See you tomorrow, bright and early."

"Bright and early," Jake echoed. And he closed the door.

The president turned his gaze to Jean. "It's been an outstanding day."

She thought, And now you want to give it a big finish. But the president didn't move from his desk chair. Instead, he said, "Jean, you're a very attractive woman."

Lowering her eyes, she said softly, "Thank you."

"But I'm a married man."

"I know."

"If I weren't …." He left the rest of the statement unfinished.

Jean felt a lurch in the pit of her stomach. For a long moment absolute silence hung in the Oval Office. At last Jean said, in a small voice, "You mean you don't want to …?"

With an almost sheepish smile, the president answered, "Oh, I want to. But I can't. I'm not like Clinton or Grimaldi or some of those other men .... I take my marriage vow seriously."

Jean stared at him.

"I'm sorry," Tomlinson went on. "I just wanted you to know that I think you're a wonderful woman, Jean."

"But not wonderful enough."

"If I weren't married ...."

"But you are."

"Yes."

"Amy's a very lucky woman."

The president nodded.

Jean Donofrio slowly got up from her chair, her mind spinning. He doesn't want me. Not enough to be unfaithful to his wife.

As she headed slowly, uncertainly, toward the door, the president called after her. "You can blame my father, Jean. He drilled this god-damned faithfulness into me."

She nodded, and silently left the Oval Office. It wasn't until she was safely out in the empty, unattended anteroom that she allowed her tears to flow.

# The *Athena* Program

"Athena was the ancient Greek goddess of war," Kevin O'Donnell said.

"But not offensive, brutal war, where you invade a neighboring country," Adam Westerly amended.

"Defensive war," O'Donnell agreed.

"Like Britain against Hitler," Jake added.

Westerly nodded.

Westerly and Kevin O'Donnell had congregated in Jake's office. It was the end of the working day, officially, time for most of the staff to head home. But for these three it was time for what O'Donnell called "a bullshit session."

"This is going to be a major effort," Westerly said, as he sat down in one of the chairs arranged around the small, round conference table in the corner, his tie pulled loose, his jacket sagging around his corpulent body.

O'Donnell, trim and sharp as usual, said, "Getting every major power on Earth to work together on this? That won't be a major effort, Adam, it'll be a goddamn miracle."

Jake said, "The president's already called for an international conference."

"Jawboning," said Westerly.

With the beginnings of a grin, Jake said, "Wasn't it Churchill who said, "Jaw, jaw is better than war, war?"

"Yeah," said Westerly. "And World War II started shortly afterward."

Jake's budding smile vanished.

The international conference was held in Geneva, of course. Switzerland was known as an island of peace and tranquility, where diplomats could meet and discuss their nations' affairs without resorting to armed conflict. Sometimes. Jake was surprised that the conference went so smoothly. More than thirty nations attended, including Russia and China, as well as the United States, most of Europe, and many of the developing nations of Asia and Africa.

There were the usual wrangles and disagreements, but after more than two weeks of meetings and discussions, a seemingly workable agreement was hammered out.

A new organization was created: the International Peacekeeping Force. Its mission was to protect every nation on Earth against missile attack from any nation on Earth. Its power would be based on a network of laser-armed satellites, capable of destroying ballistic missiles within minutes after they were launched.

Every nation represented at the meeting agreed to register each of its rocket launches with the IPF. Each launch would be inspected by IPF agents before it would be allowed to lift off.

"They're actually going to sign the agreement," Jake told Tami, with more than a little wonderment in his voice.

From the kitchen of their apartment, Tami offered her newswoman's insight, "You've led them into a new world, Jake."

He grinned at her. "I had a lot of help."

Politicians dictated the general format of the Peacekeepers' operation. A network of at least fifty robotic laser-armed satellites would be placed in low orbit around the Earth. That would be enough to ensure that every square inch of territory on the planet was covered by at least three of the satellites every moment of the day or night. No one could launch a ballistic missile from anywhere on Earth without it being targeted and destroyed within minutes by the orbiting lasers.

While the laser-armed satellites were robotic, they would be controlled by a network of twelve crewed satellites in higher orbits, each of them controlling at least five of the killer satellites—but only for the half hour it took for the command birds to swing past on their higher orbits and take over control of the next set of killer satellites.

That way, the politicians reasoned, none of the command satellites would have control over the same group of killer birds for more than half an hour. The decision complicated the engineers' work, but not impossibly so.

Within months of the diplomats' conference conclusion, the first antimissile satellites began launching from the United States, Russia, China, the European Union, and several smaller countries in Asia and Africa.

The president went to the U.S. Air Force's launch facility at Vandenberg Base, in California, for the launch of the first antimissile satellite. Jake and Tami accompanied him.

"This is a historic occasion," said President Tomlinson, speaking to the crowd standing before his podium in the California sunshine. "We are making the world safer for our children and our children's children."

Standing in the front row of the listening crowd, clutching Tami's hand in his own, Jake felt an inner glow of pride that he had been part of this step toward world peace. But it's only one step, he reminded himself. There are still plenty of ways for nations to make war on one another. And terrorists are still a threat. But the threat of nuclear devastation, the fear of wiping out civilization within half an hour, that's going to be a thing of the past. We're moving beyond that, heading toward a better, safer world.

He hoped he was right.

Once back in Washington, things quickly settled into their normal routines. A proposal by the Democrats for a government-funded assured wage for every working-age citizen was passed by the House of Representatives but shot down in the Senate after a bitter debate. The budget request for the air force—almost double the previous year's budget, due to the *Athena* program's needs—squeaked past a surprisingly strong opposition.

"It's an old political tactic," counseled Adam Westerly. "Get credit for passing the program but starve its funding."

Jake nodded his understanding, but inwardly he felt a smoldering hostility against such maneuvers.

*Athena* began to take shape. Jake thought it was probably a good thing that the program was largely in orbital space. After the first few rocket launches the news media grew tired of reporting about it. The massive underground control stations being built in Wyoming, Hunan, Archangel, Hyderabad, and Kimberly were closed to the news media.

As far as Jake was concerned, no news was good news. The *Athena* network of laser-armed satellites was growing steadily, as were the crewed space stations that were to control them.

It's going smoothly, Jake told himself, time and again. But a voice in his head always responded, Too smoothly.

# Winter: Two Years Later

## ■ The Oval Office

President Tomlinson looked worried as he leaned back in his desk chair. As usual, his jacket was hung on the back of the chair, revealing his fire-engine-red suspenders. But his tie was still knotted at his throat.

He's not happy, Jake thought, as he studied the president. Kevin O'Donnell, sitting next to Jake in front of the president's desk, looked equally gloomy. Adam Westerly was on his feet, a sheaf of crumpled papers in his ham-sized first. The latest poll results, Jake knew.

"It's not that bad," Westerly was saying. "Hell, it's still more than a year 'til the election."

"But we're not doing as well as we should," O'Donnell said, almost accusingly.

"Not in the major metropolitan areas," Westerly admitted.

The president shook his head. "The polls didn't look very good for Harry Truman in forty-eight."

"This isn't nineteen forty-eight," grumbled Westerly.

O'Donnell shrugged. "The economy's doing well. The antimissile program is moving ahead as planned. Crime rates are down pretty much all over the country. Why the hell aren't we doing better in the goddamned polls?"

Westerly shrugged massively. "I'm open to suggestions."

"I think it's the Russians," said the president.

"The Russians?" yelped Jake, surprised. "But they've been working with us on *Athena*."

"Yes, but the voters don't trust them. For nearly a century they've pictured the Russians as our enemy, and now we want the American people to accept them as friends."

"Partners," muttered O'Donnell.

Westerly nodded. "It's a big change. Maybe too big. Too soon."

"Not to mention the Chinese," O'Donnell added.

"It's a lot to accept," said the president.

"What can we do about it?" Westerly asked.

"You tell me," Tomlinson said.

Jake said, "Mr. President, it's time for you to speak to the American people. Time to build their trust. The *Athena* program is the keystone to a new era. You've got to explain that to the voters."

"Will they listen to me?"

"You're their leader," O'Donnell began.

"But I wasn't elected. I became president because Sebastian died in office."

Westerly, still standing before the president's desk, quickly counseled, "Water under the bridge, Mr. President. You've been the nation's leader for more than three years now. The people expect you to be their president."

"Which means," O'Donnell took up, "they expect you to lead them."

"But if they don't like the direction I'm leading them in ...."

Jake spoke up. "You tell them why you're leading them in that direction. You show them what's at stake."

"World peace or nuclear holocaust," said Westerly.

O'Donnell shook his head wearily. "It'll be a tough sell. They've spent damned near four generations thinking of the Russians as our enemy. Now you're asking the nation to trust them."

Westerly said, "There can't be real peace without trust."

President Tomlinson nodded solemnly. "We've got to trust the Russians."

"And they have to trust us," Jake added.

O'Donnell's face twisted into a doubtful frown. "Lotsa luck, fellas."

The president trekked across the country, giving speeches extolling the benefits of peace and international cooperation. His poll ratings inched upward slowly. Russian artists and performers were invited to the United States, while American dance troupes and musical groups toured Moscow and other major Russian cities. Teams of Chinese acrobats and musicians traveled from Maine to California. American families visited the homelands of their ancestors, all expenses paid by Washington.

Still the support for the International Peacekeeping Force and the antimissile satellites remained depressingly low. The mood in the Oval Office turned grim.

"They're just not buying it," Westerly admitted sadly.

"They don't trust the Russkies," agreed O'Donnell. "Or the Chinese."

Jake added dolefully, "They don't trust anybody who wasn't born in the US of A."

Tomlinson agreed. "This is a big pill for them to swallow."

"Maybe too big."

"It's like when Wilson tried to get the country to accept the League of Nations, after World War I."

"Gave him a stroke."

"Set up the conditions for World War II."

"So what can we do about it?" asked the president.

Dead silence answered his question.

## ■ Space Station *Hunter*

The first laser beam caught them unaware, slicing through the station's thin aluminum skin exactly where the main power trunk and air lines fed into the bridge. A sputtering fizz of sparks, a moment of heart-wrenching darkness, and then the emergency dims came on. The electronics consoles switched to their internal batteries with barely a microsecond's hesitation, but the air fans sighed to a stop and fell silent.

The four men and two women on duty in the bridge had about a second to realize they were under attack. Enough time for the breath to catch in your throat, for the sudden terror to hollow out your guts.

The second laser hit was a high-energy pulse deliberately aimed at the bridge's observation port. It cracked the impact-resistant plastic as easily as a hammer smashes an egg; the air pressure inside the bridge blew the port open. The six men and women became six exploding bodies spewing blood. There was not even time enough to scream.

The station was named *Hunter*, although only a handful of its crew knew why. It was not one of the missile-killing satellites, nor one of the sensor-laden observation birds. It was a command-and-control station, manned by a crew of twenty, orbiting some one thousand kilometers high, below the densest radiation zone of the inner Van Allen belt. It circled the Earth in about one hundred and five minutes. By design, the station was not hardened against laser attack. The attackers knew this perfectly well.

Commander Hazard was almost asleep when the bridge was destroyed. He had just finished his daily inspection of the space station. Satisfied that the youngsters of his crew were reasonably sharp, he had returned to his coffin-sized personal cabin and wormed out of his sweaty fatigues. He was angry with himself.

Two months aboard the station and he still felt the nausea and unease of space adaptation syndrome. It was like the captain of an ocean vessel being seasick all the time. Hazard fumed inwardly as he stuck another timed-release medication plaster on his neck, slightly behind his left ear. The old one had fallen off. Not that they did much good. His neck was faintly spotted with the rings left by earlier medication patches. Still his stomach felt fluttery, his palms slippery with perspiration.

Clinging grimly to a handgrip, he pushed his weightless body from the mirrored sink to the mesh sleep cocoon fastened against the opposite wall of his cubicle. He zipped himself into the bag and slipped the terry-cloth restraint across his forehead.

Hazard was a bulky, dour man with iron-gray hair still cropped Academy close, a weather-beaten squarish face built around a thrusting spade-like nose, a thin slash of a mouth that seldom smiled, and eyes the color of a stormy sea. Those eyes seemed suspicious of everyone and everything, probing, inquisitory. A closer look showed that they were weary, disappointed with the world and the people in it. Disappointed most of all with himself.

He was just dozing off when the emergency klaxon started blaring. For a disoriented moment he thought he was back in a submarine and something had gone wrong with a dive. He felt his arms pinned by the mesh sleeping bag, as if he had been bound by unknown enemies. He almost panicked as he heard hatches slamming automatically and the terrifying wailing of the alarms. The communications unit on the wall added its urgent shrill to the clamor.

The comm unit's piercing whistle snapped him to full awareness. He stopped struggling against the mesh and unzippered it with a single swift motion, slipping out of the head restraint at the same time.

Hazard slapped at the wall comm's switch. "Commander here," he snapped. "Report."

"Varshni, sir. CIC. The bridge is out. Apparently destroyed."

"Destroyed?"

"All life-support functions down. Air pressure zero.

No communications," replied the information officer in a rush. His slightly singsong Oxford accent was trembling with fear.

"It exploded, sir. They are all dead in there."

Hazard felt the old terror clutching at his heart, the physical weakness, the giddiness of sudden fear. Forcing his voice to remain steady, he commanded, "Full alert status. Ask Mr. Feeney and Ms. Yang to meet me at the CIC at once. I'll be down there in sixty seconds or less."

## ■ IPF Command Center

Worland, Wyoming, was not exactly at the end of the Earth, thought Captain Phil Lansing, but it was close enough.

Almost in the middle of the Bighorn Basin, the command center was mostly underground, the beauties of the basin's distant mountains and high prairie perpetually out of sight.

The mountain goats can enjoy the scenery out there, thought Captain Lansing. All we have to look at is the goddamned view-screens. He was surrounded by the flickering screens. They showed the entire Earth—cities and snow-covered mountains; restless oceans surging across thousands of empty miles; highways and air-ports and military bases.

Nearly eight billion people out there, Lansing grumbled to him-self, and the closest bit of civilization is a rundown asshole of a town that looks like an outtake from *High Noon*.

"Anomaly on screen A-seven," announced one of the noncoms monitoring the surveillance screens.

Lansing swiveled his command chair to face the screen, and the young woman sitting before it.

"Anomaly?" he asked.

"It's gone dead, sir."

Lansing stared at the screen. Nothing but a flickering washed-out gray.

He stood up and stepped closer to the seated noncom. Bending slightly, he stared at the dead screen. "What about the backup?"

"Also nonoperative, sir." The young tech sergeant was wide-eyed, alarmed.

"Which station is it supposed to be linked with?"

"*Hunter*."

"Try the comm link."

"I did, sir. No go."

"Try it again," Lansing commanded.

The sergeant swiveled her spindly chair to face the screen and tapped on the keyboard. The screen remained blank.

"No go," the sergeant repeated, in a thin, hushed voice.

Irritated, Lansing snapped, "I can see that."

From across the crowded, hushed room another tech sergeant called out, "Sir, my link's down too!"

Lansing turned to see another blank communications screen. Then the one next to it blanked out, as well. Before he could say anything, or even think of what he should say, every screen in the crowded control center went dead. Lansing stood in the middle of the suddenly silent room, pivoting slowly, staring at the blank screens.

This isn't supposed to be happening! he told himself. We're cut off from all the orbiting stations!

His air force training exerted its influence. "Get Colonel Iseminger on the intercom," he yelled at his communications officer. "*Now!*"

When in doubt, Lansing reminded himself, kick the problem upstairs.

## ■ *Hunter* Combat Information Center

The *Hunter* was one of nine orbiting battle stations that made up the command-and-control system of the newly created International Peacekeeping Force's strategic-defense network. In lower orbits, fifty-three unmanned ABM satellites armed with multimegawatt lasers and hypervelocity missiles crisscrossed the Earth's surface, with more being added every month.

In theory, these satellites could destroy thousands of ballistic missiles within minutes of their launch, no matter where on Earth they rose from.

In theory, each battle station controlled fifteen of the ABM satellites, but never the same fifteen for very long. The battle station's higher orbits were deliberately picked so that the crewless satellites passed through their field of view as they hurried by in their lower orbits. At the insistence of the fearful politicians of a hundred nations, no ABM satellites were under the permanent control of any one particular battle station.

In theory, each battle station patrolled one-ninth of the Earth's surface as it circled the globe. The sworn duty of its carefully chosen international crew was to make certain that any missiles launched from that part of the Earth would be swiftly and efficiently destroyed.

In theory.

The International Peacekeeping Force was new, untried except for computerized simulations and war games. Its purpose was to make certain that nuclear devastation would no longer threaten humankind. The Peacekeepers had the power and the authority to prevent any nuclear strike from reaching its targets.

Their authority extended completely across the Earth, even to the superpowers themselves.

In theory.

Hazard hurriedly tugged on a fresh set of coveralls, then pulled aside the privacy curtain of his cubicle and launched himself down the narrow passageway with a push of his meaty hands against the cool metal of the bulkheads. His stomach lurched at the sudden motion and he squeezed his eyes shut for a moment.

The Combat Information Center was buried deep in the middle of the station, protected by four levels of living and working areas plus the station's storage magazines for water, food, air, fuel for the maneuvering thrusters, power generators, and other equipment. Fighting down the queasy fluttering of his stomach as he sailed along the passageway toward the CIC, Hazard told himself that at least he did not suffer the claustrophobia that affected some of the station's younger crew members. To a man who had spent most of his career aboard nuclear submarines; in contrast, the station was roomy, almost luxurious.

He had to yank open four airtight hatches along the short way. Each automatically clanged shut behind him. At last Hazard floated into the dimly lit combat center. It was a tiny, womblike circular chamber, its walls studded with display screens that glowed a sickly green in the otherwise darkened compartment. No desks or chairs in zero gravity; the CIC's work surfaces were chest-high consoles, most of them covered with keyboards.

Varshni and the Norwegian officer, Stromsen, were on duty. Varshni, wearing the uniform patch that ID'd him as an officer from India, was small, slim and dark—and right now he was wide-eyed with anxiety. His face shone with perspiration and his fatigues were dark at the armpits and between his shoulders. In the greenish glow from the display screens he looked positively ill. Stromsen looked tense, her strong jaw clenched, her ice-blue eyes fastened on Hazard, waiting for him to tell her what to do.

"What happened?" Hazard demanded.

"It simply blew out," said Varshni. "I had just spoken with Michaels and D'Argencour when … when … ." His voice choked off.

"The screens went blank." Stromsen pointed to the status displays. "Everything suddenly zeroed out." She was controlling herself carefully, Hazard saw, her every nerve taut to the point of snapping.

"The rest of the station?" Hazard asked.

She gestured again toward the displays. "No other damage."

"Everybody on full alert?"

"Yes, sir."

Lieutenant Feeney ducked through the hatch, his eyes immediately drawn to the row of burning red malfunction lights where the bridge displays should have been.

"Mother of Mercy, what's happened?"

Before anyone could reply, Susan Yang, the chief communications officer, pushed through the hatch and almost bumped into Feeney. She saw the displays and immediately concluded, "We're under attack!"

"That is impossible!" Varshni blurted.

Hazard studied their faces for a swift moment. They all knew what had happened; only Yang had the guts to say it aloud. She seemed cool and in control of herself. How could someone who looks so young appear so unruffled, Hazard wondered—well, probably older than she looks. Feeney's pinched, narrow-eyed face failed to hide the fear that they all felt, but the Irish officer held himself well and returned Hazard's gaze without a tremor.

The only sound in the CIC was the hum of the electrical equipment and the soft sighing of the air fans. Hazard felt uncomfortably warm with the five of them crowding the cramped little chamber. Perspiration trickled down his ribs. They were all staring at him, waiting for him to tell them what must be done, to bring order out of the numbing fear and uncertainty that swirled around them. Four youngsters from four different nations, wearing the blue-gray fatigues of the IPF, with colored patches denoting their technical specialties on their left shoulders and the flag of their national origin on their right shoulders.

Hazard said, "We'll have to control the station from here. Mr. Feeney, you are now my number one; Michaels was on duty in the bridge. Mr. Varshni, get a damage-control party to the bridge. Full suits."

"No one's left alive in there," Varshni whispered. "Yes, but their bodies must be recovered. We owe them that. And their families." He glanced toward Yang. "And we've got to determine what caused the blowout."

Varshni's face twisted unhappily at the thought of the mangled bodies.

"I want a status report from each section of the station," Hazard went on, knowing that activity was the key to maintaining discipline. "Start with ...."

A beeping sound made all five of them flinch, then turn toward the communications console. Its orange demand light blinked for attention in time with the angry beeps. Hazard reached for a handgrip to steady himself as he swung toward the comm console. He noted how easily the youngsters handled themselves in zero *gee*. For him it still took a conscious, gut-wrenching effort.

Stromsen touched the keyboard with a slender finger.

A man's unsmiling face appeared on the screen: light-brown hair clipped as close as Hazard's gray, lips pressed together in an uncompromising line. He wore the blue-gray of the IPF with a commander's silver star on his collar.

"This is Buckbee, commander of station *Graham*. I want to speak to Commander Hazard."

Sliding in front of the screen, Hazard grasped the console's edge with both white-knuckled hands. He knew Buckbee only by reputation, a former U.S. Air Force colonel, from the Space Command until it had been disbanded, but before that he had put in a dozen years with SAC.

"This is Hazard."

Buckbee's lips moved slightly in what might have been a smile, but his eyes remained cold. "Hazard, you've just lost your bridge."

"And six lives."

Unmoved, Buckbee continued as if reading from a prepared script, "We offer you a chance to save the lives of the rest of your crew. Surrender the *Hunter* to us—"

"Us?"

Buckbee nodded, a small economical movement. "We will bring order and greatness out of this farce called the IPF."

A wave of loathing so intense that it almost made him vomit swept through Hazard. He realized that he had known all along, with a certainty that had not needed conscious verification, that his bridge had been destroyed by deliberate attack, not by accident.

"You killed six kids," he said, his voice so low that he barely heard it himself. It was not a whisper but a growl.

"We had to prove that we mean business, Hazard. Now surrender your station or we'll blow you all to hell. Any further deaths will be on your head, not ours."

Jonathan Wilson Hazard, captain, U.S. Navy (ret.). Marital status: divorced. Two children: Jonathan Jr., twenty-six; Virginia Elizabeth, twenty. Served twenty-eight years in U.S. Navy, mostly in submarines. Commanded fleet ballistic-missile submarines *Ohio, Corpus Christi*, and *Utah*. Later served as technical advisor to Joint Chiefs of Staff and as naval liaison to NATO headquarters in Brussels. Retired from navy after hostage crisis in Brussels. Joined International Peacekeeping Force and appointed commander of orbital battle station *Hunter*.

"I can't just hand this station over to a face on a screen," Hazard replied, stalling, desperately trying to think his way through the situation. "I don't know what you're up to, what your intentions are, who you really are."

"You're in no position to bargain, Hazard," said Buckbee, his voice flat and hard. "We want control of your station. Either you give it to us or we'll eliminate you completely."

"Who the hell is 'we'?"

"That doesn't matter."

"The hell it doesn't! I want to know who you are and what you're up to."

Buckbee frowned. His eyes shifted away slightly, as if looking to someone standing out of range of the video camera.

"We don't have time to go into that now," he said at last.

Hazard recognized the crack in Buckbee's armor. It was not much, but he pressed it. "Well, you goddamned well better make time, mister. I'm not handing this station over to you or anybody else until I know what in hell is going on."

Turning to Feeney, he ordered, "Sound general quarters. ABM satellites on full automatic. Ms. Yang, contact IPF headquarters and give them a full report of our situation."

"We'll destroy your station before those idiots in Geneva can decide what to do!" Buckbee snapped.

"Maybe," said Hazard. "But that'll take time, won't it? And we won't go down easy, I guarantee you. Maybe we'll take you down with us." Buckbee's face went white with fury. His eyes glared angrily.

"Listen," Hazard said more reasonably, "you can't expect me to just turn this station over to a face on a screen. Six of my people have been killed. I want to know why, and who's behind all this. I won't deal until I know who I'm dealing with and what your intentions are."

Buckbee growled, "You've just signed the death warrant for yourself and your entire crew."

The comm screen went blank.

## ■ White House Switchboard

Fiddling with her earphone with one hand, the switchboard operator frowned at her display screen.

"Executive mansion," she said into her microphone.

"This is IPF Command Center, Wyoming. I need to speak to the president. Emergency priority alpha-one-one."

The operator blinked. The switchboard seemed normal, all the other operators going through their usual routines. But the face on her screen looked taut with tension. Almost anger. And why is this IPF officer calling in on a civilian line? Don't they have their own phone system? Nevertheless, she automatically replied, "Yes, sir," as she tapped out the Oval Office's code.

The executive assistant working just outside the Oval Office recognized the two stars on the collar of the officer on her screen. Alpha-one-one was the top emergency priority code. Something big must be happening, she realized. She routed the call directly to the president's desk.

President Tomlinson picked up the phone on its first ring. Before he could say anything, the man on the line blurted, "We're under attack!"

"What?"

There were two senators and a pair of congressmen in the Oval Office with the president. They looked at each other, puzzled by the sudden tension that gripped the president's face.

"The whole network is out!" the caller said, loud enough for the president's visitors to hear. "Somebody's knocked out the whole system!"

"Calm down," said the president, as he stared at the printout beneath his caller's image in the phone's miniature screen: Major General Quentin Fitzgerald, IPFHQ, Wyoming.

It took more than a quarter hour for General Fitzgerald to explain that all communications with the command centers in orbit had been cut off.

"You mean you've had a tech failure?" the president asked.

"No sir!" General Fitzgerald shouted so loudly that the president's visitors could hear him clearly. "Somebody's cut off all the radio links. It's not a tech failure, sir, it's deliberate!"

"You're sure?"

"Yessir."

Tomlinson sat frozen for an instant. Then he asked, "Isn't there a backup system?"

"Yessir," said the general. "Laser links. But—"

"See if you can reach the *Hunter* or any other of our satellites. Keep your phone linked to this White House line."

"Yessir," the general repeated.

The president replaced his phone's receiver, then said to his visitors, "Some communication snarl-up with the IPF birds in orbit."

The senator from Missouri said, "The more complex a system is, the more ways it can get fouled up."

Getting to his feet, President Tomlinson said, "I suppose you're right. But I've got to get in touch with the Russians and the other governments involved with the IPF. If you'll excuse me …."

The visitors got to their feet. "Certainly, Mr. President."

As they headed for the door, Tomlinson picked up the red phone on his desk. "Put me through to Minister Grigor Medvedev, in Moscow," he commanded.

## ■ Space Station *Hunter*

For a moment Hazard hung weightlessly before the dead screen, struggling to keep the fear inside him from showing. Putting a hand out to the edge of the console to steady himself, he turned slowly to his young officers.

Their eyes were riveted on him, waiting for him to tell them what to do, waiting for him to decide between life and death.

Quietly, but with steel in his voice, Hazard commanded, "I said general quarters, Mr. Feeney. Now!"

Feeney flinched as if suddenly awakened from a dream. He pushed himself to the command console, unlatched the red cover over the "general quarters" button, and banged it eagerly with his fist. The action sent him recoiling upward and he had to put up a hand against the overhead to push himself back down to the deck. The alarm light began blinking red and they could hear its blaring even through the airtight hatches of the CIC.

"Geneva, Ms. Yang," Hazard said sternly, over the howl of the alarm. "Feeney, see that the crew is at their battle stations. I want the satellites under our control on full automatic, prepared to shoot down anything that moves if it isn't in our precleared data bank. And Mr. Varshni, has that damage-control party gotten under way yet?"

The two young men rushed toward the hatch, bumping each other in their eagerness to follow their commander's orders. Hazard almost smiled at the Laurel-and-Hardy aspect of it. Lieutenant Yang pushed herself to the comm console and anchored her softboots on the Velcro strip fastened to the deck there.

"Ms. Stromsen, you are the duty officer. I am depending on you to keep me informed of the status of all systems."

"Yes, sir!"

Keep them busy, Hazard told himself. Make them concentrate on doing their jobs and they won't have time to be frightened.

"Encountering interference, sir," reported Yang, her eyes on the comm displays. "Switching to emergency frequency."

Jamming, thought Hazard.

"Main comm antenna overheating," Stromsen said. She glanced down at her console keyboard, then up at the displays again. "I think they're attacking the antennas with lasers, sir! Main dish out. Secondaries ...." She shrugged and gestured toward the baleful red lights strung across her keyboard. "They're all out, sir."

"Set up a laser link," Hazard commanded. "They can't jam that. We've got to let Geneva know what's happening."

"Sir," said Yang, "Geneva will not be within our horizon for another forty-three minutes."

"Try signaling the commsats. Topmost priority."

"Yes, sir."

Got to let Geneva know, Hazard repeated to himself.

If anybody can help us, they can. If Buckbee's pals haven't put some of their own people into the comm center down there. Or staged a coup. Or already knocked out the commsats. They've been planning this for a long time.

They've got it all timed down to the microsecond.

He remembered the dinner, a month earlier, the night before he left to take command of the *Hunter*. I've known about it since then, Hazard said to himself. Known about it but didn't want to believe it. Known about it and done nothing. Buckbee was right. I killed those six kids. I should have seen that the bastards would strike without warning.

It had been in the equatorial city of Belém, where the Brazilians had set up their space launching facility. The IPF was obligated to spread its launches among all its space-capable member nations, so Hazard had been ordered to assemble his crew at Belém for their lift into orbit. The night before they left, Hazard had been invited to dinner by an old navy acquaintance who had already put in three months of orbital duty with the Peacekeepers and was on Earthside leave.

His name was Cardillo. Hazard had known him, somewhat distantly, as a fellow submariner, commander of attack boats rather than the missile carriers Hazard himself had captained. Vincent Cardillo had a reputation for being a hardnose who ran an efficient boat, if not a particularly happy one. He had never been really close to Hazard—their chemistries were too different. But on this specific sweltering evening in a poorly air-conditioned restaurant in downtown Belém, Cardillo acted as if they shared some old fraternal secret between them.

Hazard had worn his IPF summer-weight uniform: pale blue with gold insignia bordered by space black. Cardillo came in casual civilian slacks and a beautifully tailored Italian silk jacket. Through drinks and the first part of the dinner their conversation was light, inconsequential. Mostly reminiscences by two gray-haired ex-submariners about men they had known, women they had chased, sea tales that grew with each retelling. But then:

"Damn shame," Cardillo muttered, halfway through his entrée of grilled eel.

The restaurant was one of the dozens that had sprung up on the waterfront in Belém since the Brazilians had made the city their major spaceport. Outside the floor-to-ceiling windows, the muddy Parã River widened into the huge bay that eventually fed into the Atlantic. Hazard had spent his last day on Earth touring around the tropical jungle on a riverboat.

The makeshift shanties that stood on stilts along the twisting mud-brown creeks were giving way to industrial parks and cinderblock housing developments. Air conditioning was transforming the region from rubber plantations to a modern space-launching facility. The smell of cement dust blotted out the fragrance of tropical flowers. Bulldozers clattered in raw clearings slashed from the forest where stark steel frameworks of new buildings rose above the jungle growth. Children who had splashed naked in the brown jungle streams were being rounded up and sent to air-conditioned schools.

"What's a shame?" Hazard asked. "Seems to me these people are starting to do all right for the first time in their lives. The space business is making a lot of jobs around here."

Cardillo took a forkful of eel from his plate. It never got to his mouth.

"I don't mean them, Johnny. I mean us. It's a damn shame about us."

Hazard had never liked being called "Johnny." His family had addressed him as "Jon." His navy associates knew him as "Hazard" and nothing else. A few very close friends used "J. W."

"What do you mean?" he asked. His own plate was already wiped clean. The fish and its dark spicy sauce had been marvelous. So had the crisp-crusted bread.

"Don't you feel nervous about this whole IPF thing?" Cardillo asked, trying to look earnest. "I mean, I can see Washington deciding to put boomers like your boats in mothballs, and the silo missiles, too. But the attack subs? Decommission our conventional weapons systems? Leave us disarmed?"

Hazard had not been in command of a missile submarine in more than three years. He had been allowed, even encouraged, to resign his commission after the hostage fiasco in Brussels.

"If you're not in favor of what the American government is doing, then why did you agree to serve in the Peacekeepers?"

Cardillo shrugged and smiled slightly. It was not a pleasant smile. He had a thin, almost triangular face with a low, creased brow tapering down to a pointed chin. His once-dark hair, now peppered with gray, was thick and wavy. He had allowed it to grow down to his collar. His deep-brown eyes were always narrowed, crafty, focused so intently he seemed to be trying to stare through you.

There was no joy in his face, even though he was smiling; no pleasure. It was the smile of a gambler, a con artist, a used-car salesman.

"Well," he said slowly, putting his fork back down on the plate and leaning back in his chair, "you know the old saying, 'If you can't beat 'em, join 'em.'"

Hazard nodded, although he felt puzzled. He groped for Cardillo's meaning. "Yeah, I guess playing space cadet up there will be better than rusting away on the beach."

"Playing?" Cardillo's dark brows rose slightly. "We're not playing, Johnny. We're in this for keeps."

"I didn't mean to imply that I don't take my duty to the IPF seriously," Hazard answered.

For an instant Cardillo seemed stunned with surprise. Then he threw his head back and burst into laughter. "Jesus Christ, Johnny," he gasped. "You're so straight-arrow it's hysterical."

Hazard frowned but said nothing. Cardillo guffawed and banged the table with one hand. Some of the other diners glanced their way. They seemed to be mostly Americans or Europeans, a few Asians. Some Brazilians, too, Hazard noticed as he waited for Cardillo's amusement to subside. Probably from the capital or Rio.

"Let me in on the joke," Hazard said at last.

Cardillo wiped at his eyes. Then, leaning forward across the table, his grin fading into an intense, penetrating stare, he whispered harshly, "I already told you, Johnny. If we can't avoid being members of the IPF—if Washington's so fucking weak that we've got to disband practically all our defenses—then what we've got to do is take over the Peacekeepers ourselves."

"Take over the Peacekeepers?" Hazard felt stunned at the thought.

"Damn right! Men like you and me, Johnny. It's our duty to our country."

"Our country," Hazard reminded him, "has decided to join the International Peacekeeping Force and has encouraged its military officers to obtain commissions in it."

Cardillo shook his head. "That's our stupid goddamn government, Johnny. Not the country. Not the people who really want to *defend* America instead of selling her out to a bunch of fucking foreigners."

"That government," Hazard reminded him, "won a big majority last November."

Cardillo made a sour face. "Ahh, the people. What the fuck do they know?"

Hazard said nothing.

"I'm telling you, Johnny, the only way to do it is to take over the IPF."

"That's crazy."

"You mean if and when the time comes, you won't go along with us?"

"I mean," Hazard said, forcing his voice to remain calm, "that I took an oath to be loyal to the IPF. So did you."

"Yeah, yeah, sure. And what about the oath we took way back when—the one to preserve and protect the United States of America?"

"The United States of America *wants* us to serve in the Peacekeepers," Hazard insisted.

Cardillo shook his head again, mournfully. Not a trace of anger. Not even disappointment. As if he had expected this reaction from Hazard. His expression was that of a salesman who could not convince his stubborn customer of the bargain he was offering.

"Your son doesn't feel the same way you do," Cardillo said.

Hazard immediately clamped down on the rush of emotions that surged through him. Instead of reaching across the table and dragging Cardillo to his feet and punching in his smirking face, Hazard forced a thin smile and kept his fists clenched on his lap.

"Jon Jr. is a grown man. He has the right to make his own decisions."

"He's serving under me, you know." Cardillo's eyes searched Hazard's face intently, probing for weakness.

"Yes," Hazard said tightly. "He told me." Which was an outright lie.

## ■ Wyoming: IPF Command Center

Captain Lansing was sweating as he stood at attention before Colonel Iseminger's desk.

The colonel—his face like chiseled granite, his dark eyes boring into Lansing's soul—asked again, "The entire system is down?"

"Yessir."

"What about the laser backups?"

"They're only good for contacting any birds that're above our horizon, sir."

"So use them!" Iseminger snapped. "What the hell do you think they're for?"

"Now, sir?"

"Right now! At once!"

"Yessir." Lansing snapped a salute and scurried from the colonel's office.

Iseminger leaned back in his desk chair. The system's too complex, he said to himself. I told them when they first showed me the plans. Too damned complicated. Hundreds of satellites up there: the killers with their fancy lasers, the crewed command stations, and a gaggle of commsats linking them all together. Too damned complicated. Got to expect failures. Only natural.

But a slim threat of fear wormed into his consciousness. The whole system has gone down? he asked himself. The entire damned system? Grim-faced, he reached for the phone that automatically connected to his superiors in Washington.

Jake was reviewing the latest status reports on the *Athena* system when the president's aide phoned.

"He wants to see you," the woman's voice said, tight with tension. "*Now.*"

"Right," said Jake.

He hurried through the sea of desks toward the Oval Office. Everything seemed normal enough. People hunched over phones or computer screens. The buzz and crackle of everyday business.

He spotted a trio of military officers hotfooting it toward the Oval Office ahead of him. Two air force generals and an army man. Enough brass on their uniform shoulders to weigh down a good-sized ship.

One of the president's aides was holding the door to the Oval Office wide open. Jake followed the generals inside. The president was sitting tensely at his desk, talking to someone—on the red phone. Jake recognized the face on the phone's screen: Grigor Medvedev, from Moscow.

"We have established a laser link with the one of the command stations above our horizon." Medvedev's squarish, high-foreheaded face was beaded with perspiration.

"All our radio links are out," the president replied, his voice tight with tension.

"Ours too."

"And the commsats are down." Medvedev nodded unhappily.

"What's your assessment?" the president asked.

With a shrug, the Russian replied, "It can't be an accidental failure. It's much too … too *complete* for that."

"Somebody's trying to take over the system?"

Standing by the office's half-open door, Jake saw one of the air force generals nodding agreement.

Medvedev agreed too. "That is what it looks like to me, too."

"What do we do about it?" the president asked.

No one had an answer.

## ■ Space Station *Hunter* Combat Information Center

"Missiles approaching, sir!"

Stromsen's tense warning snapped Hazard out of his thoughts about his son. He riveted his attention to the main CIC display screen. Three angry red dots were working their way from the periphery of the screen toward the center, which marked the location of the *Hunter*.

"Now we'll see if the ABM satellites are working or not," Hazard muttered.

"Links with the ABM sats are still good, sir," Yang reported from her station, a shoulder's width away from Stromsen. "The integral antennas weren't knocked out when they hit the comm dishes."

Hazard gave her a nod of acknowledgment. The two young women could not have looked more different: Yang was small, wiry, dark, her straight black hair cut like a military helmet; Stromsen was willowy yet broad in the beam and deep in the bosom, as blonde as butter.

"Lasers on 024 and 025 firing," the Norwegian reported.

Hazard saw the display lights. On the main screen the three red dots flickered orange momentarily, then winked out altogether.

Stromsen pecked at her keyboard. Alphanumerics sprang up on a side screen. "Got them all while they were still in first-stage burn. They'll never reach us." She smiled with relief. "They're tumbling back into the atmosphere. Burn-up within seven minutes."

Hazard allowed himself a small grin. "Don't break out the champagne yet. That's just their first salvo. They're testing to see if we actually have control of the lasers."

It's all a question of time, Hazard knew. But how much time? What are they planning? How long before they start slicing us up with laser beams? We don't have the shielding to protect against lasers. The stupid politicians wouldn't allow us to armor these stations. We're like a sitting duck up here.

"What are they trying to accomplish, sir?" asked Yang. "Why are they doing this?"

"They want to take over the whole defense network. They want to seize control of the entire IPF."

"That's impossible!" Stromsen blurted.

"The Russians won't allow them to do that," Yang said. "The Chinese and the other members of the IPF will stop them."

"Maybe," said Hazard. "Maybe." He felt a slight hint of nausea ripple in his stomach. Reaching up, he touched the slippery plastic of the medicine patch behind his ear.

"Do you think they could succeed?" Stromsen asked. "What's important is, do *they* think they can succeed? There are still hundreds of ballistic missiles on Earth. Thousands of hydrogen warheads. Buckbee and his cohorts apparently believe that if they can take control of a portion of the ABM network, they can threaten a nuclear strike against the nations that don't go along with them."

"But the other nations will strike back and order their people in the IPF not to intercept their strikes," said Yang.

"It will be nuclear war," Stromsen said. "Just as if the IPF never existed."

"Worse," Yang pointed out, "because first there'll be a shoot-out on each one of these battle stations."

"That's madness!" said Stromsen.

"That's what we've got to prevent," Hazard said grimly.

The orange light on the comm console began to blink again. Yang snapped her attention to it. "Incoming message from the *Graham*, sir."

Hazard nodded. "Put it on the main screen."

Cardillo's crafty features appeared on the screen. He should have still been on leave back on Earth, but instead he was in uniform, aboard *Graham*, smiling crookedly at Hazard.

"Well, Johnny, I guess by now you've figured out that we mean business."

"And so do we. Give it up, Vince. It's not going to work."

With a small shake of his head Cardillo answered, "It's already working, Johnny boy. Two of the Russian battle stations are with us. So's the *Wood*. The Chinese and Indians are holding out but the European station is going along with us."

Hazard said, "So you've got four of the nine stations."

"So far."

"Then you don't really need *Hunter*. You can leave us alone."

Pursing his lips for a moment, Cardillo replied, "I'm afraid it doesn't work that way, Johnny. We want *Hunter*. We can't afford to have you rolling around like a loose cannon. You're either with us or against us."

"I'm not with you," Hazard said flatly.

Cardillo sighed theatrically. "John, there are twenty other officers and crew on your station ...."

"Fourteen now," Hazard corrected.

"Don't you think you ought to give them a chance to make a decision about their own lives?"

Despite himself, Hazard broke into a malicious grin. "Am I hearing you straight, Vince? You're asking the commander of a vessel to take a damned *vote?*"

Grinning back at him, Cardillo admitted, "I guess that was kind of dumb. But you do have their lives in your hands, Johnny."

"We're not knuckling under, Vince. And you've got twenty-some lives aboard the *Graham*, you know. Including your own. Better think about that."

"We already have, Johnny. One of those lives is Jonathan Hazard Jr. He's right here on the bridge with me. A fine officer, Johnny. You should be proud of him."

A hostage, Hazard realized. They're using Jon Jr. as a hostage.

"Do you want to talk with him?" Cardillo asked.

Hazard nodded.

Cardillo slid out of view and a younger man's face appeared on the screen. Jon Jr. looked tense, strained. This isn't any easier for him than it is for me, Hazard thought. He studied his son's face. Youthful, clear-eyed, a square-jawed honest face. Hazard was startled to realize that he had seen that face before, in his own Academy graduation photo.

"How are you, son?"

"I'm fine, Dad. And you?"

"Are we really on opposite sides of this?"

Jon Jr.'s eyes flicked away for a moment, then turned back to look squarely at his father's. "I'm afraid so, Dad."

"But why?" Hazard felt genuinely bewildered. "The IPF is dangerous," Jon Jr. said. "It's the first step toward a world government. The Third World countries want to bleed the industrialized nations dry. They want to grab all our wealth for themselves. The first step is to disarm us, under the pretense of preventing nuclear war. Then, once we're disarmed, they're going to take over everything—using the IPF as *their* armed forces."

"That's what they've told you," Hazard said.

"That's what I know, Dad. It's true. I know it is."

"And your answer is to take over the IPF and use it as *your* armed forces to control the rest of the world, is that it?"

"Better us than them."

Hazard shook his head. "They're using you, son. Cardillo and Buckbee and the rest of those maniacs; you're in with a bunch of would-be Napoleons."

Jon Jr. smiled pityingly at his father. "I knew you'd say something like that."

Hazard put up a beefy hand. "I don't want to argue with you, son. But I can't go along with you."

"You're going to force us to attack your station."

"I'll fight back."

His son's smile turned sardonic. "Like you did in Brussels?"

Hazard felt those words like a punch in his gut. He grunted with the pain of it. Wordlessly he reached out and clicked off the comm screen.

Brussels.

They had thought it was just another one of those endless Sunday demonstrations. A peace march. The Greens, the Nuclear Winter freaks, the Neutralists, peaceniks of one stripe or another. Swarms of little old ladies in their finest frocks, limping old war veterans, kids of all ages. Teenagers, lots of them, in blue jeans and denim jackets. Young women in shorts and tight T-shirts.

The guards in front of NATO's headquarters complex took no particular note of the older youths of both sexes mixed in with the teens. They failed to detect the hard, calculating eyes and the snub-nosed guns and grenades hidden under their jackets and sweaters.

Suddenly the peaceful parade dissolved into a mass of screaming wild people. The guards were cut down mercilessly as the cadre of terrorists fought their way into the main building of NATO headquarters. They forced dozens of peaceful marchers to go in with them, as shields and hostages.

Captain Jonathan W. Hazard, USN, was not on duty that Sunday, but he was in his office nevertheless, attending to some paperwork that he wanted out of the way before the start of business on Monday morning.

Unarmed, he was swiftly captured by the terrorists, beaten bloody for the fun of it, and then locked in a toilet. When the terrorists realized that he was the highest-ranking officer in the building, Hazard was dragged out and commanded to open the security vault where the most sensitive NATO documents were stored.

Hazard refused. The terrorists began shooting hostages. After the second murder Hazard opened the vault for them. Top-secret battle plans, maps showing locations of nuclear weapons, and hundreds of other documents were taken by the terrorists and never found, even after an American-led strike force retook the building in a bloody battle that killed all but four of the hostages.

Hazard stood before the blank comm screen for a moment, his softbooted feet not quite touching the deck, his mind racing.

They've even figured that angle, he said to himself. They know I caved in at Brussels and they expect me to cave in here. Some sonofabitch has grabbed my psych records and come to the conclusion that I'll react the same way now as I did then. Some sonofabitch. And they got my son to stick the knife in me.

The sound of the hatch clattering open stirred Hazard. Feeney floated through the hatch and grabbed an overhead handgrip.

"The crew's at battle stations, sir," he said, slightly breathless. "Standing by for further orders."

It struck Hazard that only a few minutes had passed since he himself had entered the CIC.

"Very good. Mr. Feeney," he said. "With the bridge out, we're going to have to control the station from here. Feeney, take the con. Ms. Stromsen, how much time before we can make direct contact with Geneva?"

"Forty minutes, sir," she sang out, then corrected, "Actually, thirty-nine fifty."

Feeney was worming his softboots against the Velcro strip in front of the propulsion-and-control console.

"Take her down, Mr. Feeney."

The Irishman's eyes widened with surprise. "Down, sir?"

Hazard made himself smile. "Down. To the altitude of the ABM satellites. Now."

"Yes, sir." Feeney began carefully pecking out commands on the keyboard before him.

"I'm not just reacting like an old submariner," Hazard reassured his young officers. "I want to get us to a lower altitude, so we won't be such a good target for so many of their lasers. Shrink our horizon. We're a sitting duck up here."

Yang grinned back at him. "I didn't think you expected to outmaneuver a laser beam, sir."

"No, but we can take ourselves out of range of most of their satellites." Most, Hazard knew, but not all.

"Ms. Stromsen, will you set up a simulation for me? I want to know how many unfriendly satellites can attack us at various altitudes, and what their positions would be compared to our own. I want a solution that tells me where we'll be safest."

"Right away, sir," Stromsen said. "What minimum altitude shall I plug in?"

"Go right down to the deck," Hazard said. "Low enough to boil the paint off."

"The station isn't built for reentry into the atmosphere, sir!"

"I know. But see how low we can get."

The old submariner's instinct: run silent, run deep. So the bastards think I'll fold up, just like I did at Brussels, Hazard fumed inwardly. Two big differences, you wiseasses. Two very big differences. In Brussels the hostages were civilians, not military men and women. And in Brussels I didn't have any weapons to fight back with.

## ■ White House Situation Room

As he entered the room, Jake recognized General Harmon about to seat himself in the straight-backed leather chair positioned squarely in the middle-length of the long conference table. God, there's enough brass around the table to capsize a battleship, he thought. The president sat tensely at the head of the table. No one spoke. The Situation Room was dimly lit, the glow from the display screens that lined the walls made the room almost ghostly.

"So what's going on?" the president asked without preamble.

General Harmon cleared his throat. "This is a coup, Mr. President. We're seizing control of the IPF satellites."

The president snapped, "We?"

"The air force, sir," Harmon replied. "We're acting in cooperation with the Russian IPF commanders and several of the smaller nations."

At that moment, the main door of the Situation Room opened and Vice President Eugene McMasters stepped in. He fixed General Harmon with a hard stare. "Why wasn't I informed of this meeting?"

Harmon frowned at the vice president. "You were informed. Why else are you here?"

"Because one of my flunkies told me there was 'a meeting of the minds,' as he put it, going on in the Situation Room."

Obviously suppressing a smile, General Harmon said, "Sit down, Mr. McMasters. You haven't missed anything. We're just getting started."

As the vice president pulled out a chair near the end of the conference table, President Tomlinson said, "General, do you mean to tell me you've initiated a coup d'état?"

"No sir," Harmon snapped. "You're still the president and you can remain so—as long as you don't get in our way."

"In the way of what?"

"We're taking control of the *Athena* antimissile system. We're going to make a new world order."

"You ... and the Russians?" The president's tone quavered with shocked disbelief.

"And any other nation that's willing to cooperate with us."

Folding his hands on the tabletop, the president asked, "And what happens to the nations that don't want to cooperate with you?"

Harmon's usually dour face broke into a tight grin. "They'll cooperate. Or get nuked."

Jake saw Tomlinson's jaw set. Staring unflinchingly at General Harmon, the president said, "General, you are relieved of duty. Retire to your quarters, right now."

Harmon laughed aloud. "You've got it backwards, sir. I can relieve *you* of duty if you don't go along with us."

Tomlinson's eyes flicked up and down the long conference table. Jake saw what he saw, a lineup of the nation's top brass, many of them looking uncomfortable, but not one of them saying a word. The silence was awesome.

## ■ Space Station *Hunter*

Hazard knew that the micropuffs of thrust from the maneuvering rockets were hardly strong enough to be felt, yet his stomach lurched and heaved suddenly.

"We have retro burn," Feeney said. "Altitude decreasing."

My damned stomach's more sensitive than his instruments, Hazard grumbled to himself.

"Incoming message from *Graham*, sir," said Yang.

"Ignore it."

"Sir," Yang said, turning slightly toward him, "I've been thinking about the minimum altitude we can achieve. Although the station is not equipped for atmospheric reentry, we do carry the four emergency evacuation spacecraft and they *do* have heat shields."

"Are you suggesting we abandon the station?"

"Oh, no, sir! But perhaps we could move the evac-craft to positions where they would be between us and the atmosphere. Let their heat shields protect us from any reentry heating—sort of like riding a surfboard."

Feeney laughed. "Trust a California girl to come up with a solution like that!"

"It might be a workable idea," Hazard said. "I'll keep it in mind."

"We're being illuminated by a laser beam," Stromsen said tensely. "Low power—so far."

"They're tracking us." Hazard ordered, "Yang, take over the simulation problem. Stromsen, give me a wide radar sweep. I want to see if they're moving any of their ABM satellites to counter our maneuver."

"I have been sweeping, sir. No satellite activity yet."

Hazard grunted. Yet. She knows that all they have to do is maneuver a few of their satellites to higher orbits and they'll have us in their sights.

To Yang he called, "Any response from the commsats?"

"No, sir," she replied immediately. "Either their laser receptors are not functioning or the satellites themselves are inoperative."

They couldn't have knocked out all the goddamned commsats, Hazard told himself. How would they communicate with one another? Cardillo claims the *Wood* and two of the Soviet stations are on their side. And the Europeans. He put a finger to his lips unconsciously, trying to remember Cardillo's exact words. *The Europeans are going along with us*. That's what he said. Maybe they're not actively involved in this. Maybe they're playing a wait-and-see game.

Either way, we're alone. They've got four, maybe five, out of the nine battle stations. We can't contact the Chinese or Indians. We don't know which Russian satellites haven't joined in with them—if any. It'll be more than a half hour before we can contact Geneva, and even then what the hell can they do?

Alone. Well, it won't be for the first time. Submariners are accustomed to being on their own.

"Sir," Yang reported, "the *Wood* is still trying to reach us. Very urgent, they're saying."

"Tell them I'm not available but you will record their message and personally give it to me." Turning to the Norwegian lieutenant, he snapped, "Ms. Stromsen, I want all crew members in their pressure suits. Levels one and two of the station are to be abandoned. No one above level three except the damage-control team. We're going to take some hits and I want everyone protected as much as possible."

She nodded and glanced at the others. All three of them looked tense, but not afraid. The fear was there, of course, underneath. But they were in control of themselves. Their eyes were clear, their hands steady.

"Should I have the air pumped out of levels one and two—after they're cleared of personnel?"

"No," Hazard said. "Let them outgas when they're hit.

Might fool the bastards into thinking they're doing more damage than they really are."

Feeney smiled weakly. "Sounds like the boxer who threatened to bleed all over his opponent."

Hazard glared at him. Stromsen took up the headset from her console and began issuing orders into the pin-sized microphone.

"The computer simulation is finished, sir," said Yang. "Put it on my screen here."

He studied the graphics, sensing Feeney peering over his shoulder. Their safest altitude was the lowest, where only six ABM satellites could "see" them.

The fifteen laser-armed satellites under their own control would surround them like a cavalry escort.

"There it is, Mr. Feeney. Plug that into your navigation program. That's where we want to be."

"Aye, sir."

The CIC shuddered. The screens dimmed, then came back to their full brightness.

"We've been hit!" Stromsen called out.

"Where? How bad?"

"Just aft of the main power generator. Outer hull ruptured. Storage area eight—medical, dental, and food—supplemental supplies."

"So they got the Band-Aids and vitamin pills," Yang joked shakily.

"But they're going after the power generator," said Hazard. "Any casualties?"

"No, sir," reported Stromsen. "No personnel stationed there during general quarters."

He grasped Feeney's thin shoulder. "Turn us over, man. Get that generator away from their beams!"

Feeney nodded hurriedly and flicked his stubby fingers across his keyboard. Hazard knew it was all in his imagination, but his stomach rolled sickeningly as the station rotated. Hanging grimly to a handgrip, he said, "I want each of you to get into your pressure suits, starting with you, Ms. Stromsen. Yang, take over her console until she …."

The chamber shook again. Another hit.

"Can't we strike back at them?" Stromsen cried.

Hazard asked, "How many satellites are firing at us?"

She glanced at her display screens. "It seems to be only one—so far."

"Hit it."

Her lips curled slightly in a Valkyrie's smile. She tapped out commands on her console and then leaned on the final button hard enough to lift her boots off the Velcro.

"Got him!" Stromsen exulted. "That's one laser that won't bother us again."

Yang and Feeney were grinning. Hazard asked the communications officer, "Let me hear what the *Graham* has been saying."

It was Buckbee's voice on the tape. "Hazard, you are not to attempt to change your orbital altitude. If you don't return to your original altitude immediately, we will fire on you."

"Well, they know by now that we're not paying any attention to them," Hazard said to his three young officers. "If I know them, they're going to take a few minutes to think things over, especially now that we've shown them we're ready to hit back. Stromsen, get into your suit. Feeney, you're next, then Yang. Move!"

It took fifteen minutes before the three of them were back in the CIC inside the bulky space suits, flexing gloved fingers, glancing about from inside their helmets. They all kept their visors up, and Hazard said nothing about it. Difficult enough to work inside the damned suits, he thought. They can snap the visors down fast enough if it comes to that.

The compact CIC became even more crowded. Despite decades of research and development, the space suits still bulked nearly twice as large as an unsuited person.

Suddenly Hazard felt an overpowering urge to get away from the CIC, away from the tension he saw in their young faces, away from the sweaty odor of fear, away from the responsibility for their lives.

"I'm going for my suit," he said, "and then a fast inspection tour of the station. Think you three can handle things on your own for a few minutes?"

Three heads bobbed inside their helmets. Three voices chorused, "Yes, sir."

"Fire on any satellite that fires at us," he commanded. "Tape all incoming messages. If there's any change in their tune, call me on the intercom."

"Yes, sir."

"Feeney, how long until we reach our final altitude?"

"More than an hour, sir."

"No way to move her faster?"

"I could get outside and push, I suppose."

Hazard grinned at him. "That won't be necessary, Mr. Feeney." Not yet, he added silently.

Stepping through the hatch into the passageway, Hazard saw that there was one pressure suit hanging on its rack in the locker just outside the CIC hatch. He passed it and went to his personal quarters and grabbed his own suit. It's good to leave them on their own for a while, he told himself. Build up their confidence. But he knew that he had to get away from them, even if only for a few minutes.

His personal space suit smelled of untainted plastic and fresh rubber, like a new car. As Hazard squirmed into it, its joints felt stiff—or maybe it's me, he thought. The helmet slipped from his gloved hands and went spinning away from him, floating off like a severed head. Hazard retrieved it and pulled it on. Like the youngsters, he kept the visor open.

His first stop was the bridge. Varshni was hovering in the companionway just outside the airtight hatch that sealed off the devastated area. Two other space-suited men were zippering an unrecognizably mangled body into a long black plastic bag. Three other bags floated alongside them, already filled and sealed.

Even inside a pressure suit, the young man seemed small, frail, like a skinny child. He was huddled next to the body bags, bent over almost into a fetal position. There were tears in his eyes. "These are all we could find. The two others must have been blown out of the station completely."

Hazard put a gloved hand on the shoulder of his suit. "They were my friends," Varshni said.

"It must have been painless," Hazard heard himself say. It sounded stupid.

"I wish I could believe that."

"There's more damage to inspect, over by the power generator area. Is your team nearly finished here?"

"Another few minutes, I think. We must make certain that all the wiring and air lines have been properly sealed off."

"They can handle that themselves. Come on, you and I will check it out together."

"Yes, sir." Varshni spoke into his helmet microphone briefly, then straightened up and tried to smile. "I am ready, sir."

The two men glided up a passageway that led to the outermost level of the station, Hazard wondering what would happen if a laser attack hit the area while they were in it. Takes a second or two to slice the hull open, he thought. Enough time to flip your visor down and grab on to something before the air blowout sucks you out of the station.

Still, he slid his visor down and ordered his companion to do the same. He was only mildly surprised when the Indian officer replied that he already had.

Wish the station were shielded. Wish they had designed it to withstand attack. Then he grumbled inwardly, Wishes are for losers; winners use what they have. But the thought nagged at him. What genius put the power generator next to the unarmored hull? Damned politicians wouldn't allow shielding; they *wanted* the stations to be vulnerable. A sign of goodwill, as far as they're concerned. They thought nobody would attack an unshielded station because the attacker's station is also unshielded. We're all in this together, try to hurt me and I'll hurt you. A hangover from the old mutual-destruction kind of dogma. Absolute bullshit.

There ought to be some way to protect ourselves from lasers. They shouldn't put people up here like sacrificial lambs.

Hazard glanced at Varshni, whose face was hidden behind his helmet visor. He thought of his son. Sheila had ten years to poison Jon's mind against me. Ten years. He wanted to hate her for that, but he found that he could not. He had been a poor husband and a worse father. Jon Jr. had every right to loathe his father. But dammit, this is more important than a family argument! Why can't the boy see what's at stake here? Just because he's sore at his father doesn't mean he has to take total leave of his senses.

They approached a hatch where the red warning light was blinking balefully. They checked the hatch behind them, made certain it was airtight, then used the wall-mounted keyboard to start the pumps that would evacuate the section of the passageway where they were standing, turning it into an elongated air lock.

Finally they could open the farther hatch and glide into the wrecked storage magazine.

Hazard grabbed a handhold. "Better use tethers here," he said.

Varshni had already unwound the tether from his waist and clipped it to a hold.

It was a small magazine, little more than a closet. In the light from their helmet lamps, they saw cartons of pharmaceuticals securely anchored to the shelves with toothed plastic straps. A gash had been torn in the hull, and through it Hazard could see the darkness of space. The laser beam had penetrated into the cartons and shelving, slicing a neat burned-edge slash through everything it touched.

Varshni floated upward toward the rent in the outer hull. It was as smooth as a surgeon's incision, and curled back slightly where the air pressure had pushed the thin metal outward in its rush to escape to vacuum.

"No wiring here," Varshni's voice said in Hazard's helmet earphones. "No plumbing either. We were fortunate."

"They were aiming for the power generator."

The young man pushed himself back down toward Hazard. His face was hidden behind the visor. "Ah, yes, that is an important target. We were very fortunate that they missed."

"They'll try again," Hazard said.

"Yes, of course."

## ■ White House Situation Room

From his seat almost at the end of the long conference table, Jake saw President Tomlinson and General Harmon glaring at each other. On Jake's right, sitting a few chairs ahead of him, was Vice President McMasters, a crooked smile on his narrow, pinched face.

Jake's eyes shifted to the double doors at the head of the situation room. The president's guard of Secret Service agents was outside those doors, he knew. And McMasters's, too, most likely.

While Tomlinson and Harmon jawed back and forth, Jake slowly worked his hand to the phone on the table in front of him. With a sudden move he jabbed the red emergency button.

The double doors burst open and a small phalanx of Secret Service agents—most of them men—burst into the situation room.

General Harmon spun around to see what the clatter was all about. President Tomlinson rose to his feet.

"Pete," the president said to the gangling agent who was apparently the agents' leader, "please take General Harmon to the Red Room, upstairs. See that he's disarmed and keep him under guard until I join you there."

Harmon's eyes went wide, then he reached inside his tunic and pulled out a pistol. "You're not—" But he was staring at an assortment of handguns and Uzis in the hands of the Secret Service guards.

"Disregard that order!" shouted McMasters, jumping up from his chair at the conference table. Pete and his cohorts cast startled looks at the vice president, then turned to face President Tomlinson again.

"Disarm the general," Tomlinson repeated, his voice tight with tension, "and escort him to the Red Room."

Pete stepped up to General Harmon and took the pistol from his hand. The others seated around the table, military officers and civilians, stared, slack-jawed.

"I'm afraid there's been something of a disagreement here," Tomlinson said, more coolly. Nodding toward General Harmon, he commanded, "Keep him in the Red Room until I join you there."

"Yessir," said Pete. And he motioned Harmon toward the door.

President Tomlinson resumed his chair at the head of the table. Glaring toward McMasters, he asked, "Anyone else have something to say?"

Absolute silence answered him.

## ■ Space Station *Hunter*

"Commander Hazard!" Yang's voice sounded urgent. "I think you should hear the latest message from *Graham*, sir."

Nodding unconsciously inside his helmet, Hazard said, "Patch it through."

He heard a click, then Buckbee's voice. "Hazard, we've been very patient with you. We're finished playing games. You bring the *Hunter* back to its normal altitude and surrender the station to us or we'll slice you to pieces. You've got five minutes to answer."

The voice shut off so abruptly that Hazard could picture Buckbee slamming his fist against the Off key.

"How long ago did this come through?"

"Transmission terminated forty-two seconds ago, sir," said Yang.

Hazard looked down at Varshni's slight form. He knew that Varshni had heard the ultimatum just as he had. He could not see the man's face, but the slump of his shoulders told him how Varshni felt.

Yang asked, "Sir, do you want me to set up a link with *Graham*?"

"No," said Hazard.

"I don't think they intend to call again, sir," Yang said. "They expect you to call them."

"Not yet," he said. He turned to the wavering form beside him. "Better straighten up, Mr. Varshni. There's going to be a lot of work for you and your damage-control team to do. We're in for a rough time."

Ordering Varshni back to his team at the ruins of the bridge, Hazard made his way toward the CIC. He spoke into his helmet mic as he pulled himself along the passageways, hand over hand, as fast as he could go:

"Mr. Feeney, you are to fire at any satellites that fire on us. And at any ABM satellites that begin maneuvering to gain altitude so they can look down on us. Understand?"

"Understood, sir!"

"Ms. Stromsen, I believe the fire-control panel is part of your responsibility. You will take your orders from Mr. Feeney."

"Yes, sir."

"Ms. Yang, I want that simulation of our position and altitude updated to show exactly which ABM satellites under hostile control are in a position to fire upon us."

"I already have that in the program, sir."

"Good. I want our four lifeboats detached from the station and placed in positions where their heat shields can intercept incoming laser beams."

For the first time, Yang's voice sounded uncertain. "I'm not sure I understand what you mean, sir."

Hazard was sweating and panting with the exertion of hauling himself along the passageway. This suit won't smell new anymore, he thought.

To Yang he explained, "We can use the lifeboats' heat shields as armor to absorb or deflect incoming laser beams. Not just shielding, but *active* armor. We can move the boats to protect the most likely areas for laser beams to come from."

"Like the goalie in a hockey game!" Feeney chirped. "Cutting down the angles."

"Exactly."

By the time he reached the CIC they were already working the problems. Hazard saw that Stromsen had the heaviest workload: all the station systems' status displays, fire control for the laser-armed ABM satellites, and control of the lifeboats now hovering dozens of meters away from the station.

"Ms. Stromsen, please transfer the fire-control responsibility to Mr. Feeney."

The expression on her strong-jawed face, half hidden inside her helmet, was pure stubborn indignation.

Jabbing a gloved thumb toward the lightning-slash insignia on the shoulder of Feeney's suit, Hazard said, "He *is* a weapons specialist, after all."

Stromsen's lips twitched slightly and she tapped at the keyboard to her left; the fire-control displays disappeared from the screens above it, only to spring up on screens in front of Feeney's position.

Hazard nodded as he lifted his own visor. "Okay, now.

Feeney, you're the offense. Stromsen, you're the defense. Ms. Yang, your job is to keep Ms. Stromsen continuously advised as to where the best placement of the lifeboats will be."

Yang nodded, her dark eyes sparkling with the challenge. "Sir, you can't possibly expect us to predict all the possible paths a laser beam might take and get a lifeboat's heat shield in place soon enough ...."

"I expect—as Lord Nelson once said—each of you to do your best. Now get Buckbee or Cardillo or whoever on the horn. I'm ready to talk to them."

It took a few moments for the communications laser to lock onto the distant *Graham*, but when Buckbee's face finally appeared on the screen, he was smiling—almost gloating.

"You've still got a minute and a half, Hazard. I'm glad you've come to your senses before we had to open fire on you."

"I'm only calling to warn you: any satellite that fires on us will be destroyed. Any satellite that maneuvers to put its lasers in a better position to hit us will also be destroyed."

Buckbee's jaw dropped open. His eyes widened. "I've got fifteen ABM satellites under my control,"

Hazard continued, "and I'm going to use them."

"You can't threaten us!" Buckbee sputtered. "We'll wipe you out!"

"Maybe. Maybe not. I intend to fight until the very last breath."

"You're crazy, Hazard!"

"Am I? Your game is to take over the whole defense system and threaten a nuclear-missile strike against any nation that doesn't go along with you. Well, if your satellites are exhausted or destroyed, you won't be much of a threat to anybody, will you? Try impressing the Chinese with a beat-up network. They've got enough missiles to wipe out Europe and North America, and they'll use them. If you don't have enough left to stop those missiles, then who's threatening whom?"

"You can't . . . ."

"Listen!" Hazard snapped. "How many of your satellites will be left by the time you overcome us? How much of a hole will we rip in your plans? Geneva will be able to blow you out of the sky with ground-launched missiles by the time you're finished with us."

"They'd never do such a thing."

"Are you sure?"

Buckbee looked away from Hazard, toward someone off-camera. He moved off, and Cardillo slid into view. He was no longer smiling.

"Nice try, Johnny, but you're bluffing and we both know it. Give up now or we're going to have to wipe you out."

"You can try, Vince. But you won't win."

"If we go, your son goes with us," Cardillo said.

Hazard forced his voice to remain level. "There's nothing I can do about that. He's a grown man. He's made his choice."

Cardillo huffed out a long, impatient sigh. "All right, Johnny. It was nice knowing you."

Hazard grimaced. Another lie, he thought. The man must be categorically unable to speak the truth.

The comm screen went blank.

"Are the lifeboats in place?" he asked.

"As good as we can get them," Yang said, her voice doubtful.

"Not too far from the station," Hazard warned. "I don't want them to show up as separate blips on their radar."

"Yes, sir, we know."

He nodded at them. Good kids, he thought. Ready to fight it out on my say-so. How far will they go before they crack? How much damage can we take before they scream to surrender?

They waited. Not a sound in the womb-shaped chamber, except for the hum of the electrical equipment and the whisper of air circulation. Hazard glided to a position slightly behind the two women. Feeney can handle the counterattack, he said to himself. That's simple enough. It's the defense that's going to win or lose for us.

On the display screens he saw the positions of the station and the hostile ABM satellites. Eleven of them in range. Eleven lines straight as laser beams converged on the station. Small green blips representing the four lifeboats hovered around the central pulsing yellow dot that represented the station. The green blips blocked nine of the converging lines. Two others passed between the lifeboat positions and reached the station itself.

"Ms. Stromsen," Hazard said softly.

She jerked as if a hot needle had been stuck into her flesh.

"Easy now," Hazard said. "All I want to tell you is that you should be prepared to move the lifeboats to intercept any beams that are getting through."

"Yes, sir, I know."

Speaking as soothingly as he could, Hazard went on, "I doubt that they'll fire all eleven lasers at us at once. And as our altitude decreases, there will be fewer and fewer of their satellites in range of us. We have a good chance of getting through this without too much damage."

Stromsen turned her whole space-suited body so that she could look at him from inside her helmet. "It's good of you to say so, sir. I know you're trying to cheer us up, and I'm certain we all appreciate it. But you are taking my attention away from the screens."

Yang giggled, whether out of tension or actual humor at Stromsen's retort, Hazard could not tell.

Feeney sang out, "I've got a satellite climbing on us!"

Before Hazard could speak, Feeney's hands were moving on his console keyboard. "Our beasties are now programmed for automatic, but I'm tapping in a backup manually, just in—ah! Got her! Scratch one enemy."

Smiles all around. But behind his grin, Hazard wondered, Can they gin up decoys? Something that gives the same radar signature as an ABM satellite but really isn't? I don't think so—but I don't know for sure.

"Laser beam … two of them," called Stromsen.

Hazard saw the display screen light up. Both beams were hitting the same lifeboat. Then a third beam from the opposite direction lanced out.

The station shuddered momentarily as Stromsen's fingers flew over her keyboard and one of the green dots shifted slightly to block the third beam.

"Where'd it hit?" he asked the Norwegian as the beams winked off.

"Just aft of the emergency oxygen tanks, sir."

Christ, Hazard thought, if they hit the tanks, enough oxygen will blow out of here to start us spinning like a top. "Vent the emergency oxygen."

"Vent it, sir?"

"Now!"

Stromsen pecked angrily at the keyboard to her left. "Venting. Sir."

"I don't want that gas spurting out and acting like a rocket thruster," Hazard explained to her back. "Besides, it's an old submariner's trick to let the attacker think he's caused real damage by jettisoning junk."

If any of them had reservations about getting rid of their emergency oxygen, they kept their doubts quiet.

There was plenty of junk to jettison over the next quarter of an hour. Laser beams struck the station repeatedly, although Stromsen was able to block most of the beams with the heat-shielded lifeboats. Still, despite the mobile shields, the station was being slashed apart, bit by bit.

Chunks of the outer hull ripped away, clouds of air blowing out of the upper level to form a brief fog around the station before dissipating into the vacuum of space. Cartons of supplies, pieces of equipment, even spare space suits, went spiraling out, pushed by air pressure as the compartments in which they had been housed were ripped apart by the incessant probing beams of energy.

Feeney struck back at the ABM satellites, but for every one he hit, another maneuvered into range to replace it.

"I'm running low on fuel for the lasers," he reported. "So must they," said Hazard, trying to sound calm.

"Aye, but they've got a few more than fifteen to play with."

"Stay with it, Mr. Feeney. You're doing fine." Hazard patted the shoulder of the Irishman's bulky suit. Glancing at Stromsen's status displays, he saw rows of red lights glowering like accusing eyes. They're taking the station apart, piece by piece. It's only a matter of time before we're finished.

Aloud, he announced, "I'm going to check with the damage-control party. Call me if anything unusual happens."

Yang quipped, "How do you define 'unusual,' sir?"

Stromsen and Feeney laughed. Hazard wished he could, too. As a response, he manufactured a grin for Yang, thinking, At least their morale hasn't cracked. Not yet.

## ■ White House Situation Room

The president was speaking with the head of the *Athena* antimissile system, in his headquarters in Brussels.

"They've apparently taken over four of the crewed space stations," said the general—a spare, thin-faced South African. "That means they can control nearly a third of the laser satellites."

The general seemed calm, in control of his emotions, in the oversized display screen at the head of the situation room. Except for his right eyebrow, which ticked like a metronome.

Still sitting at the far end of the conference table, Jake saw that the president's face was sheened with perspiration. But his voice was steady, unshaken.

"What are you doing about it?" Tomlinson asked, his voice tense, tight.

"We've issued a stand-down order, but they've ignored it, of course."

"What else?"

"We're preparing four launches of multinational military crews, with orders to take control of the space stations. Your own people are starting a countdown at your base in California."

"Do you think the rebels might fire at those rockets?"

With a barely noticeable dip of his chin, the general replied, "They might. But one of the space stations—the *Hunter*—seems to be shooting at the ABM satellites, and the rebel-held stations are directing laser fire at it."

Jake called from his chair, "*Hunter*'s fighting against them?"

"It appears that way," the South African replied. "It's all a bit murky; we haven't been able to establish a communications link with *Hunter*."

"But *Hunter*'s shooting at the ABM birds?" President Tomlinson asked.

"It appears that way," the general repeated.

The president asked, "Who's in command of the *Hunter*?"

From halfway down the long conference table one of the admirals answered, "Captain J. W. Hazard, United States Navy." Jake heard the pride in his voice.

Tomlinson let a small grin light his lips. "Score one for the navy."

## ■ Station *Hunter*

Encased in his space suit, Hazard watched the damage-control party working on level three, reconnecting a secondary power line that ran along the overhead through the main passageway. A laser beam had burned through the deck of the second level and severed the line, cutting backup power to the station's main computer. A shaft of brilliant sunlight lanced down from the outer hull through two levels of the station and onto the deck of level three.

One space-suited figure dangled upside down halfway through the hole in the overhead, splicing the cable carefully with gloved hands, while a second hovered nearby with a small welding torch. Two more were working farther down the passageway, where a larger hole had been burned halfway down the bulkhead.

Through that jagged rip Hazard could see clear out to space and the rim of the Earth, glaring bright with swirls of white clouds.

He recognized Varshni by his small size even before he could see the India flag on his shoulder or read the name stenciled on the front of his suit.

"Mr. Varshni, I want you and your crew to leave level three. It's getting too dangerous here."

"But, sir," Varshni protested, "our duty is to repair damage."

"There'll be damage on level four soon enough."

"But the computer requires power."

"It can run on its internal batteries."

"But for how long?"

"Long enough," said Hazard grimly.

Varshni refused to be placated. "I am not risking lives unnecessarily, sir."

"I didn't say you were."

"I am operating on sound principles," he insisted, "exactly as required in the book of regulations."

"I'm not faulting you, man. You and your crew have done a fine job."

The others had stopped their work. They were watching the exchange between their superior and the station commander.

"I have operated on the principle that lightning does not strike twice in the same place. In old-fashioned naval parlance this is referred to, I believe, as 'chasing salvos.' "

Hazard stared at the diminutive officer. Even inside the visored space suit, Varshni appeared stiff with resentment.

Chasing salvos, Hazard thought—that's what a little ship does when it's under attack by a bigger ship: run to the spot where the last shells splashed, because it's pretty certain that the next salvo won't hit there. I've insulted his abilities, Hazard realized. And in front of his team. Damned fool!

"Mr. Varshni," Hazard explained slowly, "this battle will be decided, one way or the other, in the next twenty minutes or so. You and your team have done an excellent job of keeping damage to a minimum. Without you, we would have been forced to surrender."

Varshni seemed to relax a little. Hazard could sense his chin rising a notch inside his helmet.

"But the battle is entering a new phase," Hazard went on. "Level three is now vulnerable to direct laser damage. I can't afford to lose you and your team at this critical stage. Moreover, the computer and the rest of the most sensitive equipment are on level four and in the Combat Information Center. Those are the areas that need our protection and those are the areas where I want you to operate. Is that understood?"

A heartbeat's hesitation. Then Varshni said, "Yes, of course, sir. I understand. Thank you for explaining it to me."

"Okay. Now finish your work here and then get down to level four."

"Yes, sir."

Shaking his head inside his helmet, Hazard turned and pushed himself toward the ladderway that led down to level four and the CIC.

A blinding glare lit the passageway and he heard screams of agony. Blinking against the burning afterimage, Hazard turned to see Varshni's figure almost sliced in half. A dark burn line slashed diagonally across the torso of his space suit. Tiny globules of blood floated out from it. The metal overhead was blackened and curled now. A woman was screaming. She was up by the overhead, thrashing wildly with pain, her backpack ablaze. The other technician was nowhere to be seen.

Hazard rushed to Varshni while the other two members of the damage-control team raced to the wounded woman and sprayed extinguisher foam on her backpack.

Over the woman's screams he heard Varshni's gagging whisper. "It's no use, sir … no use …."

"You did fine, son." Hazard held the little man in his arms. "You did fine."

He felt the life slip away. Lightning does strike in the same place, Hazard thought. You've chased your last salvo, son.

Both the man and the woman who had been working on the power cable had been wounded by the laser beam. The man's right arm had been sliced off at the elbow, the woman badly burned on her back when her life-support pack exploded. Hazard and the two remaining damage-control men carried them to the sick bay, where the station's one doctor was already working on three other casualties.

The sick bay was on the third level. Hazard realized how vulnerable that was. He made his way down to the CIC, at the heart of the station, knowing that it was protected not only by layers of metal but by human flesh as well.

The station rocked again, and Hazard heard the ominous groaning of tortured metal as he pushed weightlessly along the ladderway.

He felt bone weary as he opened the hatch and floated into the CIC. One look at the haggard faces of his three young officers told him that they were on the edge of defeat as well. Stromsen's status display board was studded with glowering red lights.

"This station is starting to resemble a piece of swiss cheese," Hazard quipped lamely as he lifted the visor of his helmet.

No one laughed. Or even smiled.

"Varshni bought it," he said, taking up his post between Stromsen and Feeney.

"We heard it," said Yang.

Hazard looked around the CIC. It felt stifling hot, dank with the smell of fear.

"Mr. Feeney," he said, "discontinue all offensive operations."

"Sir?" The Irishman's voice squeaked with surprise. "Don't fire back at the sonsofbitches," Hazard snapped. "Is that clear enough?"

Feeney raised his hands up above his shoulders, like a croupier showing that he was not influencing the roulette wheel.

"Ms. Stromsen, when the next laser beam is fired at us, shut down the main power generator. Ms. Yang, issue instructions over the intercom that all personnel are to place themselves on level four—except for the sick bay. No one is to use the intercom. That is an order."

Stromsen asked, "Shut down the power generator?"

"We'll run on the backup fuel cells and batteries. They don't make so much heat."

There were more questions in Stromsen's eyes, but she turned back to her consoles silently.

Hazard explained, "We are going to run silent. Buckbee, Cardillo, and company have been pounding the hell out of us for about half an hour. They have inflicted considerable damage. However, they don't know that we've been able to shield ourselves with the lifeboats. They think they've hurt us much more than they actually have."

"You want them to think that they've finished us off, then?" asked Feeney.

"That's right. But, Mr. Feeney, let me ask you a hypothetical question ...." The chamber shook again and the screens dimmed, then came back to their normal brightness.

Stromsen punched a key on her console. "Main generator shut down, sir."

Hazard knew it was his imagination, but the screens seemed to be slightly dimmer.

"Ms. Yang?" he asked.

"All personnel have been instructed to move down to level four and stay off the intercom."

Hazard nodded, satisfied. Turning back to Feeney, he resumed, "Suppose, Mr. Feeney, that you are in command of *Graham*. How would you know that you've knocked out *Hunter*?"

Feeney absently started to stroke his chin and bumped his fingertips against the rim of his helmet instead. "I suppose … if *Hunter* stopped shooting back, and I couldn't detect any radio emissions from her …."

"And infrared!" Yang added. "With the power generator out, our infrared signature goes way down."

"We appear to be dead in the water," said Stromsen. "Right."

"But what does it gain us?" Yang asked.

"Time," answered Stromsen. "In another ten minutes or so we'll be within contact range of Geneva."

Hazard patted the top of her helmet. "Exactly. But more than that. We get them to stop shooting at us. We save the wounded up in the sick bay."

"And ourselves," said Feeney.

"Yes," Hazard admitted. "And ourselves." For long moments they hung weightlessly, silent, waiting, hoping.

"Sir," said Yang, "a query from *Graham*, asking if we surrender."

"No reply," Hazard ordered. "Maintain complete silence."

The minutes stretched. Hazard glided to Yang's comm console and taped a message for Geneva, swiftly outlining what had happened. "I want that tape compressed into a couple of milliseconds and burped by the tightest laser beam we have down to Geneva."

Yang nodded. "I suppose the energy surge for a low-power communications laser won't be enough for them to detect."

"Probably not, but it's a chance we'll have to take. Beam it at irregular intervals as long as Geneva is in view."

"Yes, sir."

"Sir!" Feeney called out. "Looks like *Graham*'s detached a lifeboat."

"Trajectory analysis?"

Feeney tapped at his navigation console. "Heading straight for us," he reported.

Hazard felt his lips pull back in a feral grin.

"They're coming over to make sure. Cardillo's an old submariner; he knows all about running silent. They're sending over an armed party to make sure we're finished."

"And to take control of our satellites," Yang suggested.

Hazard brightened. “Right! There’re only two ways to control the ABM satellites—either from the station on patrol or from Geneva.” He spread his arms happily. “That means they’re not in control of Geneva! We’ve got a good chance to pull their cork!”

But there was no response from Geneva when they beamed their data-compressed message to IPF headquarters. *Hunter* glided past in its unusually low orbit, a tattered wreck desperately calling for help. No answer reached them.

And the lifeboat from *Graham* moved inexorably closer.

## ■ White House Red Room

His face grim, President Tomlinson strode into the Red Room.

The first-floor room had served many purposes over the decades, mainly as an antechamber for the Cabinet Room or the president’s library, next door. A large portrait of Theodore Roosevelt—tense and impatient—hung on one of the deep-red walls. The furniture was mainly Empire style.

General Harmon was seated on one of the dainty French sofas. He shot to his feet automatically as the president entered the room. The three Secret Service men in the room got to their feet, too.

Tomlinson waved a hand at the general and said, “Sit down, Harold.”

Harmon remained standing. “You can’t stop this,” he said, his voice edgy, brittle.

“But you can,” said the president. “I want you to call it off.”

“I can’t. Not now. Nobody can.”

“Bullshit.”

“You don’t seem to realize, Mr. President, what’s happening here.”

“Yes I do. You and your colleagues are trying to take over the world. It’s a military coup, in orbital space.”

“We have control of the antimissile system—”

“No, you don’t. I’ve spoken with Medvedev and Chang.

And several of the other members—”

“And you believe what they’re telling you? You’re a bigger fool than I thought.”

Tomlinson's hands clenched into fists, but he caught himself and instead took in a deep breath. Then, "Hazard's still in control of the *Hunter*. He's fighting back."

"He won't be for much longer."

"Long enough," said the president.

With a shake of his head, the general said, "You can't stop us. Nobody can."

The president repeated, "Bullshit."

## ■ Space Station *Hunter*

The gloom in *Hunter*'s CIC was thick enough to stuff a mattress as Geneva disappeared over the horizon and the boat from *Graham* glided toward them. Hazard watched the approaching boat on one of Stromsen's screens: it was bright and shining in the sunlight, not blackened by scorching laser beams, unsullied by splashes of human blood.

We could zap it into dust, he thought. One word from me and Feeney could focus half a dozen lasers on it. The men aboard her must be volunteers, willing to risk their necks to make certain that we're finished. He felt a grim admiration for them. Then he wondered, Is Jon Jr. aboard with them?

"Mr. Feeney, what kind of weapons do you think they're carrying?"

Feeney's brows rose toward his scalp. "Weapons, sir? You mean, like sidearms?"

Hazard nodded.

"Personal weapons are not allowed aboard station, sir. Regulations forbid it."

"I know. But what do you bet they've got pistols, at least. Maybe some submachine guns, Uzis."

"Damned dangerous stuff for a space station," said Feeney.

Hazard smiled tightly at the Irishman. "Are you afraid they'll put a few more holes in our hull?"

Yang saw what he was driving at. "Sir, there are no weapons aboard *Hunter*—unless you want to count butter knives."

"They'll be coming aboard with guns, just to make sure," Hazard said. "I want to capture them alive and use them as hostages. That's our last remaining card. If we can't do that, we've got to surrender."

"They'll be in full suits." said Stromsen. "Each on his own individual life-support system."

"How can we capture them? Or even fight them?" Yang wondered aloud.

Hazard detected no hint of defeat in their voices. The despair of a half hour earlier was gone now. A new excitement had hold of them. He was holding a glimmer of hope for them, and they were reaching for it.

"There can't be more than six of them aboard that boat," Feeney mused.

I wonder if Cardillo has the guts to lead the boarding party in person, Hazard asked himself.

"We don't have any useful weapons," said Yang.

"But we have some tools," Stromsen pointed out.

"Maybe …"

"What do the lifeboat engines use for propellant?" Hazard asked rhetorically.

"Methane and oh-eff-two," Feeney replied, looking puzzled.

Hazard nodded. "Ms. Stromsen, which of our supply magazines are still intact—if any?"

It took them several minutes to understand what he was driving at, but when they finally saw the light, the three young officers went speedily to work. Together with the four unwounded members of the crew, they prepared a welcome for the boarders from *Graham*.

Finally, Hazard watched on Stromsen's display screens as the *Graham*'s boat sniffed around the battered station. Strict silence was in force aboard *Hunter*. Even in the CIC, deep at the heart of the battle station, they spoke in tense whispers.

"I hope the bastards like what they see," Hazard muttered.

"They know that we used the lifeboats for shields," said Yang.

"Active armor," Hazard said. "Did you know the idea was invented by the man this station's named after?"

"They're looking for a docking port," Stromsen pointed out.

"Only one left," said Feeney.

They could hang their boat almost anywhere and walk in through the holes they've put in us, Hazard said to himself. But they won't. They'll go by the book and find an intact docking port. They've got to! Everything depends on that.

He felt his palms getting slippery with nervous perspiration as the lifeboat slowly, slowly moved around *Hunter* toward its Earth-facing side, where the only usable port was located. Hazard had seen to it that all the other ports had been disabled.

"They're buying it!" Stromsen's whisper held a note of triumph.

"Sir!" Yang hissed urgently. "A message just came in—laser beam, ultracompressed."

"From where?"

"Computer's decrypting," she replied, her snub-nosed face wrinkled with concentration. "Coming up on my center screen, sir."

Hazard slid over toward her. The words on the screen read:

> From: *IPF Regional HQ, Lagos.*
> To: *Commander, battle station* Hunter
>
> *Message begins. Coup attempt in Geneva a failure, thanks in large part to your refusal to surrender your command. Situation still unclear, however. Imperative you retain control of* Hunter, *at all costs. Message ends.*

He read it aloud, in a guttural whisper, so that Feeney and Stromsen understood what was at stake.

"We're not alone," Hazard told them. "They know what's happening, and help is on the way." That was stretching the facts, he knew. And he knew they knew. But it was reassuring to think that someone, somewhere, was preparing to help them. Hazard watched them grinning to one another. In his mind, though, he kept repeating the phrase, *Imperative you retain control of* Hunter, *at all costs.*

At all costs, Hazard said to himself, closing his eyes wearily, seeing Varshni dying in his arms and the others maimed. At all costs.

The bastards, Hazard seethed inwardly. The dirty, power-grabbing, murdering bastards. Once they set foot inside my station, I'll kill them like the poisonous snakes they are. I'll squash them flat. I'll cut them open just like they've slashed my kids.

He stopped abruptly and forced himself to take a deep breath. Yeah, sure. Go for personal revenge. That'll make the world a better place to live in, won't it?

"Sir, are you all right?"

Hazard opened his eyes and saw Stromsen staring at him. "Yes, I'm fine. Thank you."

"They've docked, sir," said the Norwegian.

"They're debarking and coming up passageway C, just as you planned," Yang added.

Looking past her to the screens, Hazard saw that there were six of them, all in space suits, visors down. And pistols in their gloved hands.

"Nothing bigger than pistols?"

"No, sir. Not that we can see, at least."

Turning to Feeney. "Ready with the aerosols?"

"Yes, sir."

"All crew members evacuated from the area?"

"They're all back on level four, except for the sick bay."

Hazard never took his eyes from the screens. The six space-suited boarders were floating down the passageway that led to the lower levels of the station, which were still pressurized and held breathable air. They stopped at the air lock, saw that it was functional. The leader of their group started working the wall unit that controlled the lock.

"Can we hear them?" he asked Yang. Wordlessly, she touched a stud on her keyboard.

"... use the next section of the passageway as an air lock," someone was saying. "Standard procedure. Then we'll pump the air back into it once we're inside."

"But we stay in the suits until we check out the whole station. That's an order," said another voice.

Buckbee? Hazard's spirits soared. Buckbee will make a nice hostage, he thought. Not as good as Cardillo, but good enough.

Just as he had hoped, the six boarders went through the airtight hatch, closed it behind them, and started the pump that filled the next section of passageway with air once again.

"Something funny here, sir," said one of the space-suited figures.

"Yeah, the air's kind of misty."

"Never saw anything like this before. Christ, it's like Mexico City air."

"Stay in your suits!"

It *was* Buckbee's voice, Hazard was certain of it.

"Their life-support systems must have been damaged in our bombardment. They're probably all dead."

You wish, you sonofabitch, Hazard thought. To Feeney, he whispered, "Seal that hatch."

Feeney pecked at a button on his console.

"And the next one."

"Already done, sir."

Hazard waited, watching Stromsen's main screen as the six boarders shuffled weightlessly to the next hatch and found that it would not respond to the control unit on the bulkhead.

"Damn! We'll have to double back and find another route."

"Ms. Yang, I'm ready to hold converse with our guests," said Hazard.

She flashed a brilliant smile and touched the appropriate keys, then pointed at him. "You're on the air!"

"Buckbee, this is Hazard."

All six of the boarders froze for an instant, then spun weightlessly in midair, trying to locate the source of the new voice.

"You are trapped in that section of corridor," Hazard said. "The mist that you see in the air is oxygen difluoride from our lifeboat propellant tanks. Very volatile stuff. Don't strike any matches."

"What the hell are you saying, Hazard?"

"You're locked in that passageway, Buckbee. If you try to fire those popguns you're carrying, you'll blow yourselves to pieces."

"And you too!"

"We're already dead, you prick. Taking you with us is the only joy I'm going to get out of this."

"You're bluffing!"

Hazard snapped, "Then show me how brave you are, Buckbee. Take a shot at the hatch."

The six boarders hovered in the misty passageway like figures in a surrealist painting. Seconds ticked by, each one stretching excruciatingly. Hazard felt a pain in his jaw and realized he was clenching his teeth hard enough to chip them.

He took his eyes from the screen momentarily to glance at his three youngsters. They were just as tense as he was. They knew how long the odds of their gamble were.

The passageway was filled with nothing more than aerosol mists from every spray can the crew could locate in the supply magazines.

"What do you want, Hazard?" Buckbee said at last, his voice sullen, like a spoiled little boy who had been denied a cookie.

Hazard let out his breath. Then, as cheerfully as he could manage, "I've got what I want. Six hostages. How much air do your suits carry? Twelve hours?"

"What do you mean?"

"You've got twelve hours to convince Cardillo and the rest of your pals to surrender."

"You're crazy, Hazard."

"I've had a tough day, Buckbee. I don't need your insults. Call me when you're ready to deal."

"You'll be killing your son!"

Hazard had half expected it, but still it hit him like a blow. "Jonnie, are you there?"

"Yes I am, Dad."

Hazard strained forward, peering hard at the display screen, trying to determine which one of the space-suited figures was his son.

"Well, this is a helluva fix, isn't it?" he said softly.

"Dad, you don't have to wait twelve hours."

"Shut your mouth!" Buckbee snapped.

"Fuck you," snarled Jon Jr. "I'm not going to get myself killed for nothing."

"I'll shoot you!" Hazard saw Buckbee level his gun at Jon Jr.

"And kill yourself? You haven't got the guts," Jonnie sneered.

Hazard almost smiled. How many times had his son used that tone on him?

Buckbee's hand wavered. He let the gun slip from his gloved fingers. It drifted slowly, weightlessly, away from him.

Hazard swallowed. Hard.

"Dad, in another hour or two the game will be over. Cardillo lied to you. The Russians never came in with us. Half a dozen ships full of troops are lifting off from IPF centers all over the globe."

"Is that the truth, son?"

"Yes, sir, it is. Our only hope was to grab control of your satellites. Once the coup attempt in Geneva flopped, Cardillo knew that if he could control three or four sets of ABM satellites, he could at least force a stalemate. But all he's got is *Graham* and *Wood*. Nobody else."

"You damned little traitor!" Buckbee screeched.

Jon Jr. laughed. "Yeah, you're right. But I'm going to be a *live* traitor. I'm not dying for the likes of you."

Hazard thought swiftly. Jon Jr. might defy his father, might argue with him, even revile him, but he had never known the lad to lie to him.

"Buckbee, the game's over," he said slowly. "You'd better get the word to Cardillo before there's more bloodshed."

## ■ White House Red Room

The president and General Harmon stood in the middle of the room, staring wordlessly at each other.

Jake watched the uneasy confrontation on the display screen where he still sat at the Situation Room conference table. The phone at his place buzzed. He blinked at it once, then grabbed the receiver.

"Ross here."

A high-pitched singsong voice said, "I wish to speak to the president of the United States. This is General Lakshmi, of the International Peacekeeping Force, in Geneva."

"The president is in conference," Jake improvised. "I can take a message to him."

For a nerve-stretching moment Genera Lakshmi was silent. Then, "Please tell the president that three of the four vessels carrying troops to the space stations have been launched successfully and are scheduled to reach their planned orbits in forty-four … no, make that forty-three minutes."

"And the fourth vessel?" Jake asked.

"Its launch is on temporary hold. A mechanical problem. It is scheduled to launch in twenty-three minutes."

"Good," said Jake. "I'll tell the president."

Lakshmi's voice became querulous. "And you are?"

"I'm Jacob Ross, science advisor to the president."

"Ah. I see."

"I'll have the president phone you as soon as he's free of his conference."

"Very good. Tell him that the situation in orbit is still very tense. Very tense."

"I will," Jake promised. "Thank you." The line went dead. As he hung up the phone Jake saw the table full of brass hats staring at him. "Troops are on their way to the space stations," he told them.

"What about *Hunter*?" asked the admiral who had identified Captain Hazard.

Jake shook his head.

## ■ Space Station *Hunter*

It took another six hours before it was all sorted out. A shuttle filled with armed troops and an entire replacement crew finally arrived at the battered hulk of *Hunter*. The relieving commander, a stubby, compactly built Black man from New Jersey who had been a U.S. Air Force fighter pilot, made a grim tour of inspection with Hazard.

From inside his space suit he whistled in amazement at the battle damage.

"Shee-it, you don't need a new crew, you need a new station!"

"It's still functional," Hazard said quietly, then added proudly, "and so is my crew, or what's left of them. They ran this station and kept control of the ABM satellites."

"The stuff legends are made of, my man," said the new commander.

Hazard and his crew filed tiredly into the waiting shuttle, thirteen grimy, exhausted men and women in the pale-blue fatigues of the IPF. Three of them were wrapped in mesh cocoons and attended by medical personnel. Two others were bandaged but ambulatory.

He shook hands with each and every one of them as they stepped from the station's only functional air lock into the shuttle's passenger compartment. Hovering there weightlessly, his creased, craggy face unsmiling, to each of his crew members he said, "Thank you. We couldn't have succeeded without your effort."

The last three through the hatch were Feeney, Stromsen, and Yang. The Irishman looked embarrassed as Hazard shook his hand.

"I'm recommending you for promotion. You were damned cool under fire."

"Frozen stiff with fear, you mean."

To Stromsen, "You, too, Ms. Stromsen. You've earned a promotion."

"Thank you, sir," was all she could say.

"And you ..." he said to Yang, "you were outstanding."

She started to say something, then flung her arms around Hazard's neck and squeezed tight. "I was so frightened!" she whispered in his ear. "You kept me from cracking up."

Hazard held her around the waist for a moment. As they disengaged, he felt his face turning flame red. He turned away from the hatch, not wanting to see the expressions on the rest of his crew members.

Buckbee was coming through the air lock. Behind him were his five men. Including Jon Jr.

They passed Hazard in absolute silence, Buckbee's face as cold and angry as an Antarctic storm. Jon Jr. was the last in line. None of the would-be boarders was in handcuffs, but they all had the hangdog look of prisoners. All except Hazard's son. He stopped before his father and met the older man's gaze. Jon Jr.'s gray eyes were level with his father's, unswerving, unafraid.

He made a bitter little smile. "I still don't agree with you," he said without preamble. "I don't think the IPF is workable—and it's certainly not in the best interests of the United States."

"But you threw your lot in with us when it counted," Hazard said.

"The hell I did!" Jon Jr. looked genuinely aggrieved. "I just didn't see any sense in dying for a lost cause."

"Really?"

"Cardillo and Buckbee and the rest of them were a bunch of idiots. If I had known how stupid they are I wouldn't ...."

He stopped himself, grinned ruefully, and shrugged his shoulders. "This isn't over, you know. You've won the battle, but the war's not ended yet."

"I'll do what I can to get them to lighten your sentence," Hazard said.

"Don't stick your neck out for me! I'm still dead set against you on this."

Hazard smiled wanly at the younger man. "And you're still my son."

Jon Jr. blinked, looked away, then ducked through the hatch and made for a seat in the shuttle.

Hazard formally turned the station over to its new commander, saluted one last time, then went into the shuttle's passenger compartment. He hung there weightlessly a moment as the hatch behind him was swung shut and sealed. Most of the seats were already filled. There was an empty one beside Yang, but after their little scene at the hatch Hazard was hesitant about sitting next to her. He glided down the aisle and picked a seat that had no one next to it. Not one of his crew. Not Jon Jr. There's a certain amount of loneliness involved in command, he told himself. It's not wise to get too familiar with people you have to order into battle.

He felt, rather than heard, a thump as the shuttle disengaged from the station's air lock. He sensed the winged hypersonic spaceplane turning and angling its nose for reentry into the atmosphere.

Back to ... Hazard realized that *home*, for him, was no longer on Earth. For almost all of his adult life, home had been the submarines where his command was. Now his home was in space. The time he spent on Earth would be merely waiting time, suspended animation until his new command was ready.

"Sir, may I intrude?"

He looked up and saw Stromsen floating in the aisle by his seat.

"What is it, Ms. Stromsen?"

She pulled herself down into the seat next to him but did not bother to latch the safety harness. From a breast pocket in her sweat-stained fatigues she pulled a tiny flat tin. It was marked with a red cross and some printing, hidden by her thumb.

Stromsen opened the tin. "You lost your medication patch," she said. "I thought you might want a fresh one." She was smiling at him, shyly, almost like a daughter might.

Hazard reached up and felt behind his left car. She was right, the patch was gone.

"I wonder how long ago …"

"It's been hours, at least," said Stromsen.

"Never noticed."

Her smile brightened. "Perhaps you don't need it anymore."

He smiled back at her. "Ms. Stromsen, I think you're absolutely right. My stomach feels fine. I believe I have finally become adapted to weightlessness."

"It's rather a shame that we're on our way back to Earth. You'll have to adapt all over again the next time out."

Hazard nodded. "Somehow I don't think that's going to be much of a problem for me anymore."

He let his head sink back into the seat cushion and closed his eyes, enjoying for the first time the exhilarating floating sensation of weightlessness.

## ■ White House Oval Office

This is the most somber victory party I've ever seen, Jake said to himself as he stood by the long windows that looked out at the White House lawn.

It was a dreary autumn day, the trees stretching bare arms toward a gray overcast sky. Inside the Oval Office it was almost as morose. President Tomlinson was on his feet, his jacket carefully buttoned instead of thrown across the back of his chair, a heavy glass of scotch in his right hand.

But the president wasn't smiling. His usual charming smile was nowhere in sight. Standing next to him, in dress navy blues, was

Captain Jonathan W. Hazard, tightly gripping a glass of bourbon, as somber-faced as the president.

Jake counted eight other men and women in the Oval Office, including Amy, the president's wife, plus his own wife, Tami, looking comfortably at home amidst the great and powerful.

Kevin O'Donnell raised his voice. "Everybody ready?" Nods and murmurs of assent.

O'Donnell turned toward the president and dipped his chin. Tomlinson went to his desk, put down his drink, and picked up a flat oblong box resting by his telephone console, then turned toward Hazard, who snapped to spine-popping attention. The others in the Oval Office stood up straighter and gathered around the two men.

"Captain Hazard," the president began, "I should have a formal speech prepared for this, but all I can say is … thank you, sir. You saved the world from a possible nuclear confrontation."

His face a mask of iron, Hazard replied, "I had the help of my crew. They were indispensable."

With a nod and the beginnings of a smile, the president replied, "They'll all be getting medals, too. And promotions." As if he suddenly remembered what he was about to do, the president opened the slim box and pulled a dangling medal out of it.

"The Navy Cross is awarded for gallantry above the call of duty. I can't think of anyone who deserves it more than you, Captain Hazard."

Hazard gulped visibly. But all he said was, "Thank you, sir."

Then the captain bowed enough for the president to drape the medal's colorful ribbon over his head.

"Congratulations, captain." "Thank you, sir. I'm honored."

The little group clustered around them broke into applause.

Jake turned to Tami, standing beside him, and whispered, "Shame this is all classified."

She had tears in her eyes. "Saving the world from nuclear war is too important for headlines."

## ■ Home

Jake sat wearily on their bed, his head buzzing from the excitement of the long, happy day—and the glasses of liquor he had consumed. Tami was sitting in front of the dresser's mirror, brushing her hair.

As Jake bent down to pull off his shoes, Tami asked, "And what about McMasters? Is he going to go quietly?"

Straightening up as if a spring in his back and been pulled, Jake answered, "Our ambitious vice president has already written his letter of resignation. It's on Frank's desk."

Turning toward her husband, Tami snapped her fingers as she asked, "Just like that? He's quitting?"

"For his health." Jake's face eased into a bitter grin. "He realized that's better than being arrested and tried for treason."

"Better for him."

"Better for everybody," Jake said.

"The people have a right to know."

With a patient sigh, Jake replied, "After next year's election. After Frank's won four more years."

She frowned at her husband and said, "We do have a First Amendment, you know. Freedom of the press and all that."

Jake got up from the bed and went over to the dresser. Sitting next to her on a thin slice of the upholstered bench, he said, "Let it rest, Tami. It's better this way."

"The people have a right to know."

"Will I have to bribe you to keep quiet about McMasters?"

"Bribe me?"

"How'd you like to be the first news reporter to go to the Moon?"

Tami's eyes widened. "The Moon?"

"Scott Base. You can spend a week there. I'll go with you."

"To the Moon?"

"In return for your silence about McMasters and the attempted coup up there in orbit."

"The Moon," Tami repeated.

Jake took her gently by the shoulders and turned her toward their bedroom window. Out there a full Moon was rising, bright and beckoning, over Washington's homes and monuments and government buildings.

In a half-whisper Tami said, "There's a whole new world waiting for us out there, isn't there, Jake?"

Gently, Jacob Ross smiled and corrected, "Worlds, Tami. Worlds. Plural."

**The End**

CPSIA information can be obtained
at www.ICGtesting.com
Printed in the USA
LVHW030008220421
685173LV00006B/6/J

6-22-21
6-27-21
3